5 4

Sophie was halfway to the door when a hand closed gently but firmly over her arm.

'The gentleman asked that you stay where you are,' a voice said close to her ear. 'I advise you to heed his request. You will only serve as a distraction if you venture outside now.'

The man's voice was as inflexible as his grip, but his high-handed assumption that Sophie would just be in the way rankled. 'You don't understand! Someone may have been injured.'

'I'm sure someone has, but your going out there now isn't going to help. If you promise to stay here, I shall endeavour to find out what has taken place.'

The man did not let go of her arm, and when Sophie finally raised her eyes to look at him she realised he probably wasn't going to. He stood with legs firmly planted, radiating power and authority in a manner that suggested he was used to being in control. Dark brown hair fell across a broad forehead, over eyes bright with intelligence, and while his features were too rugged to be called handsome he was still a very good-looking man. All of which meant nothing, given that he was still holding her captive against her will.

'Kindly release my arm, sir.'

Author Note

Have you ever read a story in which a minor character totally captured your imagination? One that made you long to know what happened to that character *after* the story ended? I know I have. And when I briefly introduced Sophie Vallois, a young French girl whose courage and compassion made her such an engaging character in one of my earlier books, I knew I had to bring her back.

But Sophie is no longer the naïve young girl she once was. Irrevocably changed by the events of the past, she arrives in London an astonishingly beautiful young woman, but one determined to follow her own path. *And* to avoid marriage at all costs.

Enter Robert Silverton. A man whose only reason for being in London is to settle his crippled sister in marriage. A man who earned society's condemnation by breaking his engagement to a well-born young lady. A man whose deeply personal conflict with the French will always stand as a barrier between him and Sophie. Or so an aristocratic competitor for Sophie's hand would have her believe…

I love the elegance of the Regency period, and I'm delighted to be sharing it with you through Robert and Sophie's story. I hope it makes you smile. And that you'll take a moment to visit my website at www.gailwhitiker.com for news about forthcoming releases.

COURTING MISS VALLOIS

Gail Whitiker

First published in Great Britain 2010
Paperback edition 2011
Harlequin Mills & Boon Limited,
Eton House, 18-24 Paradise Road, Richmond, Surrey TW9 1SR

© Gail Whitiker 2010

ISBN: 978 0 263 87841 7

Harlequin Mills & Boon policy is to use papers that are natural,
renewable and recyclable products and made from wood grown in
sustainable forests. The logging and manufacturing process conform
to the legal environmental regulations of the country of origin.

Printed and bound in Spain
by Litografia Rosés, S.A., Barcelona

Gail Whitiker was born on the west coast of Wales and moved to Canada at an early age. Though she grew up reading everything from John Wyndham to Victoria Holt, frequent trips back to Wales inspired a fascination with castles and history, so it wasn't surprising that her first published book would be set in Regency England. Now an award-winning author of both historical and contemporary novels, Gail lives on Vancouver Island, where she continues to indulge her fascination with the past, as well as enjoying travel, music, and spectacular scenery. Visit Gail at www.gailwhitiker.com

Previous novels by this author:

A MOST IMPROPER PROPOSAL*
THE GUARDIAN'S DILEMMA*
A SCANDALOUS COURTSHIP
A MOST UNSUITABLE BRIDE
A PROMISE TO RETURN

*part of *The Steepwood Scandal* mini-series

To Klas, always.
Thank you for introducing me
to all things Swedish.

To my agent, Sally Harding,
for opening doors, and for being there
with a keen eye, a wealth of patience,
and an excellent sense of humour.

And to Kimberley Young,
who made me dig deeper,
but in the nicest possible way.
Thank you for guiding me safely through
the perils of the London Underground!

Chapter One

'We've found them, my lord,' Inspector Rawlings said in a voice of quiet satisfaction. 'And by all accounts, in good health and fine spirits.'

For a moment, no one spoke. Not the portly detective whose long-awaited words brought to an end a search that had begun nearly eighteen months ago. Not the beautiful, dark-haired lady whose briefly closed eyes spoke more eloquently of her feelings than words ever could. And not the tall, slender gentleman whose clandestine missions in France had been the reason for the investigation in the first place. Nothing disturbed the silence of the April afternoon but the steady ticking of the mantel clock and the rattle of carriage wheels on the cobblestones below.

'And there is no doubt in your mind that it is Sophie Vallois and her brother, Antoine?' Nicholas Grey, Viscount Longworth, asked at length.

Rawlings shook his head. 'None whatsoever. I've

had my best man on it for months. There can be no mistake.'

'Thank heavens!' Lavinia Grey said with relief. 'To know they have finally been located. I cannot imagine what their life has been like.'

'Neither can I,' the inspector admitted. 'But I suspect they did what was necessary in order to protect themselves from those who would have murdered them in their beds.'

Lavinia's slender fingers tightened on the arm of the loveseat. 'Surely it was not as dire as that.'

'I wish I could say otherwise, but to those loyal to Bonaparte, what Miss Vallois and her brother did would have been viewed as an act of treason. The two would have had no choice but to lose themselves in the back streets of Paris.'

'Which they did most effectively for the best part of three years,' Nicholas murmured. 'Are they aware of having been followed?'

'No, my lord. Budge is my best man. He could follow the Prince Regent into the privy and not arouse suspicion. Begging your pardon, my lady.'

Lavinia inclined her head, though the dimple in her cheek suggested amusement rather than annoyance. 'And my husband's letter. Was it delivered?'

'According to my information, it was put into Miss Vallois's hands at half past four on the afternoon of the tenth,' the inspector said, checking his notepad. 'That being the case, you should be receiving an answer very soon.'

'*If* the young lady has any intention of replying.'

Nicholas moved towards the fireplace, seeing in the flames the sweetly innocent face of the child he remembered. 'She might not even remember who I am. And if she does remember, she may wish to have nothing more to do with a man who was so instrumental in ruining her life.'

'You did *not* ruin her life, Nicholas,' Lavinia said with a touch of exasperation. 'Miss Vallois and her brother helped you of their own accord. It isn't fair that you should shoulder all the blame for what happened as a result.'

Nicholas smiled, touched as always by his wife's unconditional support of his actions. She was a remarkable woman, able to comprehend the rationale behind what he did without convoluted explanations or lengthy justifications. Her quick, intuitive mind would have made her an excellent intelligence agent had she chosen to turn her hand to it. And as he walked across the room towards the brocade loveseat where she sat, he thanked God—and his commanding officer—that she had not. 'You are, as always, the voice of reason and logic. Even if the logic is somewhat prejudiced in my favour.'

'Of course it's prejudiced, darling. I am your wife. How could it be otherwise?'

'Not all wives agree with their husbands.'

'Not all husbands are worth agreeing with.' She smiled up at him. 'You have always been a most delightful exception.'

Nicholas bent to press a kiss against her dark, shining hair. 'And you the reason for it.'

Across the room, Inspector Rawlings cleared his

throat. 'Excuse me, my lord, but shall I inform my man that his continued surveillance is no longer required?'

Nicholas glanced at his wife. 'Well?'

Lavinia raised her shoulders in a gesture as eloquent as it was elegant. 'I suppose there is nothing to be gained by leaving the poor man in France now. Miss Vallois and her brother have been found and your letter delivered. There is nothing we can do but sit back and wait for her reply.'

Nicholas glanced at the inspector to see if he had anything to add, but assumed from the expression on his face that he agreed with Lavinia. They had all waited a long time for news that Sophie and Antoine Vallois had been found. Now that they had, and an initial contact had been made, there was nothing any of them could do but sit back and wait for her answer. It was frustrating, to be sure, but it seemed that once again, fate had placed his well-being squarely into someone else's hands. All he could do now was hope it would smile as favourably upon him today as it had all those years ago, when, but for a chance meeting with a young French girl and her brother in the darkened countryside of war-torn France, he wouldn't have been here at all.

The lumbering coach drew to a halt in the bustling yard of the Black Swan Inn; within minutes, a stable boy ran forwards to grab the reins of the lead horse. Carriage doors were thrown open, stairs were let down and a stream of weary passengers began to make their way into the inn.

Sophie Vallois was amongst the first to disembark and

as she waited for her brother to join her, she smoothed her hands over the rumpled skirts of her well-worn travelling outfit. Thank goodness she had not worn one of her new ensembles. Quarters on board ship had been cramped, and cleanliness was not an issue with which the captain had concerned himself. Added to that, the rough crossing had been enough to test the mettle of even the hardiest sailor. Fortunately, the wind-swept sea had not sent them to their beds as it had so many others and, come morning, Sophie had been on deck to see the spectacular sight of the sun glinting off the white cliffs of the southern coast of England. Now, countless hours and even more miles later, they had arrived at the coaching inn where they were to spend the night before continuing on to London in the morning.

'So, we are to break our journey here.' Antoine Vallois stepped down from the carriage and cast a dubious glance at the exterior of the inn. 'I hope the accommodation is better than the inn's appearance would suggest.'

'It will be fine,' Sophie replied with confidence. 'Lord Longworth would not have recommended it to us otherwise.'

'Unless it has been some time since the gentleman had occasion to stay here himself,' Antoine murmured as he stepped around a steaming pile of fresh horse droppings. Thankfully, the interior of the inn turned out to be far more pleasant than the weathered timbers and muddy yard might suggest, and the fragrant smells wafting up from the kitchen did much to restore their spirits, as did the roaring fire burning in the grate. Instinctively

Sophie moved towards it, anxious to banish the chill of the unseasonably cool April evening.

'Wait here while I see to our rooms and enquire about dinner,' Antoine said, placing their two small bags on the floor beside her. 'If Lord Longworth was unable to secure accommodations, we may find ourselves bedding down with the horses. And while sleeping in a barn is nothing new, I would rather not be plucking bits of straw from my clothes when we arrive in London tomorrow.'

Sophie's mouth twitched as she held her gloved hands out to the flames. 'I'm sure Lord Longworth would not care if you arrived looking like *l'épouvantail*. As long as we arrive safely.'

'The scarecrow, eh?' Antoine chuckled. '*Tiens*, you have no respect for your brother and far too much for this English lord. You seem to forget that our acquaintance with the man was brief and the repercussions far reaching. I would have expected you to be more suspicious of his reasons for asking us to come to England after all this time.'

'I admit, the circumstances are curious,' Sophie agreed, 'but I do not believe he would have asked us to come all this way if his motives were anything but honourable.'

'I hope you're right,' Antoine said, though his eyes remained guarded. 'Wait here and speak to no one. I do not trust these English around my beautiful sister.'

Sophie resisted the urge to smile. 'Do you not believe your sister capable of defending herself?'

'Having seen the way you handle a pistol, I think my

sister is *more* than capable of defending herself. It is the well-being of the English I worry about now.'

The remark was typical of the close relationship they shared, and as her brother headed towards the bar, Sophie realised how glad she was that he had agreed to make the trip with her. The last few years hadn't been easy for either of them. The strain of constantly having to move had been exhausting, and when at the beginning of last year they had finally settled into affordable rooms near the centre of Paris, she had nearly wept with relief. It was the first time since leaving home they had enjoyed anything close to a normal existence, so it was only natural that when the letter from Viscount Longworth had arrived, inviting them to come to England, Antoine would be suspicious. After all, what did they really know about the man whose life they had saved all those years ago? The fact of his having stayed in their barn for two weeks meant nothing given that he had been either delirious or unconscious for much of the time.

It certainly hadn't been the time to ask him what had brought him to France—or why he had been lying in a ditch with a bullet lodged in his side.

Because of her preoccupation with what lay ahead, it was a few minutes before Sophie realised that something was happening in the yard outside. An argument by the sounds of things, though the words were muffled by the thickness of the stone walls. Several of the inn's patrons glanced towards the door, but none seemed inclined to move, reluctant perhaps to involve themselves in something that might have untimely consequences. But when the sharp retort of a pistol split the night air, followed by a woman's high-pitched scream, Sophie knew the argument had turned deadly.

She turned to look for Antoine—and felt her heart stop when she saw him running towards the door. 'Antoine!'

'Stay where you are, Sophie. I have to see if I can help.'

'Then I'll come too—'

'No! If you would do anything, see to our rooms, then wait for me upstairs.'

For the space of a heartbeat, Sophie hesitated. If someone was seriously injured, Antoine would need her by his side. It would be almost impossible for him to do what was necessary without an assistant or the proper equipment. 'Wait, I'm coming with you!'

She was halfway to the door when a hand closed gently but firmly over her arm.

'The gentleman asked that you stay where you are,' a voice said close to her ear. 'I advise you to heed his request. You will only serve as a distraction if you venture outside now.'

The man's voice was as inflexible as his grip, but his high-handed assumption that Sophie would just be in the way rankled. 'You don't understand! Someone may have been injured.'

'I'm sure someone has, but your going out there now isn't going to help. If you promise to stay here, I shall endeavour to find out what has taken place.'

The man did not let go of her arm, and when Sophie finally raised her eyes to look at him, she realised he probably wasn't going to. He stood with legs firmly planted, radiating power and authority in a manner that suggested he was used to being in control. Clearly a man of means, he wore a well-tailored jacket and light-coloured breeches beneath his greatcoat, and though his leather boots were scuffed and in need of a polish, the quality of the workmanship was unmistakable. Dark brown hair fell across a broad forehead, over eyes bright with intelligence, and while his features were too rugged to be called handsome, he was still a very good-looking man. All of which meant nothing given that he was still holding her captive against her will. 'Kindly release my arm, sir.'

'Have I your word you won't do anything foolish?'

'You think a desire to go to the aid of an injured person foolish?'

'I think the intention noble, but the deed reckless.' Nevertheless, his hand dropped away. 'Your husband asked that you see to your accommodation. If you will wait for me at the bar, I shall offer what assistance I can and then return with any details I am able to uncover.'

'Oh, but Antoine is not—'

But the man was already gone, his greatcoat billowing around him as he stepped into the night. Other men followed him to the door, but none ventured out, and, inexplicably annoyed, both with their cowardice and by the high-handed treatment of the stranger, Sophie walked briskly towards the bar. She wasn't used to being cast aside like some helpless female who swooned at the sight of blood. She had often assisted Antoine with his work. Why would he not look to her for help now?

Her mood did not improve when she had to raise her voice to gain the innkeeper's attention.

'All right, all right, you needn't shout,' the old fellow grumbled, shuffling back from the window where he'd been trying to see what was going on outside. 'What do you want?'

'I'd like to see about our rooms. The name is Vallois.'

The innkeeper, whose grizzled eyebrows looked more like slivers of metal than natural hair, opened a well-worn book and ran his finger down the list. 'Nothing like that here.'

Surprised, Sophie said, 'Perhaps they were reserved under the gentleman's name. Viscount Longworth?'

If she had hoped to impress him with the use of a title, her gambit failed. 'No. Nothing like that either.'

'But I was told the arrangements would be made. His lordship sent me a letter, and said a copy would be sent here. Did you not receive it?'

The old man grunted. 'Mr Rastley might have.'

'Mr Rastley?'

'Him what owns the place. But he had to go off to see to his dying sister and there's no reservation in your name or the toff's.' The man closed the book. 'I can give you a blanket and you can sleep in the stable if you like—'

'Sleep in the stable? Good God, man, what kind of establishment are you running here?'

The remark was uttered by a tall, well-dressed man who came to stand beside her. He was obviously a gentleman. A shiny black beaver sat atop golden curls and a diamond pin was tucked securely into the folds of an elaborately tied cravat. Unlike the first gentleman who'd come to her aid, there wasn't a speck of dust on his boots, and the heavy gold rings on his fingers indicated a degree of wealth most often associated with the aristocracy. But while it was clear he intended to intervene on her behalf, Sophie knew better than to encourage the acquaintance. For all his fine appearance, his expression was cold, his mouth possessed of a cynical twist, his eyes hooded like those of a cat eyeing the helpless bird it intended having for dinner.

'Thank you, sir, but I have no doubt the situation can be resolved to the satisfaction of all concerned,' she told him. 'There has obviously been some confusion over the reservations.'

'Indeed. Confusion that has left you without a comfortable bed in which to spend the night.' The man flicked a contemptuous glance at the innkeeper. 'And to cause so beautiful a lady such a degree of inconvenience is an unconscionable crime.'

The old man blanched. 'Begging your pardon, Mr Oberon, but we don't have any rooms—'

'So you said,' the gentleman drawled. 'However, you cannot expect this young woman to spend the night alone and unprotected.' He turned to her and, as he leaned his elbow on the bar, Sophie saw the expression in his eyes change. 'Who knows what manner of harm might befall her? Better you spend the night with me, my dear, than take your chances elsewhere.'

The ploy was so obvious that Sophie almost laughed. 'Fortunately, I am neither alone nor unprotected. As soon as my brother returns, we will settle this matter to the satisfaction of all involved.'

'Your *brother?*'

'Yes. He ran outside after the first shot was fired...' Sophie faltered, painfully reminded of what had taken place only moments ago. She had no way of knowing if Antoine was all right because she had no way of knowing what manner of contretemps he had stumbled into. Innocent bystanders often came to harm when force was used to settle differences between men. But barely had the thought crossed her mind than it was laid to rest— and by the very man who had prevented her from going to Antoine's side in the first place.

'You will be glad to know that all is well, *madame*,' the gentleman said. 'The matter is settled and the injured man will recover, thanks to the timely intervention of your husband.'

'Her husband?' Mr Oberon turned to regard Sophie with an expression of reproach. 'I thought you said you were travelling with your brother?'

'I am. This gentleman mistakenly *assumed* he was my husband.'

'Perhaps because you made no attempt to correct me,' the first man said.

'How could I?' Sophie fired back. 'You ran outside before I had a chance to say anything.'

'By the by, Silverton,' Mr Oberon cut in carelessly, 'what *was* going on outside?'

'An argument, over a lady,' said the man so addressed, his slight hesitation enough to cast doubt as to the lady's respectability. 'An insult was tendered, an apology demanded, and when the offending gentleman refused to give it, the lady's companion took out a whip and struck the man across the face. The first gentleman responded by shooting the second in the leg. A nasty wound, but not life threatening, thanks to the prompt attention of this young lady's brother, whom I assume to be a doctor?'

'He is studying to become one,' Sophie was stung into replying. 'And I would *not* have been in the way. I often help my brother in such situations.'

'But I wasn't to know that, was I?' Mr Silverton said. 'I only heard him ask you to stay where you were. And detecting the note of concern in his voice, I deigned to intervene. Perhaps I should have left well enough alone and let you rush headlong into the fray.'

The reprimand was faint but unmistakable—enough to inspire guilt, but not harsh enough to wound. Sophie was still considering her reply when the door opened and Antoine walked in, his face grim, the front of his jacket spattered with blood. 'Antoine! Are you all right?'

'Yes, which is more than I can say for the fellow outside.' He glanced at the two men standing beside her and, to Sophie's surprise, offered his hand to her adversary. 'I am in your debt, *monsieur*. Without your help in holding the man down, I doubt I would have been able to staunch the flow of blood. *Merci beaucoup.*'

Mr Silverton's hesitation was so brief as to be almost imperceptible, but Sophie noticed. She watched him take Antoine's hand, shake it briefly, then release it almost immediately. 'I'm sure you would have managed.'

'Yes, I'm sure he would.' Mr Oberon's mouth pulled into a thin line. 'The French are nothing if not resourceful when it comes to dealing with matters of life and death.'

His words fell into a strained silence and Sophie wondered at the look that passed between the two Englishmen. But, more concerned with her own plight, she turned to her brother and said, 'It seems we must look for alternate accommodations, Antoine. Rooms have not been reserved for us and the inn is full.'

His surprise was as great as her own. 'Did you not show the man the letter?'

'There wasn't any point. He said there were no rooms available.'

'Then you will take mine,' Mr Silverton said at once. 'It is not large, but it has two beds and is relatively quiet. I shall make myself comfortable in the bar.'

'Oh, no,' Sophie said quickly. 'We couldn't possibly—'

'Thank you, Mr Silverton,' Antoine cut in. 'My sister has had a long day and is anxious to look her best on the morrow. We are most grateful for your offer.'

Sophie's mouth dropped open. They were *grateful* for his offer? Since when had they resorted to accepting help from strangers? Especially from a man who hadn't even wanted to shake her brother's hand!

'*Ce n'est pas une bonne idée, Antoine,*' she whispered urgently. '*Nous serons mieux lotis dans la grange avec les chevaux!*'

It was an indication of how distraught Sophie was that she allowed herself to fall back into French. Before leaving Paris, she and Antoine had agreed to speak English whenever they found themselves in the company of others. And while sleeping in the barn with the horses was not what she *wished* to do, it was far preferable to putting herself in a position of debt to this man. She had learned that offers of kindness always came with terms—and that payment was never negotiable.

Unfortunately, Mr Silverton obviously thought it a *fait accompli.* 'The room is at the top of the stairs, second on the left. If you will give me a moment, I shall remove my things and then return to give you the key. Oberon, may I store my valise in your room?'

'If you must, but don't think to spend the night. *I* have only the one bed and I certainly don't intend sharing it with you.'

Mr Silverton's voice was heavy with sarcasm. 'Rest assured, the thought never entered my mind. I'll see you at dinner.'

'Fine. All this high drama has left me with an appetite. In fact…' Mr Oberon glanced at Sophie, his gaze skimming over her with a thoroughness she found insulting. 'Perhaps you would care to join us, *mademoiselle*? The innkeeper has assured us of a decent meal in his private dining room and I can assure you, it will be far preferable to sitting cheek to jowl with the riff-raff out here.'

Resisting the urge to tell him the riff-raff would be *in* the private dining room, Sophie said, 'Thank you, but, no. My brother and I will be fine out here.'

'Very well. Then I bid you a good evening. And may I say that it has been…a pleasure.'

His eyes said everything his words did not and as he turned and walked away Sophie felt her face burn with humiliation. If such was a display of upper-crust English manners—

'You must forgive Oberon's lack of tact,' Mr Silverton said drily. 'He tends to speak before he thinks.'

'You owe us no apology, sir,' Antoine replied stiffly. 'Your conduct more than made up for his.'

Mr Silverton bowed. 'I would not wish you to think English chivalry dead.' His glance rested on Sophie for the briefest of moments before he touched the brim of his beaver and walked towards the narrow staircase.

Sophie followed him with her eyes, not at all pleased with the events of the past half-hour. 'You should not have accepted his offer, Antoine. We know nothing about him.'

'Nevertheless, I wasn't about to see you spend your first night in England sleeping in a barn.'

'Better that than finding ourselves beholden to a man who clearly doesn't like us.'

'I don't care if he likes us,' Antoine said. 'All that matters is that you have a proper bed in which to sleep and hot water in which to bathe. Lord Longworth wasn't able to provide that for you so I wasn't about to turn Mr Silverton down when he did. Besides, I doubt the loss of one night's sleep is going to trouble him unduly.'

Of course it wasn't. Mr Silverton was clearly a man of means, Sophie told herself. If he slept poorly in the bar tonight, he would simply go home and sleep it off tomorrow, no doubt in the comfort of a very fine house with his wife and servants to attend him. He certainly wouldn't be thinking about her. She was just one more person he'd met along the way.

And that's all he was to her. One more anonymous face in the crowd. She knew nothing about his life, so what did it matter if he thought her ill mannered for having refused his offer of help? Thanks to him, she would be clean and well rested when she arrived in London for her reunion with Nicholas tomorrow. Surely that was more important than worrying about what kind of impression she'd made on a man she was never going to see again.

Chapter Two

'So, who do you think she was?' Montague Oberon enquired between bites of underdone potato and overcooked beef.

Robert Silverton didn't look up from his plate of steak-and-kidney pie, hoping his apparent preoccupation with his meal would discourage Oberon from continuing to talk about her. 'Why would you not think she was his sister?'

'Because you heard what he said about it being important she look her best tomorrow.'

'Perhaps she is meeting with a prospective employer. Or a long-lost relation.'

'Or her new protector. You know what they say about French women.'

'I know what *you* say about French women,' Robert said, reaching for the salt cellar. "But I fear they are not all whores, strumpets or ballet dancers.'

'Pity.' Oberon took a piece of bread, his brow

furrowing. 'I suppose she could have been his mistress. There seemed to be a deal of affection between them, and God knows, I've never looked at *my* sister that way.'

'Why would you? You've told me countless times that you despise Elaine.'

'Of course. You would too if she were *your* sister. But I've never seen you look at Jane that way and the two of you are very close.'

'You're imagining things.' Finishing his meal, Robert picked up his glass. 'There were marked similarities in their appearance. The slenderness of the nose, the firm line of the jaw, the shape of the eyes...' *The seductive curve of the lady's mouth. Oh, yes, he'd noticed that. And he'd stared at it far too many times during their brief conversation...* 'I have no doubt they were related. But I could ask the gentleman on your behalf and leave you to the consequences.'

The viscount's son nearly choked. 'And find myself on the other end of a Frenchie's blade? No, thank you. I haven't your skill with the foil.'

'You could if you showed more inclination to learn.'

'I've little inclination to do anything that involves hard work or strenuous exercise,' Oberon said, pausing to flick a remnant of charred crust from the bread. 'Still, I'd give a year's allowance to have her in my bed for one night.'

'It seems to me your money would be better spent on the pursuit of a respectable bride,' Robert said, sitting back in his chair. 'Was that not a requirement of your continuing to receive the exceedingly generous allowance your father doles out to you twice a year?'

'Damned if it wasn't,' Oberon muttered. 'The old codger knows me too well. I cannot afford to live without the allowance, so I am forced to legshackle myself to some simpering heiress or some horse-faced widow long past her prime in order to assure its continuation.'

Robert smiled, aware that even under the most dire of circumstances, Oberon would never settle for anything less than a diamond of the first water. 'I'm sure such desperate measures will not be called for. No doubt you'll find at least one young lady amongst this year's crop of blushing débutantes to tempt you.'

'Tempt *us,* don't you mean?'

'No. I've had my brush with marriage, thank you,' Robert said. 'My only goal is to settle my sister in marriage and I intend to devote all of my energies to that.'

Oberon frowned. 'You may have a difficult task there, Silver. Jane's a delightful girl, but there is her affliction to consider.'

'I wouldn't call a misshapen foot an affliction, and I certainly don't consider it an impediment to her making a good marriage.'

'Of course not. You're her brother and honour bound to defend her. But what man would not wish his wife to be the most beautiful woman of his acquaintance?'

Robert raised his glass and studied his companion over the rim. The remark came as no surprise. It was exactly what he expected from a man who valued physical perfection above all and saw anything less as flawed. 'Jane *is* an acknowledged beauty.'

'But she *limps*, Silver. She cannot walk without the use of a cane and is hard pressed even to ride as well as other young ladies her age.'

'But she rides nevertheless.'

'Only when in the country where no one can see her. Be reasonable, old man. Jane's chances of making a good match in London are about as remote as ours of finding a man of wit and intelligence amongst the rabble out there,' Oberon said bluntly. 'Perhaps if you left her in the country, introduced her to the local clergyman—'

'Jane's chances of making a good match in London are no better or worse than any one else's,' Robert said mildly. 'Love enables one to overlook what others see as faults.'

'Blinds one to them, you mean. It sets up ridiculous expectations and does nothing more than pave the way for marital strife. I don't expect the woman I marry to love me, any more than I expect to love her.'

'Then what do you expect?'

'Loyalty, obedience and good breeding skills. I expect her to sit at my table and entertain my guests, manage my households to make sure the servants don't rob us blind and provide me with an heir at the earliest opportunity so I can go off and indulge my other interests.'

'Those being?'

'To find myself in bed with a different woman every night.'

Robert snorted. 'If that's all you require, you may as well marry your housekeeper and spend your nights at a brothel.'

'And pay for the pleasure of bedding a woman? I'd

rather eat bad oysters for breakfast,' Oberon said. 'I could give you the names of a *dozen* young ladies happy to warm my bed for nothing more than the pleasure they receive in return.'

'Then why not marry one of them?'

'Because I want a flower of rare perfection. A woman as virginal as Hestia, as amusing as Thalia, as—'

'As exquisite as Aphrodite?'

'That would be my first choice, though if she is not, I shall simply snuff the candles and do the deed as quickly as possible.' Oberon shrugged. 'London is full of tempting young chits only too happy to do what a man likes. Take that stunning young woman we just met. I'd wager even *you* wouldn't mind a tumble with her, despite your stated aversion to all things French.'

'That has nothing to do with it,' Robert said, aware that it wasn't entirely true, but wishing he'd never told Oberon of his antipathy. 'As a result of what happened between Lady Mary Kelsey and myself, I have no intention of involving myself with *any* woman, whether she be well born or otherwise.'

'Ah, yes, the broken engagement. Pity about that,' Oberon reflected. 'Unlike you, Lady Mary is not keeping quiet about her feelings. Last week she called you a heartless bastard for breaking things off without a word of explanation.'

'Trust me, it is better I do not vouchsafe the reasons,' Robert murmured.

'Be that as it may, she is threatening to sue you for breach of promise and society has taken her side. You have been cast out, my friend. Abandoned. Thrown to the murderous hordes. Which means you may as well find yourself a nice little mistress to keep you warm at night—in fact, what say you to a little wager? Whoever establishes the most beautiful woman in London as his mistress before the end of the Season shall be declared the winner.'

'I'd say that apart from it being a totally iniquitous undertaking, it makes absolutely no sense. Have you any idea how many beautiful women there are in London?'

'Ah, but I said the *most* beautiful.'

'By whose standards? Jane is considered a beauty, yet you are offended by her handicap and label her unattractive as a result.'

The viscount's son had the decency to blush. 'I did not say she offended me—'

'Not in so many words, but we both know that is what you meant.'

'Then we shall let a panel of our peers make the decision. And the stakes of the wager will show that he who loses must give the other that which he desires most. I'm willing to put up my stallion,' Oberon said, stabbing the last piece of beef with his fork. 'I recall you once saying that were I to offer you a chance to buy him, you'd take it without second thought. Now you can have him for free.'

Robert sighed. 'Let it go, Oberon. You know this is a complete waste of time.'

'On the contrary, it could be very interesting. We just have to come up with something of equal value for you to put forward.' Oberon tapped his finger against his chin.

'I have it! Your sapphire ring. I've always been partial to it and that is what I claim as my prize.'

Robert stared. 'You think I would risk a priceless family heirloom on something as feeble as this?'

'Why not? A wager must always have a prize *and* a consequence or it is not worth the trouble. So what do you say? Are you in?'

There were times, Robert reflected, when it was impossible to find the words that would adequately describe how he felt about some of the things Oberon did. Just as it was equally hard to imagine that one day, the man sitting opposite him would wear a viscount's coronet and own a veritable fortune in property and wealth. Robert picked up his glass and shook his head. 'No.'

'But why not? It is a harmless enough wager.'

'Not if the terms of the wager become known to the ladies involved.'

'Faith, Silver, when did you acquire such pretty manners? I remember a time when you would have wagered a month's allowance on something as inconsequential as in which direction a flock of pigeons took off.'

'That was before my father shot himself over gambling debts he couldn't afford to repay,' Robert said quietly. 'I swore then I wouldn't follow in his footsteps. And I won't have Jane ending up the same way as our poor mother.'

'But she wouldn't, old man. Unlike your father, *you* never lose!'

'A man's luck can change. Fortune is a fickle mistress.'

'For others, perhaps, but not you. Your prowess at the tables is legendary.'

'Count me out,' Robert said. 'I want nothing to do with it.'

Oberon sat back, rapping his fingers on the table and looking thoroughly peeved. 'Really, Silver, if I didn't like you so well, I'd pass you over for Welton. Unfortunately even he's begun to bore me of late. Twice now he's stood me up for lunch, and the last time I called round, he wouldn't even see me.'

Robert frowned. That didn't sound like Lawrence. When they had all been at Oxford together, it was most often Lawrence Welton to whom Oberon had gravitated. Likely because the affable Lawrence was the only one who had not been openly critical of Oberon's debauched lifestyle. 'Are you sure he's well?'

'Well enough to attend a social engagement the same afternoon he stood me up,' Oberon said. 'No, I've washed my hands of him. He used to be such good fun. Now he's become as staid and as boring…as you.'

Robert was unmoved by the criticism. So what if Oberon thought him boring? *He* knew what was important and it certainly wasn't deceiving innocent young women for the sake of someone else's pleasure or gain. 'Play the game if you must, but I'll have nothing to do with it. However, I will offer a toast. To your future wife,' Robert said, raising his glass. 'May she be as beautiful as Aphrodite, as gentle as Hestia—'

'And as lusty as an Irish farmer's daughter,' Oberon said. 'A toast to the dear lady's health…wherever she may be!'

* * *

It was late the following afternoon when Sophie finally stepped down from the carriage into the quiet of the respectable English street, and as far as she was concerned it wasn't a moment too soon. Her serviceable brown jacket and skirt were hopelessly creased, her half-boots were covered in dust, and there was a stain on the palm of her left glove from having touched something black and oily. Added to that, the unsettling events of the previous evening had made it impossible to sleep, leaving her feeling overly tired and decidedly on edge. If it weren't for Antoine, she would have climbed back into the carriage and turned the horses in the direction of home.

A long row of tall, white houses stretched before her, each with four stone steps leading to a shiny black door. From the centre of each door, a brass lion roared a warning to those who came near, and to either side and above, rows of windows glinted in the last rays of sunlight. A square ran the length of the street, bordered by trees newly covered in green, and in front of each house, black wrought-iron posts stood waiting to receive horses and carriages.

It was a far cry from the crowded *Rue de Piêtre* and the three small rooms she and Antoine called home.

'Buy some sweet violets, miss?' asked a young girl passing by with a tray. She was petite and dark haired, and the sweet smell rising from the flowers brought back bittersweet memories of home. Mama had always loved violets....

'*Non, merci,*' Sophie murmured, forgetting the girl

wouldn't be able to speak French. Forgetting they weren't in France. They were in England, and suddenly it all seemed like a huge mistake. What in the world had made her think this was the right thing to do? Too much time had passed. They should never have come—

'Upon my word, Sophie, is it really you?'

And then it was too late. The past caught up with the present and the moment of reckoning was at hand. Sophie looked up to see the door standing open and a swarm of black-coated servants emerge, like bees flying out of a hive. A couple stood on the top step, and while the beautiful woman in the exquisite silk gown was not known to her, the man…oh, yes, she knew the man. There might be lines around his mouth that hadn't been there before, and traces of grey peppering the dark, wavy hair, but his eyes were still the clear bright blue of a summer sky and his smile was still as warm as an August day in Provence. She would have recognised him anywhere. 'Lord Longworth,' Sophie said, breathing an audible sigh of relief. 'It has been…a long time.'

'A *very* long time.' Nicholas Grey started down the stairs. 'So long I scarcely recognise the beautiful young woman you've become. And I'm not sure exactly what to say except…welcome to England, dear Sophie. And may I say how very, very happy I am to see you again.'

It was almost like coming home. Sophie stepped into his embrace, feeling as though a weight had been lifted from her shoulders. 'No happier than I, for you look much better than when last we parted.'

'I dare say it would have been difficult to look worse. But even the deepest of cuts and bruises heal and I am

pleased to say I had exceptionally good care.' Nicholas
glanced at the young man standing quietly on the street
behind her, and slowly extended his hand. 'Antoine. I was
afraid you would not remember who I was. Or choose
not to come if you did.'

'Under the circumstances, you would be a hard man
to forget,' Antoine said, his greeting more reserved than
his sister's, but his tone cordial as he shook the viscount's
hand. 'I take it your memory is fully restored?'

'It is, though it was several months after the accident
before I could claim a complete recovery.'

'I have learned that injuries like yours often induce
temporary memory loss.'

'So it would seem.' Nicholas smiled. 'I understand
you are apprenticed to a surgeon in Paris.'

Sophie glanced at him in surprise. 'To Monsieur
Larocque, yes, but…how could you know that?'

'I suspect there is very little Lord Longworth doesn't
know about us,' Antoine said. 'No doubt he has had us
thoroughly investigated.'

'Antoine!'

'No, it's all right, Sophie,' Nicholas said quietly. 'I
regret that such duplicity was necessary, but it would
serve no purpose to lie and I will not insult your intelligence by doing so. Yes, I hired someone to find you
and they did what was necessary in order to uncover
your whereabouts. But the investigation was discreet
and nothing of its undertaking made public. So unless
you told anyone of your reasons for coming to England,
I can assure you that no one here knows.'

It was a moment before Antoine said, 'I told the

gentleman to whom I am apprenticed that I was coming to visit an old friend, and that time was of the essence given the precarious state of his health. However…' he looked at Nicholas and began to smile '…you appear uncommon well for a man on his deathbed, my lord.'

In full understanding of the situation, Nicholas chuckled. 'I'm glad I was able to hang on until your arrival.' He reached up to scratch his ear. 'Am I in imminent danger of expiring?'

'Not imminent, but the prognosis isn't good.'

'In that case, I suggest we go inside before I take a turn for the worst.'

'Thank heavens,' Lady Longworth said. 'I thought the entire visit was to be conducted on our doorstep.'

Making a sound of disgust, Nicholas said, 'Forgive my abominable manners. Sophie, Antoine, my beautiful wife, Lavinia, who, I can assure you, has been as anxious about your arrival as I.'

'Of course I've been anxious. But you must both be weary after your long journey,' Lavinia said. 'Why don't we retire to the drawing room? I've asked Banyon to set out refreshments.' She extended a slender white hand to Antoine. *'Vous ne viendrez pas avec moi, monsieur?'*

The young man's eyebrows rose. 'Your accent is perfect, *madame. Avez-vous été née en France?'*

'No, I was born in England, but my first husband was French and we lived in Paris for several years after we married. It will be delightful to have someone to speak the language with again.'

'I am surprised you do not speak it with Lord Longworth,' Sophie said. 'I remember his French being very good.'

'Alas, that was over three years ago,' Nicholas said. 'And given that I seldom use the language any more, I am beginning to forget many words and phrases.'

'Understandable. Even my own French is not as good as it once was.' Lavinia turned to Antoine, a hint of mischief lurking in the depths of those lovely eyes. 'I look to you for help in that regard, *monsieur.*'

'Ce serait mon plaisir,' Antoine replied, and though he did not smile, Sophie thought she detected a slight thawing of his reserve. Good. If the beautiful Lady Longworth had the ability to make her brother less suspicious of the situation, so much the better. She watched them walk into the house, quietly chatting in French, and found herself alone on the steps with Nicholas.

'Tu es…très belle, mademoiselle,' he complimented her. 'And I am sorry my accent is so poor compared to my wife's.'

'Your accent is fine,' Sophie said, wondering why Nicholas still seemed so ill at ease with her. He was a great man—a viscount in the British aristocracy. He had a beautiful wife, a lovely home and was clearly a man of means.

And yet, perhaps it was only to be expected. The last time they had seen each other, she had been a naïve girl of sixteen living on a farm in the French countryside and he an Englishman fighting for his life. She had struggled to make him understand what was happening to him and had done her best to keep him alive by feeding him soup smuggled from the kitchen, and by wrapping his wounds in bandages made from her own petticoats. For that, he had called her his angel of mercy and had gripped her hand when the fever had raged and the terror of his own anonymity had settled in his eyes.

Perhaps that was the problem, Sophie reflected. He was no longer a man on the brink of death and she was no longer the child he remembered. Maybe now that she was here and so little like the person he'd left behind, he was regretting his invitation, wishing he'd left things as they were. So much had changed in both their lives.

'Lord Longworth—'

'No,' he interrupted gently. 'Let there be no formality between us, Sophie. You are the young lady who saved my life and to whom I will always be indebted. I would ask that now, and in the future, you call me Nicholas.'

She looked up at him and tilted her head to one side. 'Is such familiarity permitted in England?'

'I see no reason why not. You are a good friend, and good friends always address one another by their Christian names.'

'*D'accord,* then Nicholas it shall be. As long as I am Sophie to you.'

'You will always be that, even though I now know your full name to be Sophia Chantal Vallois.'

Sophie raised one eyebrow. 'You *have* done your homework.'

To her amusement, he actually looked embarrassed. 'I fear so.' Then, his expression changed, becoming serious. 'Our first meeting seems…a very long time ago now, Sophie. Almost as though it were another lifetime. And there are still parts of those three weeks I don't remember. But I sincerely hope I did nothing to hurt you, or say anything to which you might have taken offence. A man in pain often lashes out at those around him, and I would hate to think I had scarred the child I left behind with a callous remark or a thoughtless word.'

So, that was the reason for his reserve, Sophie reflected. It had nothing to do with the people they were now, but rather with the impression he had made all those years ago. 'You did nothing wrong, Nicholas,' she said. 'Even in the depths of pain, you could not have been more *vaillant*. And if some of your memories of that time are dim, it is probably not a bad thing. It allows you more room for the good memories. For the ones that are worth remembering.'

'I'd like to think so.' He looked at her and a smile trembled over his lips. 'What about you, Sophie? Have you happy memories of the last three years?'

Sophie knew that he wanted her to say yes. She could see in his eyes, the hope that her life had not been an ongoing series of struggles and hardships, and perhaps one day she would tell him the truth. But not today. 'I have many happy memories, but I'm quite sure this is going to be one of the happiest.'

Chapter Three

'Are you sure I cannot offer you more tea, Sophie?' Lavinia asked. 'Or another scone? Cook was most insistent that you try both the orange marmalade and the raspberry jam.'

'*Merci, non,* I have already eaten too much,' Sophie demurred, sitting back on the loveseat. Nearly an hour had passed since she and her brother had sat down with their hosts in the elegant rose drawing room, and in keeping with the spirit of the day, the formalities had long been dispensed with. 'If I continue like this, I will not fit into my clothes.'

'Nonsense, you could do with a little extra weight,' Lavinia said. 'Don't you think so, Nicholas?'

'I cannot imagine Sophie looking any better than she does.'

Lavinia's lips twitched. 'Spoken like a true diplomat. No wonder you do so well in the House.'

'It does but pass the time.' Nicholas set his cup

and saucer on the table. 'But now that we've all had a chance to become better acquainted, I think our guests would like to know why they are here. It isn't every day a stranger from one's past invites you to come to London.'

'Especially when that stranger happens to be a member of the English aristocracy *and* an intelligence agent for the British government,' Antoine added.

'*Former* intelligence agent,' Nicholas said. 'I am happy to say those days are behind me. But it does bring me to the reason for my invitation, the first and foremost being to thank you properly for having saved my life. Without your discretion and most excellent care, I would certainly have died. A man doesn't forget something like that and because I am in a position to repay you, it is my sincere hope that you will allow me to do so.'

'But there is nothing *to* repay,' Sophie said. 'We did what anyone would have done under the circumstances.'

'On the contrary, given the political instability of the time, finding an Englishman shot and left for dead should have raised any number of questions. You asked none.'

Antoine shrugged. 'By your own admission, you had no answers to give.'

'But you must have wondered.'

'*Bien sûr.* But at the time I was more concerned with keeping you alive than with trying to find out why you had been shot.'

'And therein lies the difference, Antoine.' Nicholas got to his feet. 'Where others would have waited *until* they knew why I had been shot, you went ahead and removed the bullet regardless. That is the mark of an honourable man.'

Sophie had no need to look at her brother to know that he would be uncomfortable with the praises being heaped upon him. Whatever services he had rendered had stemmed from a genuine desire to save a man's life: the natural inclination of a man who one day hoped to become a doctor. For that, he expected neither praise nor reward. But equally aware that he was a guest in the gentleman's home, Antoine said simply, 'What is it you wish to do?'

'For you,' Nicholas said, 'a letter of recommendation that will open the doors to whatever university you wish to attend, as well as a financial endowment to help offset the costs of your studies towards becoming a doctor.'

Antoine went very still. 'You are offering me… money?'

'I prefer to think of it as a means to an end.'

'*C'est la même chose*. But we are not in need of your charity, my lord. Sophie and I have managed well enough on our own.'

'Have you?' Nicholas linked his hands behind his back. 'I may not be familiar with all the ins and outs of becoming a doctor in France, but in England, there are considerable fees involved in the study of medicine. Not to mention the costs of establishing your own practice.'

'None of which, if you'll forgive me, are your responsibility.'

'But all of which *became* my responsibility the day

you saved my life and so drastically altered the course of your own. Let us not mince words, Antoine. Because of me, you and Sophie had to hide out in the French countryside with the fear of discovery hanging over your heads like the sword of Damocles; upon reaching Paris, you took whatever manner of work you could find. First as a labourer, then as a clerk, then briefly as a—'

'Thank you, my lord. I am well aware of the means by which I earned enough money to cover our expenses,' Antoine said. 'It is enough you had us investigated. Pray do not compound the injury by prying into matters that are clearly none of your concern.'

'But it *is* our concern,' Lavinia said gently. 'We care what happens to you and Sophie.'

'Of course we do,' Nicholas said. 'Why else would we have gone to all this trouble?'

'I really don't know,' Antoine said coldly. 'But we did not ask for your help and our situation is not so desperate that we are forced to come to you with our hands out. It was Sophie's wish to see you again and I agreed to make the trip with her. A decision I am now beginning to regret!' He abruptly got to his feet. 'Now, if that is all you wish to say—'

'It is *not* all I wish to say—!'

'Nicholas, please!' Lavinia said. 'Antoine. *N'ira pas faire vous s'asseoir et nous écouter jusqu'au bout.*'

Her low, quiet voice seemed to inject a note of calm into the escalating tension and Sophie was relieved to see her brother sit back down. She knew this was difficult for him. Antoine was proud. Too proud to accept what he would only see as a handout, even from a man whose life he had saved. 'Listen to what Nicholas has to say, Antoine,' Sophie urged softly. 'Then let common sense, rather than pride, dictate your answer.'

'And please understand it was never our intention to offend you,' Lavinia said.

'Indeed it was not,' Nicholas said gruffly. 'My *only* desire was to try to make things better for you. I apologise if you see that as an intrusion into your lives, but the fact is I was worried about the two of you. Those were dangerous times and hardly a day went by I didn't wonder what had become of you. I owe you my *life*, Antoine. Perhaps to a doctor that doesn't mean very much, but to me—to us,' Nicholas said, glancing at his wife, 'it meant…everything.'

There was a poignant silence as Nicholas sat down and took Lavinia's hand in his. Watching them together, Sophie knew he had spoken from the heart. Whether or not his plans for their future came to pass, his reasons for bringing them to England could not be faulted. They stemmed from a genuine desire to thank them for the most noble gesture one man could make towards another.

Sophie glanced at her brother and was relieved to see that he, too, was regretting his hastily spoken words. 'You have nothing to apologise for, my lord. Sophie's right. Sometimes a man's pride gets in the way and prevents him from seeing what is truly before him.'

'I fear we've all been guilty of that.' Nicholas offered him an apologetic smile. *'Pride goeth before destruction, and a haughty spirit before a fall.'*

'But pride can be a good thing too,' Sophie said. 'It

gives us the courage to fight for what we believe in.' She leaned over and touched her brother's arm. 'It enabled you to pursue your dream of becoming a doctor.'

'Yes, it did,' Nicholas agreed. 'But a surgeon is *not* a doctor. And if your wish is still to become a doctor, I can help you. For all the *right* reasons.'

For a moment, Antoine was silent. There was a great deal at stake and Sophie knew her brother would not make a hasty decision. He would take time to think the matter through, weighing his options before giving them his answer. 'And Sophie? What would you do for her?'

This time, it was Lavinia who answered. 'It is our wish that Sophie stay here in London with us for a while. Not only so we can get to know her better, but so that we might introduce her to English society. It is our hope she will form lasting friendships with the young men and women to whom she is introduced.'

'Naturally, we will provide her with all things necessary to a young lady entering society,' Nicholas said. 'A suitable wardrobe. A maid to attend to her needs. A carriage. Or if she prefers, a decent mare to trot around Hyde Park—'

'Why?'

Antoine's one-word question stopped Nicholas in his tracks. 'Why?' He looked at the younger man and frowned. 'Is it not obvious?'

'Not to me.'

But to Sophie, who had been listening with growing concern, the answer was suddenly all *too* clear. 'I think, Antoine, that Nicholas and Lavinia wish me to find…a husband.'

'A husband?' Then, her brother's eyes opened wide. 'An *English* husband? *C'est de la folie!* Sophie has no intention of marrying an *Englishman*! She is perfectly capable of finding a husband in France!'

'But what kind of man would he be?' Lavinia asked. 'The son of a *boulanger*? A shop assistant barely making enough to feed himself, let alone a wife and eventually a family.'

A flush darkened Antoine's cheeks. 'You assume too much, my lady.'

'Do I? You forget that I've lived in France. I am well aware of the practicalities of life as they apply to a young woman in Sophie's position and they are not without their limitations.'

'Let us speak plainly, Antoine,' Nicholas said. 'Sophie's chances of making a good marriage where she is are extremely limited. For all your noble aspirations, a surgeon is little better than a tradesman and your sister will not benefit by the association. Here, we can offer her so much more. She will move in elevated circles; accompany us to soirées and balls held at some of the best houses in London. And when a gentleman does offer for her, as I have no doubt several will, he will have to meet *my* standards as far as wealth and station go, and seek *your* approval as the man who will be your brother-in-law.'

'May I be permitted to say something?' Sophie asked, torn between annoyance and amusement at the conversation going on around her.

'But, of course, dear,' Lavinia said quickly. 'It is, after all, your future we're talking about.'

'Yes, it is. And while I appreciate what you'd like to do, I really have no wish to be married.'

She might as well have said she wanted to strap on paper wings and fly to the moon.

'No wish to be married?' Lavinia said. 'But…*every* young lady wishes to be married, Sophie. It is the only respectable option open to a woman.'

'Perhaps, but since Antoine and I left home I have seen much of relationships between men and women, and I am not convinced marriage is to my benefit. A man stands to gains much whereas a woman loses everything.'

'Not if she marries the right man,' Lavinia said.

'But she will not know if he is the right man until *after* she's married him,' Sophie said. 'And then it is too late. Besides, what gentleman of good family is going to want someone like me? A farmer's daughter, from Bayencourt?'

'Rubbish! You no more resemble a farmer's daughter than I do a tinker!' Nicholas said. 'You are an astonishingly beautiful young woman who carries herself like a duchess, and who speaks the King's English with a slight, albeit charming accent. I cannot think of *any* man who would not be proud to have you by his side.'

'There, Sophie, did I not tell you?' Antoine said. 'If you gained nothing else from your employment with Mrs Grant-Ogilvy—'

'Good Lord. *Constance* Grant-Ogilvy?' Lavinia interrupted in surprise.

Sophie sucked in her breath. *Mère de Dieu,* she had *begged* Antoine not to mention that woman's name. 'Yes. Do you…know her?'

'Not personally, but I understand she is a woman of high moral character and an absolute stickler for propriety. You could not have had a better teacher in the arts of being a lady.'

The moment passed—and Sophie breathed again. 'Nevertheless, I am *not* a lady and I did not come to London looking for a husband.' She turned to Nicholas. 'I came to see *you*. And to meet Lavinia.'

'Yes, well, why don't we talk about all this in the morning?' Nicholas said. 'After you've had a chance to settle in.' He glanced at his wife, seeking support. 'What do you think, my dear?'

'I think that's a good idea,' Lavinia said slowly, 'but we probably owe Sophie an apology as well.'

Sophie blinked. 'An apology?'

'It was never our intention to make you uncomfortable, my dear. We simply thought that if you wished to be married, we might be able to provide you with a better opportunity to do so. However, if that is not the case, will you not at least stay and give us a chance to get to know you? We have both waited a long time to say thank you.'

Sophie began to smile. 'And I have waited a long time to see Nicholas well again. But the final say must be Antoine's. He has been as much guardian as brother to me these past three years and I could not stay if he was not easy with the decision.'

'Well, Antoine,' Lavinia said, 'what do you say?'

Antoine drew a deep breath. '*En vérité, je ne sais pas*. It seems…so much to ask. A great imposition on you both—'

'Then let me tell you one more thing,' Nicholas said quietly. 'My memory of Sophie was of a child. A golden-haired angel who appeared to me through a nightmarish haze of darkness and pain. I really had no idea how old she was and in bringing her here now, I thought to give her whatever a child her age might like. But the young lady who stepped down from the carriage is not a little girl who hankers after sandcastles by the sea. She is beautiful young woman with a mind of her own, and more than anything, we would like to get to know her better. All *you* have to do is say yes.'

Antoine was quiet for a long time, longer than Sophie expected. To her, the question was straightforward, the answer, simple. 'You have concerns about leaving me here, Antoine?' she asked at length.

'No, not really,' Antoine said finally. 'I admit, it wasn't what I had in mind, but as Nicholas pointed out, I have neither the financial wherewithal nor the social connections to make life better for you. And given that I would like to see you married—'

'Antoine—!'

'*Soyez patient,* Sophie. You and I have had this conversation before. I too believe that marriage is the only respectable occupation for a woman, and your chances of making a good marriage here are far better than they would be in France. As to marrying an Englishman… well, that decision must be yours. But if you would like to stay with Nicholas and Lavinia, I won't stand in your way.'

'Please stay with us, Sophie,' Lavinia said. 'It would make us both so very happy.'

Sophie looked at the three people in the room and realised that for the second time in three years, her life was about to change—but this time it would be a change for the better. In the company of Nicholas and Lavinia, she would be able to explore London and all it had to offer. She would have access to good books and fine music, perhaps have conversations about subjects that had always been of interest to her. And if her time in London culminated with a proposal of marriage, she could always say no. But the chance to get to know these two dear people might never come again.

'Yes, I would like to stay,' Sophie said firmly. 'And, if possible, I would like Antoine to stay as well.'

'Sophie! *C'est trop demandez!*'

'No, it's not too much to ask at all,' Lavinia said quickly. 'We simply thought you would be anxious to return to France.'

'Which, of course, I must or Monsieur Larocque will look for someone to take my place.'

'But surely a few more days won't make that much of a difference,' Nicholas said. 'There are people here who would like to meet you. Friends, who know what you did and who would be proud to make your acquaintance.'

'Why not stay with us for a week?' Lavinia suggested. 'Nicholas and I will be attending a ball tomorrow evening and we would be delighted to have you come with us. It will be the perfect opportunity to introduce you and Sophie to society.'

Antoine frowned. 'If I stay, it will not be with a view to entering English society.'

'Then come for the sport,' Nicholas said. 'Lord

Bruxton plays an excellent game of billiards. I can promise you some stiff competition if you're up for it.'

'Antoine is actually quite good,' Sophie said, knowing
her brother would always downplay his abilities. 'Monsieur Larocque often invites him to play.' She got up and
crossed to his side. 'Please say you will stay, Antoine.
It will give you a chance to practise your game before
you play Monsieur Larocque again. And I would enjoy
seeing *les dames anglaises* swooning over you.'

Antoine snorted. 'They will surely have more sense
than that. But, if it will make you happy, I will stay—but
only for a week. Then I must go back.'

It was good enough for Sophie. She didn't care if it
was Nicholas's persuasiveness or her own pleas that had
finally convinced her brother to change his mind. All
that mattered was that he was to stay in London for a
week—and that she was to stay for at least a month. After
such an auspicious start, how could she look upon this as
anything but the possible start of a new and memorable
chapter in both their lives?

Robert Silverton was not in a good mood as the carriage made its way from Portman Square to Mayfair.
Not only because he had no desire to spend an evening
being given the cold shoulder by a large number of the
three hundred guests Lady Bruxton would have surely
invited to her *petite soirée,* but because of what he had
heard at his club just that afternoon.

It seemed that despite having told Montague Oberon
he had no intention of participating in his ridiculous
wager, the man had gone ahead and set it up regardless.

Now he and several of Oberon's more disreputable friends were engaged in a race to establish the most beautiful woman in London as their mistress.

'I shouldn't worry about it,' said his sister, Jane, from the seat opposite. 'You need only strike your name from the book and in a few days it will all be forgotten. It seems a silly thing upon which to wager.'

'It is, but Oberon lives to gamble and when the topic of—' Robert shot her a wry glance '—that is, when talk veered in that direction, he couldn't resist putting forward this preposterous wager.'

He watched her lips compress, knew she wanted to laugh. 'You needn't pussyfoot around the subject with me, Robert, I am well aware that most men keep mistresses. What do you think those old tabbies talk about while they are watching their young charges pirouette about the ballrooms of society?'

'How prettily they dance?'

'Not for a moment. They gossip about which gentlemen are having affairs, and about which married ladies are in love with other women's husbands. How do you think I found out about Lady Andrews and Jeremy West?'

'Yes, I did wonder about that,' Robert murmured. 'But it is hardly the kind of information an unmarried lady should be privy to.'

'Oh, my dear Robert, you have no *idea* how much scandalous information I am privy to. It is one of the highlights of my sad little life. But seriously, you must stop worrying about me all the time. You've done little else since Mama died and it really isn't fair. You should be out there looking for a wife.'

'Need I remind you that I *was* briefly engaged to Lady Mary Kelsey?' Robert said. 'And that as a result, my name has now been struck from the list of eligible bachelors.'

'Then why are we going to Lady Bruxton's tonight?'

'Because *you* still need to be exposed to good society and Lady Bruxton was kind enough to invite us both, despite my shoddy reputation.'

Jane wrinkled her nose. 'I don't care what anyone says, you were right to break off your engagement. Life would have been very unpleasant for both of us had you gone ahead and married Lady Mary. I *know* she didn't like me.' She was silent for a moment, but when she spoke again, there was a delightful wickedness in her voice. 'I'll wager Mr Oberon would never consider *me* in the running for the most beautiful ladybird in London.'

'I should damn well hope not! Apart from your being a respectable young woman, I cannot imagine you married to a man like Oberon.'

'Why not? When his father dies, Monty becomes a very rich young man. The list of ladies wishing to be his wife *or* his mistress will stretch long, of that you can be sure.'

'And I pity every one of them,' Robert said, suddenly reminded of the French girl he'd seen at the Black Swan Inn. A girl whose beautiful face lingered in the shadows of his mind. He hadn't seen her or her brother again after taking his leave of them that night, but he hadn't forgotten her—and neither had Oberon. He'd talked about nothing else the entire way back to London.

'Well, let's hope there will be a few new faces at Lady Bruxton's tonight,' Jane said. 'Otherwise, I shall be forced to marry a blind man who falls in love with the sound of my voice and does not mind that I hobble on the way to the drawing room.'

'You will marry a man who loves you *despite* the fact you hobble,' Robert informed her with amusement. 'And I have every confidence *this* will be the year you find him.'

'Goodness, such unwavering belief in my ability.'

'Do you not share it?'

'I would like to, but I fear Tykhe has chosen to bestow her favours elsewhere.'

'Then we shall seek our own good fortune,' Robert said boldly. 'Thumb our noses at the Fates.'

'Oh, no, we must never do that,' Jane said, laughing. 'Unless we wish to bring their wrath down upon our heads.'

'Nothing of the sort,' Robert said. 'But we have endured more than our fair share of bad luck, Jane. It is time the gods smiled favourably upon us for a change.'

Sophie recognised him the moment he walked into the room. Though he was far more elegantly attired than on the occasion of their first meeting, there was no mistaking the confidence in his stride or his ruggedly handsome features. He stood tall and proud, his dark hair gleaming in the candlelight, and though several women turned to look at him as he passed, his warmest smile was reserved for the young woman at his side. A slender lady wearing green and who walked with a cane in her hand. 'I know that gentleman,' Sophie said.

Lavinia's dark brows rose in surprise. 'Which one?'

'The tall one who just came in. Silverton, I believe his name is.'

'Yes. Robert Silverton. And that is his sister, Jane. Where do you know him from?'

'The Black Swan Inn. He and another gentleman were there the evening we landed.'

Sophie had purposely made no mention of the events that had taken place at the inn. Nicholas would have been furious that his arrangements had fallen through, and Lavinia would have been horrified at the thought of a lovers' quarrel erupting into gunfire in the court-yard. But with Mr Silverton in the room and the prospect of an encounter likely, Sophie thought it best to men-tion that the two of them had spoken. 'I would not have thought them brother and sister. The resemblance is not strong.'

'No. Robert tends to follow his father's side while Jane gets her fair hair and delicate colouring from her mother's. But they come from a very good family. Their father was knighted for services to the Crown, and their mother was the youngest daughter of a baronet,' Lavinia said. 'Sadly, their deaths kept Robert and Jane out of society for many years.'

'Neither of them is married?'

'No. Jane was injured in a carriage accident as a child and does not go about much. You see how she limps. As for Mr Silverton, I regret to say he is out of favour with society at the moment.'

Sophie frowned. 'Out of favour?'

Lavinia glanced around, and then lowered her voice. 'About six weeks ago, Mr Silverton asked a young lady to marry him. She accepted and wedding plans got underway. Then, a few weeks later, he broke it off without a word of explanation to anyone. Naturally the lady was terribly upset and said some very harsh things about him in public. After all, it's one thing for a lady to change her mind, but quite another for a gentleman. As a result, no self-respecting mother will allow her daughter anywhere near Mr Silverton, and many doors have been closed in his face. I'm surprised he's here tonight.'

Sophie watched the good-looking brother and sister move through the crowd and noticed that while some of the guests offered them a reserved smile, others ignored them completely. 'It seems a very harsh treatment,' she said. 'He must have had a good reason for breaking the engagement off.'

'I'm sure he did,' Lavinia agreed. 'But a gentleman simply doesn't do things like that. And the fact he won't say *why* he did it has hurt him irreparably. Lady Mary is telling her own version of the story and it is not kind. Even Jane has suffered for it.'

Sophie switched her attention to the sister. A truly lovely young woman, Jane Silverton stood a good head shorter than her brother and looked to be fairly delicate. And though the smile on her lips was cheery, the paleness of her cheeks told another story. 'I should like to meet her. I think it's cruel that she be shunned for something her brother did.'

'That's very kind of you, dear.'

'I just try to put myself in her place,' Sophie said, for in truth, she *had* been in Jane Silverton's place once, though not for the same reasons. 'And you should know that while Mr Silverton and I did have a conversation that night, we were not formally introduced. He may not even remember who I am.'

'Well, he'll remember you after tonight,' Lavinia said, discreetly raising her hand to attract the couple's attention. 'Madame Delors surpassed even *my* expectations with that gown. You are easily one of the most beautiful women in the room.'

While Sophie took leave to disagree with the latter part of Lavinia's statement, she couldn't deny that the gown of cream-coloured lace over a gold satin slip was the most glorious thing she had ever seen. Cut outrageously low in the front, it displayed a rather alarming amount of skin—which had prompted her to stitch a wide band of lace inset with pearls and tiny satin roses into the neckline—and from a raised waist, the skirt fell in elegant folds to the floor. Delicate slippers of soft kid leather, cream-coloured elbow-length gloves, and a spray of cream-and-pink roses in her hair put the finishing touches on what Sophie could only think to call a truly magnificent ensemble.

Even so, she doubted it would be enough to thaw Mr Silverton's chilly reserve.

'Mr Silverton, Jane, how lovely to see you again,' Lavinia said when the pair finally managed to reach them. 'Allow me to introduce a very dear friend of mine, Miss Sophie Vallois. Sophie, this is Miss Jane Silverton and her brother, Mr Robert Silverton.'

'How lovely to meet you, Miss Vallois,' Jane said. 'Or should I say, *enchantée*?'

The girl's voice was as delightful as her sparkling green eyes and Sophie found it hard to believe that any gentleman would find her lacking. 'How do you do, Miss Silverton,' she replied, before adding more diffidently to her brother, 'Mr Silverton.'

'Miss Vallois.' He briefly inclined his head. 'We meet again.'

So, he wasn't about to pretend ignorance of their first encounter. She awarded him a point for honesty. 'I didn't think you would remember.'

His deep brown eyes were steady on hers. 'On the contrary, I am unlikely to forget.'

'Sophie informs me the two of you met at the Black Swan Inn,' Lavinia said.

'Saying we *met* would not be entirely correct,' Mr Silverton said. 'We were brought together by circumstances less than conducive to pleasant socialising and parted soon after.'

'Then how fortunate you should both end up here tonight in order that the formalities might be observed.'

The gentleman inclined his head. 'As you say.'

'Is your husband not with you this evening, Lady Longworth?' Miss Silverton asked.

'Yes, but he and Sophie's brother just left to play billiards with Lord Bruxton. Apparently they are all quite mad for the game.'

'Your brother plays billiards?' Mr Silverton asked Sophie in surprise.

'When he has a chance, yes.'

'I thought the study of medicine was an all-consuming passion.'

Sophie raised her eyes to his, daring him to disagree. 'A man must take some time away from his studies, lest he become too weary to absorb anything new. Even God rested on the seventh day.'

Was that a hint of a smile? 'A lofty comparison.'

'But fitting under the circumstances. I admire *anyone* who has the determination to strive for something they truly believe in.'

'And I have always been impressed by people who choose to help others in such a way,' Jane spoke up. 'But tell me, how did the four of you meet?'

'Through my husband,' Lavinia said easily. 'Nicholas and Antoine met in France several years ago, and we finally persuaded him to come to London and to bring Sophie with him. Unfortunately, Antoine must shortly return home, but Sophie is to stay with us until the end of the Season.'

'Oh, how wonderful!' Jane said happily. 'Then you must pay us a visit while you are here, Miss Vallois. We will have petit fours, and speak French, and you can tell me all about the latest fashions from Paris. *J'adore la mode française.* Have you seen much of London?'

'Not yet.'

'Then why not join us tomorrow afternoon? Robert

has promised to take me for a drive around Hyde Park. It would be lovely if you and your brother could come too.'

It was an unexpectedly kind offer and one Sophie would have been happy to accept—had she not caught sight of the expression on Mr Silverton's face. Obviously he did not share his sister's enthusiasm for the outing and saw no reason to pretend he did. 'Perhaps another time,' she said. 'I have no wish to intrude.'

'Oh, but you wouldn't be intruding,' Jane said. 'My brother is always delighted to have friends come along. Aren't you, Robert?'

'Of course. I merely thought it too soon after Miss Vallois's arrival for such an outing. She might wish to rest.'

'Fudge! If she has been here since yesterday, she is well over the worst and decidedly in need of a diversion,' Jane said. 'Tell her you were only thinking of her welfare and that you would love to have her come with us.'

Sophie had a difficult time holding her tongue. Had Lavinia not been present, she would have politely but firmly declined the invitation. She had no wish to force her company on *any one* who had no desire to share it, even if it meant disappointing Jane, who obviously did. To her surprise, however, it was Mr Silverton who resolved the problem. 'You are more than welcome to join us, Miss Vallois. Jane is anxious for your company, and I am happy to oblige her. As for your own enjoyment, while it might not be as diverting as a night spent in a barn with the horses, I'm sure you will find it an amusing way to pass an hour or two.'

Jane frowned. 'A night spent in a barn with *horses*? What on earth are you talking about, Robert?'

But Sophie knew *exactly* what he was talking about. And the knowledge that he not only *understood* French, but that he *remembered* every word she'd said to Antoine that night at the inn, brought hot colour sweeping into her cheeks. No wonder he'd been so distant with her.

'Come, Jane,' Mr Silverton said. 'Miss Vallois can send a note if she wishes to join us. For now, we mustn't keep her and Lady Longworth from their evening.'

'No, of course not. Forgive me,' Jane said. 'It's just that I so seldom meet anyone I really like, I tend to get carried away. But now that we've met, I know we are all going to be great friends. Until tomorrow, then, Miss Vallois. Good evening, Lady Longworth.'

'Jane,' Lavinia said. 'Mr Silverton.'

'Lady Longworth.' He bowed, and then turned to Sophie. 'Miss Vallois.'

Sophie inclined her head, but refused to meet his eyes. Why should she when it was so obvious that he didn't like her? His words had been clipped and the warmth he had shown his sister and Lavinia had definitely not been extended to her.

'A charming pair, are they not?' Lavinia asked.

'The sister more than the brother, I think,' Sophie said. 'Imagine extending an invitation to someone she barely knows.'

'Jane has always had a good heart,' Lavinia said. 'Which is why it annoys me so that she is not yet married. At times, I feel like shaking the young men for

their fickleness. But I expect she will benefit greatly
from spending time with you and Antoine tomorrow.'

'And I look forward to introducing Antoine to her. In
fact—' Sophie broke off and slowly began to smile. 'I
have a feeling my brother might enjoy Miss Silverton's
company very much.'

Chapter Four

So she wasn't a whore, a strumpet or a ballet dancer, Robert reflected as he and Jane walked away. She was an exceptionally beautiful young woman who, thanks to the kindness of Lord and Lady Longworth, was about to be launched into English society. The prospect did not please him. His own reasons aside, it meant she was fair game for the likes of Montague Oberon, and he did not relish the thought of watching the man salivate over her every time he saw her out in public.

'Behold the prodigal son,' Jane whispered in her brother's ear a few minutes later. 'And more splendidly attired than half the ladies in the room.'

Her assessment wasn't far off. Not many gentlemen could have carried off the colourful waistcoat and elaborately folded cravat with such panache, but Oberon's height and bearing allowed him to do so magnificently. His golden curls were swept back in a manner few men could have worn to advantage and his clothes were immaculate. Pompous prig he might be, Robert reflected, but looks, breeding and a fortune allowed him to carry it off with aplomb.

'Evening, Silver,' Oberon said when he came within speaking distance. 'Jane. Lovely to see you again.'

'Mr Oberon. What a splendid waistcoat. It is surely a modern version of Joseph's coat of many colours.'

Oberon's expression was blank. 'Joseph?'

'You remember. From the bible.'

'Oh, yes, of course. The old fellow whose wife turned to stone.'

'That was Lot,' Robert said. 'And it was salt.'

'Salt?' Oberon frowned. 'What has salt to do with it? We were talking about my waistcoat.' He paused for a moment to glance around the room. 'Jupiter, what an appalling crowd. I vow there weren't this many people at the—' He broke off, his eyes frozen to one spot. 'Good God, it's *her*!'

Jane turned to look. 'Who?'

'The girl from the inn. Aphrodite reincarnated,' Oberon murmured. 'It is her, isn't it, Silver?'

Breathing a sigh of exasperation, Robert said, 'Yes.'

'Splendid. Then I must be introduced.'

'I'd like a word with you first.'

'Later.' Oberon's eyes never strayed from the object of his affection. '*After* I speak to the Goddess!'

'Now. Will you excuse us, Jane?'

'Of course. I see Lady Jennings sitting on her own and looking rather disgruntled,' Jane said. 'I shall go and keep her company. No doubt she will have a few choice things to say about some of the guests here this evening.'

'Not about me, I hope,' Oberon said.

'On the contrary, you are always one of her favourite topics, Mr Oberon.' And with a smile for him and a wink for her brother, Jane left the two of them alone.

'Impertinent minx,' Oberon said without rancour. 'Is it my imagination or is her limp less noticeable than it used to be?'

'I am hardly the one to ask given that I never thought it *was* all that noticeable,' Robert said, drawing the other man aside. 'Now, would you mind telling me what the hell you think you're doing?'

Oberon's gaze shortened and refocused. 'Doing?'

'The wager. I told you I wanted no part of it, yet you went ahead and put my name to it regardless.'

'Ah, yes, that. Yes, I did set it up because several of the lads thought it would be a great lark. All of them are in the market for a new mistress and when Mortimer wagered a month at his father's hunting lodge in Yorkshire that he would be the first to succeed, Cramby staked a thousand pounds against him, saying Mortimer had more money than sense.'

'There's a lot of that going around,' Robert muttered. 'But I won't have it, Oberon. Take my name off the bet and out of the book. My reputation doesn't need any further blackening by you.'

'Can't do it, old boy. We all put our hand to it, you see. I personally signed for you,' Oberon confided. 'And when you consider what the winner stands to gain, it really makes no sense to call it off. Now, about the French girl. Who is she and how does she come to be here tonight?'

Biting back a scathing retort, Robert said, 'I know nothing more about her than I did at the inn. Except that her name is Miss Vallois and she is here with Lord and Lady Longworth.'

'You mean she's staying with them?'

'Possibly.'

'Interesting.' Oberon's eyes assumed a speculative gleam. 'She must be well born to be moving in their circle. I wonder if the fair Lavinia has taken it upon herself to launch the girl into society.'

'I have no idea.'

'Then I'll find out for myself. Introduce us.'

'No.'

The blunt answer brought Oberon's head around. 'I *beg* your pardon?'

'I said no. If the young lady is being presented to society, she is not some light-skirt for you to trifle with.'

'My dear Robert, did it not occur to you I might have *other* things in mind for the delectable Miss Vallois?'

'It did not.' Robert smiled without warmth. 'I know your reputation, Oberon, and a leopard doesn't change his spots.'

The other man's expression cooled. 'Tread lightly, my friend. 'Tis a fine line between familiarity and contempt, and many a friendship has been lost over a careless misstep. I ask only to be introduced to the young lady. What possible harm can come of that?'

They were coming. The man who didn't like her—and the one who did in ways of which no mother would ever approve. Sophie took a deep breath and slowly opened her fan. What a pity Lavinia had chosen that very moment to go off and speak with friends.

'Miss Vallois,' Mr Silverton said, stopping in front of her. 'Pray forgive the intrusion, but my friend has asked to be made known to you.'

Sophie glanced up into his handsome face, aware of the strength in those chiselled features, and saw again the cool disinterest she had come to associate with Robert Silverton. But she also saw something else. A reserve that seemed to echo her own uncertainty. 'As you wish, Mr Silverton.'

'Miss Sophie Vallois, may I present Mr Montague Oberon.'

'Miss Vallois, what a pleasure this is,' Mr Oberon said. 'I did not think I would be fortunate enough to see you again.'

'It *is* something of a surprise,' Sophie acknowledged, not liking the way his eyes lingered on the low décolleté of her gown. She purposely raised her fan to block his view. 'So you and Mr Silverton are friends as well as travelling companions.'

'Oh, yes. Very good friends.' Mr Oberon raised guileless blue eyes to hers. 'As you saw that night at the inn, Silverton is everything a gentleman should be. Thoughtful, unselfish, steady as a rock. Sadly, all the things I am not.'

Startled by his candour, Sophie said, 'Then what qualities do you possess?'

'Wealth, humour and impeccable taste when it comes to female beauty…which is why you caught my eye the other evening. The gods themselves could not have sent a more divine creature to move amongst us. But I am well aware I owe you an apology. My behaviour was, to say the least, reprehensible. Due, no doubt, to the tedium of travel and the insufferable manners of that wretched innkeeper. Please say you will forgive me or I shall never rest easy again.'

The effusive apology surprised Sophie as much as amused her, and though she believed his words to be little more than pretty flattery, the fact he *had* offered an apology allowed her to look upon him with a touch more charity. 'I accept your apology.'

'I am relieved beyond words.'

'Ah, good evening, Mr Oberon,' Lavinia said, finally returning. 'How nice to see you again.'

'The pleasure must always be mine, Lady Longworth.' Mr Oberon's smile moved smoothly into place. 'I vow you grow more lovely with every passing day.'

'And I vow you grow more fulsome with your compliments. Have you met Miss Vallois?'

'Indeed. Silverton was kind enough to introduce us. Am I to understand the lady will be spending the Season here in London with you?'

'You are.'

'Then perhaps I might call upon you in the near future to exchange pleasantries in a less crowded venue.'

Lavinia inclined her head. 'You are, of course, welcome to call. But now I must steal Sophie away. Lord and Lady Beale are anxious to meet her. Sophie?'

Grateful for the opportunity to escape, Sophie dropped a quick curtsy. 'Mr Oberon.' Then, raising her chin, and goaded by some mischievous impulse she would no doubt regret later, she looked at the gentleman standing quietly beside him and said, 'Please tell your sister that my brother and I look forward to joining you tomorrow afternoon, Mr Silverton. If the invitation is still open.'

His expression didn't change, but Sophie heard the quiet edge of mockery in his voice. 'It is, and I shall be pleased to tell her of your acceptance.'

Sophie smiled as she tucked her arm in Lavinia's. 'Good evening, gentlemen.'

'Ladies.' Oberon barely waited until they were out of hearing before exclaiming, 'Until tomorrow? What was that all about?'

'Jane has invited Miss Vallois and her brother to come driving with us,' Robert said distantly.

'And she *agreed*?'

'Why would she not? By your own words, I am thoughtful, considerate and steady as a rock.'

'I was only trying to flatter you.'

'By making me sound like the trusted family dog?'

'Nothing of the sort. I simply wanted her to know that you and I are very different.'

'I believe she worked that one out on her own,' Robert drawled, but Oberon wasn't listening. He was following Sophie's progress across the room like a hungry lion following a sprightly gazelle.

'By God, she's exquisite,' he murmured. 'Those eyes. That hair. And that complexion! As pink as rose petals and as smooth as alabaster. Imagine her lying naked in your bed, Silver. Imagine the softness of her skin as you run your hand slowly over her throat, and then lower.' He briefly closed his eyes and made a sound deep in his throat. Seconds later, his eyes snapped open. 'I must know who she is. Where does she come from, and why is she here?'

'I have no idea,' Robert said. 'Is it not enough that she is a good friend of Lord and Lady Longworth's?'

'No. The French are as stuffy as the English when it comes to matters of class. And a well-brought-up French girl would have no need of a London Season.'

The same thought had occurred to Robert, but he had no intention of giving Oberon the satisfaction of agreeing with him. 'If you don't think she's well born, why trouble yourself to make enquiries?'

'Because I would hate to miss the opportunity of getting to know her *if* her birth is all it should be,' Oberon said. 'Look at her, man! When did you last see beauty like that? Observe the elegance of her carriage, the unconscious grace with which she carries herself. Who knows? She may well be the daughter of a French count.'

'You could ask Lady Longworth.'

'I could, but if the Longworths are using her extraordinary beauty as a means of capturing a wealthy husband, the truth may be revealed only *after* the vows are spoken. She may be an heiress—or an actress, which means I'm better off making my own enquiries.'

'Which means what? You strap Miss Vallois to the rack and turn the screws until she tells you what you want to know?'

Oberon laughed. 'Really, Silver, my methods are far more civilised. You see, in every person's life, there are secrets. And there are always people who *know* those secrets. It is simply a matter of finding the right people and asking them the right questions.'

'And if they suffer from the antiquated notion of loyalty or friendship?'

'Then they must be *encouraged* to share what they know.' Oberon smiled, but to Robert's way of thinking, it was a singularly unpleasant thing. 'Next to torture, I've always found money to be the most effective way of eliciting the truth.'

Oberon walked away and Robert made no attempt to stop him. The man was like a dog with a bone. Once he sank his teeth into something, he wouldn't let go until there was nothing left to hold on to. Such was the case with Miss Vallois. Oberon had decided she was of interest to him and he would leave no stone unturned until he knew everything there was to know about her.

A daunting prospect for anyone, let alone a young woman newly arrived in London and looking to make a successful marriage. For *her* sake, Robert hoped there was nothing in her past that would preclude that from happening.

By the time the evening came to an end, Sophie was convinced the English were indefatigable. Though it was well past two in the morning, Lavinia and Nicholas were still chatting enthusiastically about the people to whom they had spoken, and about the delight those people had expressed at having been introduced to the charming brother and sister from France.

Sophie was pleased the evening had gone so well, but her feelings of excitement had long since given way to exhaustion. The noise of so many people, the sights and sounds of a grand ball, the necessity of constantly having to be on one's guard to say the right thing, were tiring in the extreme, to say nothing of the difficulties involved in keeping everyone's titles and positions straight. What a confusing jumble of lords and ladies the English aristocracy was!

Then there was the always-disturbing behaviour of one Mr Robert Silverton…

'I think you'll sleep well tonight,' Lavinia said as they climbed the stairs to their rooms. 'I'll have Jeanette bring you a cup of chocolate in the morning.'

'Thank you, Lavinia.' Sophie was so weary she had to concentrate on putting one foot in front of the other. 'If left alone, I fear I may sleep until noon.'

'In that case, I shall have a breakfast tray sent up as well.'

Thankfully, Jeanette was waiting to help her undress and after the magnificent gown was removed and carefully hung in the closet, Sophie sat down at the dressing table and gazed longingly at the bed. 'I don't suppose I could go to bed without having my hair brushed?'

Jeanette pursed her lips. 'Her ladyship wouldn't like it, miss. She's very particular about that sort of thing.'

'Yes, I'm sure she is.' Sophie sighed as she turned to face the glass. As the maid took the pins from her hair and it came tumbling down around her shoulders, Sophie closed her eyes and let her mind drift back over the events of the evening. Ironically, she found herself thinking about Robert Silverton. Why, she couldn't imagine. The man had made no secret of the fact he didn't like her, yet she was finding it exceedingly difficult to put him from her thoughts. She had followed his progress around the room, watching as he had stopped to speak with people he knew. The young ladies had been careful to keep their distance, but several of the older ones had smiled in a way that led Sophie to believe he was still *very* attractive to women open to *une dalliance*.

'Sophie, are you awake?' Lavinia called from the other side of the door.

'Yes.' Sophie opened her eyes, glad to have something to think about other than Robert Silverton. 'Come in, Lavinia.'

Lavinia did, looking wonderfully exotic and far too wide awake in a dressing robe of deep crimson silk trimmed with layers of snowy white lace. Her long dark hair was caught in a loose knot at the nape of her neck and there was a definite twinkle in her eyes. 'Thank you, Jeanette. That will be all.'

The maid put down the silver-handled brush, bobbed a curtsy and left. Lavinia waited for the door to close before settling herself on the edge of the bed and gazing at Sophie's reflection in the glass. 'I hope you don't mind, but I couldn't wait until breakfast to hear what you thought of your first ball. And to tell you how proud Nicholas and I were of you this evening. I'm sure we will see your name in the society pages tomorrow.'

Sophie turned on the upholstered seat and her mouth lifted in a smile. 'I hope they neglect to mention that I addressed the Countess of Doncaster's eldest daughter as Lady Doncaster.'

Lavinia dismissed it with a wave. 'You apologised so

sweetly even Lady Doncaster couldn't take offence. But we could spend some time with *Debrett's* tomorrow, if you like.'

'Or we could just avoid attending any more grand balls. But I did enjoy myself this evening, Lavinia, and I think Antoine did too.'

'Good, because I noticed several young ladies watching him,' Lavinia commented. 'Miss Margaret Quilling couldn't take her eyes from him.'

'Which one was she?'

'The tall girl in white. Quite pretty, with blond hair dressed with feathers and pearls.'

Sophie nodded, remembering the ensemble rather than the lady. It had been of white tulle over satin with a rather unusual band of satin crescents forming a wide border around the bottom. The sleeves had been short and edged with a smaller band of crescents. 'Yes, I remember. She complimented me on my gown and asked if I'd had it made in Paris.'

'Really? I must pass that on to Madame Delors. She will be delighted to know that her gowns are being praised by such illustrious members of society.' Lavinia got up and wandered across to the window. 'Does the room please you, Sophie? I thought you might prefer one facing the square.'

'The room is perfect,' Sophie said, glancing around the spacious chamber. A huge four-poster bed was draped in lavender velvet, with the bedspread and pillows being of a lighter hue. A wardrobe stood against the opposite wall and a writing table was nestled under a window framed by delicate white curtains. 'My mother would have loved it. Lavender was always her favourite colour.'

'It must have been hard for you to leave her.'

'I didn't get the chance.' Sophie's eyes misted as they always did when she thought of the gentle woman who had raised her as best she could, despite the frequent bouts of debilitating illness. 'She died four years ago.'

'Oh, my dear, I'm so sorry. I didn't know.'

'That's all right. She passed peacefully in her sleep.'

Lavinia's face softened. 'And your father? Do you miss him?'

Sophie felt a return of the old disappointment, followed by the inevitable feelings of guilt. 'I wish I could say I did, but after Mama died, Papa became a very difficult man. He grew bitter and argumentative. Always looking for fault. When he found out what Antoine and I had done, he made it very clear we were not welcome in his house.'

'Gracious! How *did* he find out?'

'There was talk of it in the village,' Sophie said, unwilling to say more. 'When Papa heard, he accused Antoine of being sympathetic to the English cause and of disgracing the Vallois name. He said he was never to show his face in Bayencourt again!'

'How cruel!'

'It was, but Antoine and Papa never really got on. By the next morning, we were gone.'

'But why did you go with him, Sophie? You were so young. Surely Antoine would have preferred that you stay behind.'

'Of course, but how could I stay when it was *my* fault he had to leave?'

'Your fault?'

'I was the one who asked him to help Nicholas.'

'Oh, my dear, you must *never* reproach yourself for that,' Lavinia said. 'You should be proud that you cared enough about the life of a stranger that you would try to help him.'

'He would have died if I hadn't,' Sophie said, remembering the extent of Nicholas's injuries when she had found him lying at the side of the road. 'But I was actually more worried about him after he left. With no memory of what had happened to him, I was afraid the man who'd shot him might still be out there waiting for him.'

'He was,' Lavinia said quietly. 'Thankfully, Nicholas was able to track him down and bring him to justice before he was able to harm anyone else. But you were very brave to do what you did. And to leave home like that.'

'It was hard in the beginning,' Sophie admitted. 'We were afraid one of our neighbours might have alerted the authorities, so after we left Bayencourt, we kept to the back roads and were careful not to draw attention to ourselves. We slept in barns, ate when and where we could. Once we reached Paris, it was easy to lose ourselves in the crowds. Eventually, Antoine managed to find accommodation for us over a small shop, and after working at a number of jobs, he was offered an apprenticeship with Monsieur Larocque.'

'How did you come to be employed by Mrs Grant-Ogilvy?' Lavinia asked.

Sophie's stomach clenched, the way it always did when that name was mentioned. 'I made a gown for the daughter of one of her friends. I remember sitting for hours at a time, handstitching hundreds of tiny beads to the bodice. When Mrs Grant-Ogilvy saw it, she asked to meet the girl who had done the work. As it happens, she was also looking for someone to teach her daughters how to speak French, so I was hired to do both.'

'How long were you with her?'

'Just over a year. I left just before her eldest daughter married.' Sophie decided to keep her other reason for leaving to herself. She had no desire to talk about Eldon. Eldon, with his grasping hands and hot liquored breath...

'Well, it was certainly a valuable association for you,' Lavinia said. 'It explains how you came to speak English so well and to carry yourself with such grace. I'm quite sure you will be married before the end of the Season.'

Mon Dieu, that word again. 'Lavinia, I meant what I said about not wishing to find a husband,' Sophie said slowly. 'I know this may sound strange, but I would like to open a shop.'

'A shop? You mean…you wish to be in *trade*?'

The look of abject horror on Lavinia's face made Sophie laugh. 'Oh, Lavinia, it's not that bad. I'm a very good seamstress and I have a definite talent for design. I want to make clothes for ladies who can't afford the expensive *ateliers* of Paris.'

'But if you were married, you wouldn't *need* to work,'

Lavinia pointed out. 'You would be able to lead the life of a lady and you would have the respect of society—'

'But not the independence,' Sophie said. 'I would be subject to my husband's whims. Forever at his beck and call, with nothing to call my own. That is not how I wish to live my life.'

'But you are so very beautiful, Sophie,' Lavinia said, trying to make her understand. 'You saw how popular you were tonight.'

'What I saw were ladies far more accomplished than myself dancing with gentlemen of wealth and breeding in a world familiar to them both. That isn't *my* world, Lavinia. And no gentleman of good family is going to bother with an unsophisticated French girl like me.'

'Let me tell you something, Sophia Chantal Vallois,' Lavinia said quietly. 'The young lady I've come to know is not in the least unsophisticated. She is a beautiful young woman who is going to make a lot of men fall in love with her, and when *she* finds the right man, she is going to find out that being loved by him is the sweetest pleasure of all.'

Sophie's mouth twisted. 'I will tell you if it happens.'

'You won't have to.' Lavinia stood up, her face breaking into a smile. 'Your face will say it all.'

Chapter Five

❦

'So, did you meet anyone at Lady Bruxton's ball with whom you would like to further an acquaintance?' Robert asked his sister as he turned the landau towards Eaton Place the following afternoon.

Jane, who was looking exceedingly stylish in a deep maroon gown with a new cream-and-maroon bonnet, pulled a face. 'Not a one—and please do not suggest I encourage Mr Hemmings. He is surely the most tiresome man on earth.'

'What about Sir Bartholomew Grout?'

'For pity's sake, Robert. Even wearing spectacles, the man is constantly tripping over his own feet. I need someone sturdier than that lest we both find ourselves on the ground half the time. And though I spoke to him for almost ten minutes, he did not smile at me once!'

'A most grievous offence, I'm sure,' Robert said as he drew up before the Longworths' town house.

'It was to me,' Jane said. 'And I suspect it would be to you as well.'

'Thankfully, I'm not keeping a list of anyone's good or bad points at the moment.'

'Well, you should. That way when the right lady comes along, you will be prepared.'

Robert secured the reins. 'Fine. When she appears, I shall be sure to make a note of how many times she makes me smile.'

'Odious man!' Jane said, though she was quick to laugh. 'Perhaps you are better off with a mistress. I don't suppose it matters how many times *she* makes you smile, since smiling is not the purpose of the association.'

It was an outrageous remark for an unmarried girl to make even to her older brother, but to be made within hearing of a gentleman with whom she had no acquaintance at all was as grievous a social error as a young lady could commit. Robert glanced at the darkly handsome gentleman standing at the bottom of the steps and realised his sister had just committed an unforgivable *faux-pas* in front of Antoine Vallois.

'Oh, dear,' Jane said, clearly not sure whether to laugh or to beg an apology. 'That was extremely bad timing. I hope, sir, that you will forgive my unfortunate choice of words. My poor brother is used to such outbursts, but I fear the general public is not.'

The gentleman walked slowly towards the carriage. 'Perhaps I should claim not to have heard the remark, *mademoiselle*. That would, I expect, be the more gentlemanly thing to do.' He looked at Robert and nodded. 'We meet again, Mr Silverton.'

'Mr Vallois,' Robert said, his voice clipped. 'Allow me to introduce my sister, Jane. And while I should offer an apology for what she just said, I doubt she would thank me for doing so.'

'I most certainly would not,' Jane said tartly. 'Pray do not fear that I am always so outspoken, Mr Vallois, but Robert and I were discussing the importance of a smile in the early stages of courtship. I took leave to disagree with him in the way brothers and sisters so often do.'

The gentleman inclined his head. 'I understand perfectly. I'm sure Sophie has often despaired of me in such a way.'

'I have never despaired of you, Antoine. If anything, it is the other way around.'

Drawn by the sound of her voice, Robert glanced up to see Miss Vallois standing in the doorway. She looked radiant in a pale blue gown, her silvery blond hair tucked up under a fetching straw bonnet, her blue eyes bright with anticipation. She looked as fresh and as appealing as spring itself, but with a sensuality that seemed strangely at odds with her innocence. Robert found it a very disturbing combination. 'Good afternoon, Miss Vallois.'

'Mr Silverton.'

'*Bonjour*, dear Miss Vallois!' Jane cried. 'Haven't we a splendid afternoon for our drive?'

'We have indeed,' Miss Vallois said as she approached the carriage. 'And what a fine pair of horses you drive, Mr Silverton. So perfectly matched, even to the flash of white on their faces.'

'Robert is most particular about his cattle,' Jane said. 'Aren't you, Robert?'

'No more so than any other gentleman.' Robert jumped down from the seat. 'A well-matched pair is always to be preferred.'

'In horses and in marriage, I dare say,' Jane said. 'Which means I must marry a lame man. Isn't that so, Mr Vallois?'

His reaction was one of mild confusion. 'I cannot imagine why you would think so, Miss Silverton. You must marry as your heart dictates.'

'Ah, but my heart is not free to choose. Were I to fall in love with a prince, I should expect to be disappointed, for he would not turn a kindly eye towards me,' Jane said, her unaffected smile stealing the gravity from her words. 'Like Mr Oberon, he would wish his lady to be perfect in all ways.'

'Then I could only think the prince, like Mr Oberon, a fool,' Mr Vallois replied quietly.

Robert was astonished to see his unflappable sister momentarily at a loss for words, but the lapse was brief and, quickly recovering, she patted the vacant seat beside her. 'How droll you are, *monsieur*. I insist you come and sit next to me. It will give me an opportunity to show you that I am not as gauche as you must surely believe me to be.'

The gentleman inclined his head. 'It would be my pleasure to sit beside you, *mademoiselle*, but I will not be joining you this afternoon.'

'Why ever not? Surely your sister told you that you were included in the invitation.'

'I did,' Miss Vallois said, 'but unbeknownst to me, Antoine and Lord Longworth had already made other plans.'

'*Quel dommage.*' Jane studied Mr Vallois thoughtfully for a moment. 'I understand you are not staying long in London. I would regret not having an opportunity to show you that there is a more refined side to my nature.'

'I have no doubt you possess as refined a nature as any other young lady, Miss Silverton.'

'But she does smile a great deal more,' Robert said drily. 'Though whether that is to recommend her, I cannot say.'

'I would consider it a recommendation,' Mr Vallois said. Then, speaking quietly in rapid French, he added, '*Qu'est-ce qui est plus doux que le sourire d'une belle dame?*'

Robert watched his sister's cheeks go bright pink and turned to glare at Antoine. 'Forgive me, sir, but if you wish to converse with my sister, I would ask that you do so in English.'

'But he said nothing impertinent, Robert.' Jane's smile was as bright as a new penny. 'In fact, I do believe it is one of the nicest things anyone has ever said to me. *Merci beaucoup, Monsieur Vallois.*'

'*De rien.*' Mr Vallois held her gaze a moment longer before addressing Robert. 'Please accept my apology, Mr Silverton. It was not my intention to offend. Only to express an opinion that a beautiful lady's smile is truly a lovely thing to behold.' He touched the brim of his hat. 'Enjoy your afternoon.'

Robert stiffly inclined his head. He knew his feelings of resentment towards the French were not shared by his sister, but the strength of his conviction was such that he could not be happy about seeing her offered a compliment by one, especially one as handsome as Antoine Vallois. A man she barely knew, but who had the ability to make her blush. Damn his charming ways.

'Mr Silverton?'

And now the sister sought to distract him. He turned to see her watching him with those perceptive blue eyes, the question on her face a direct result of the confrontation that had just taken place. Had she guessed at the nature of his thoughts? Figured out that his hostility towards her brother stemmed from a natural antipathy towards her countrymen? Judging from the way her smile dimmed as he handed her into the carriage, she knew something was amiss. But he wasn't about to let it trouble him. For Jane's sake, he would be pleasant, but that was all. He wasn't looking for a wife and he certainly had no intention of making the exquisite Miss Vallois his mistress.

She had made it perfectly clear at the Black Swan Inn that she'd prefer the company of the *horses* rather than have anything to do with him.

Sophie knew they weren't off to a promising start. After settling her in the seat beside his sister, Mr Silverton had climbed back into the driver's seat, picked up the reins and set the team off without a word. It wasn't that he was rude, simply that he was distant. And whether *that* was a result of the stilted conversation he'd just had with Antoine, or of *her* unwelcome presence in the carriage, Sophie had no idea. All she knew was that the tension was as sharp as a finely honed blade—and that it cut with equal facility.

Fortunately, Miss Silverton, with her delightful sense of humour, tried to lighten the mood by alternately paying her brother no mind, or teasing him to distraction. 'I keep telling Robert that he needs to get on with his life before he becomes a doddering old fool no woman is interested in,' she confided as they drove through the gates into the Park, 'but he refuses to listen. He simply tells me I must find a husband and settle down. But really, Miss Vallois, at eight-and-twenty, what gentleman is going to look at me with marriage in mind? I do not have sufficient wealth to make up for the loss of my youth or agility—'

'Jane—'

'And now he is going to scold me for having suggested that my handicap stands in the way of my making a good marriage. He believes it does not, but you and I know better.'

'On the contrary,' Sophie said, 'I watched you at the ball last evening and though you did not dance, you got around very well in all other respects.'

'There, you see, Jane,' Mr Silverton said over his shoulder. 'Miss Vallois has not known you above a day, yet she is already of the opinion that your leg is not the handicap you claim it to be.'

'I wonder.' Miss Silverton sent a sidelong glance at Sophie. 'What would your brother say about my handicap, Miss Vallois? He is studying to be a doctor, after all, and is likely to be less emotional about such things.'

'I would venture to say it is the *last* thing Antoine would concern himself with,' Sophie said without hesitation. 'He is far more interested in how people think than with their physical appearance.'

'In which case, he and Oberon have absolutely nothing in common,' Mr Silverton muttered.

'Apart from their looks, for Mr Vallois is certainly as handsome as Mr Oberon,' Miss Silverton said, though she was careful to maintain the correct degree of indifference. 'He must be very popular with the ladies in Paris.'

'Perhaps, though none seem to have made a lasting impression.' Then, refusing to be ignored by Mr Silverton any longer, Sophie said in a voice loud enough for him to hear, 'Like your brother, Antoine is far more concerned with my well-being than he is with his own.'

She saw his back stiffen, but he did not turn around. 'I am adequately concerned with my own well-being, Miss Vallois. It simply takes less looking after than Jane's.'

'No doubt because you are a man and men are so much more self-sufficient than women.'

There was a brief but significant pause. 'Are you trying to provoke me?'

'Yes, I suppose I am,' Sophie said calmly. 'But not unkindly, I hope.'

'That depends. You should be aware that I give as good as I get.'

'Then I shall consider myself warned,' Sophie said, settling back against the cushions with a smile of satisfaction. Well, it was a start. His posture seemed slightly less rigid than it had been when they'd started out, and his tone was a fraction less chilly. If it was an unguarded moment, she hoped there could be more. Miss Silverton, who was blissfully unaware of the milestone, said, 'It must be the way of older brothers to think of everyone else before themselves. It certainly makes sisters seem a great deal of bother.'

Mr Silverton glanced back at her, and Sophie was surprised to see that he could actually smile. 'You are not a bother, as well you know.'

'Yes, but I do enjoy teasing you. Do you tease your brother in such a way, Miss Vallois?'

'Whenever I get the chance.' Sophie turned her head, her eyes narrowing slightly as she gazed across the field. 'Is that Mr Oberon I see riding towards us?'

'It would appear so.' Mr Silverton sounded less than pleased. 'I wondered if he might turn up this afternoon.'

'He rides a magnificent horse.'

'Magnificent he may be, but you would do well to keep your distance. That beast is hellfire on four legs.'

Sure enough, a few minutes later, the peer's son brought the showy black stallion to a prancing, snorting halt in front of them. 'Afternoon, all,' he called in greeting. 'What a glorious day.'

'Oberon,' Mr Silverton said, reluctantly bringing the carriage to a halt.

'Silver. Miss Silverton. And Miss Vallois. What a delightful surprise.'

'Surely not that much of a surprise, sir,' Sophie said

sweetly. 'You were there when I informed Mr Silverton of my intention to join him and Miss Silverton this afternoon.'

'True, but in a city as large as London, there are so many other places you could have gone.'

The stallion suddenly shied and Mr Oberon made a great show of restraining him.

'Oh, Robert, isn't he splendid,' Miss Silverton said softly.

Sophie knew Jane was referring to the horse, but Mr Oberon chose to take the remark as a compliment to himself. 'Thank you, Miss Silverton. Years of experience allow a man a certain ease in the saddle.' He smiled broadly, white teeth flashing. 'What about it, Silver— care to take a turn?'

Mr Silverton's smile was coolly dismissive. 'Thank you, no.'

'Rather wait for the pleasure of ownership, eh?' Mr Oberon winked. 'I understand. But we've yet to see how that game plays out. Miss Vallois, I hope we will have the pleasure of your company at Lady White's this evening.'

It was the first Sophie had heard of it. 'I don't know. Lady Longworth has made no mention of it.'

'Oh, but you must come,' Miss Silverton implored. 'An evening spent with Lady White is a treat unto itself. Robert and I are going. You and your brother really should join us.'

'Lady Longworth may already have made other plans.'

'Cancel them,' Mr Oberon said. 'I guarantee you'll have a better time with us.'

Sophie glanced up into the man's impossibly beautiful face and found herself resenting both his high-handed assumption that she would naturally fall in with his plans and his belief that an outing of *his* choosing would be more enjoyable than one of Lavinia's. She almost hoped Lavinia *had* made other arrangements. 'I shall enquire upon returning home, Mr Oberon. If we are free, I may mention it to Lady Longworth.'

'I can ask no more than that. And now, I must be off. Like the god, Thunder grows impatient if forced to stand in one place too long.' As if to prove it, the stallion reared up, its powerful front legs slicing the air, his high, shrill whinny echoing through the park.

'Easy, boy,' Mr Oberon said, bringing him back under control. 'Wouldn't want to alarm the ladies.' He touched the brim of his hat to Mr Silverton and his sister, then smiled affectionately at Sophie, his eyes lingering on her longer than was necessary or appropriate.

Sophie turned away. Odious man. What a shame that one so blessed in appearance should be so lacking in humility. For all his chilly reserve, she much preferred Robert Silverton's quiet manners to Mr Oberon's smug arrogance…

'What are you thinking, Miss Vallois?' Mr Silverton enquired as the other man trotted away. 'You suddenly look far too serious for such a lovely afternoon.'

'Only that certain gentlemen have been given so much, yet appear to do so little good with it.'

'Oh, but that's splendid!' Miss Silverton said, clapping her hands. 'I do believe you have just given Monty a set-down and he would be devastated to hear it, knowing how taken he is with you.'

'Nonsense, we are barely acquainted,' Sophie said, uncomfortably aware of Mr Silverton's gaze on her. 'Besides, he is far too flamboyant for my liking.'

'But he is rich,' Miss Silverton said. 'And his country estate is said to rival Chatsworth for opulence. You could do much worse.'

'Leave the poor girl alone, Jane,' her brother said. 'Or she will regret having agreed to come out with us.'

'She will not resent me for telling her the facts. The more she knows before having to make the decision, the better off she will be.'

'The decision?' Sophie asked.

'As to whom you will marry, of course. What other decision of importance is there for a single lady of marriageable age?'

'I can think of several,' Sophie said, less than pleased with the direction the conversation was taking. 'Fortunately, the choice of a husband will not be one of them.'

Miss Silverton gave a soft laugh. 'Do tell! Are you already engaged to a handsome young gentleman in Paris?'

'I am not, nor have I any desire to be. I've already told Lord and Lady Longworth that I have no intention of marrying.'

The remark must have been more outrageous than Sophie thought. Miss Silverton's mouth fell open and her brother actually turned around on the seat to stare at her. 'No intention of marrying?'

'But…what will you do?' his sister asked. 'Marriage is the only viable option to ladies of good birth.'

To ladies of good birth. What would they say, Sophie wondered, if they knew the truth of hers? 'I like to think there are many other things a lady might do. Fly over London in a hot-air balloon, for example. Or travel to Egypt on a camel to explore the pyramids. Float down the Amazon in a boat. When you think about it, the possibilities are endless.'

'For a man, perhaps,' Mr Silverton observed. 'Not for a woman.'

'But do you not wish to fall in love, Miss Vallois?' Miss Silverton asked.

'Not particularly.' Sophie thought about the men she had met in the course of her life. All of them had let her down in one way or another. 'Only think how disastrous it would be to fall in love with someone like…Mr Oberon.'

'I'm not sure a woman *can* fall in love with a man like that,' Mr Silverton said. 'He will always be the more demanding of the couple, and if the lady is like the rest of her sex, she will be far more interested in *receiving* love than in giving it.'

Had he intended it as a slight? Sophie wondered. Or was he simply expressing his opinion that, on the whole, women tended to be the more selfish creatures? 'I take leave to disagree with you, Mr Silverton. Women are capable of both giving and receiving love, oftimes at their own expense. A mother will always sacrifice much for her child, whereas a man will often take his pleasures at the expense of the family.'

He directed a glance over his shoulder. 'Your remark leads me to believe that you do not hold men in high esteem.'

'Only in as much as your remark leads me to believe that you hold women in contempt. Not all women are self-serving.'

'Then you have the pleasure of knowing better women than I.'

Wondering if he was thinking of the woman who was to have been his wife, Sophie said, 'Perhaps you expect too much of the ladies with whom you keep company.'

'If honesty is too much to expect, then I must enter a guilty plea,' he said. 'As for being single past my sister's expectations, she neglected to mention that our family circumstances have been such that neither of us has been free to mingle in society these past few years.'

'Indeed we have not,' Miss Silverton said, a cloud settling on her pretty features. 'First Michael was killed in France, then Papa died under the most tragic of circumstances, and not a twelvemonth later, we lost Mama as well. How can anyone think of love when grief is so fresh upon the heart?'

'Perhaps it is in the finding of love that the pain of grief eases,' Sophie said gently. 'One cannot suffer from two such strong emotions at the same time.'

'I wish that were the case, Miss Vallois,' Mr Silverton said. 'But I have learned that a person *can* suffer more than one painful emotion at a time and feel them both with equal strength.'

'Love cannot exist in the presence of hate, Mr Silverton,' she told him.

'But hate can raise its ugly head when love is threatened or destroyed.' He turned to look at her, and for a moment, it was as though there were only the two of them. 'Of that, Miss Vallois,' he said, 'I am entirely certain.'

To Sophie's relief, the rest of the carriage ride proceeded with all felicity and it concluded with the parties being in relatively good spirits. Miss Silverton had begged Sophie to call her Jane, and said how much she was looking forward to seeing Sophie and her brother at Lady White's for cards that evening.

Fortunately, upon arriving home, Sophie discovered that no plans had been made for the evening, and when she put forward the idea of attending a soirée at Lady White's, Lavinia declared that she could not think of a more entertaining way to pass a few hours.

'Lady White is, of course, the very *essence* of eccentricity,' Lavinia said, as the two sat in Sophie's bedroom going through her wardrobe to see what she might wear. 'Her husband died six years ago and left her a very wealthy widow.' She pulled out two gowns and laid them on the bed. 'She must be in her mid-sixties now, but she still rides to hounds every year. Strange. I don't remember ordering this peacock-blue silk from Madame Delors.'

Sophie glanced up. 'You didn't. I made it and brought it with me.'

'You *made* this?' Lavinia took a closer look. 'But…

this is exquisite, Sophie. The gathering along here and the beadwork down the front is quite remarkable. And the fabric is exceptional—and very expensive.'

'I know. A lady bought it for her daughter, but when the daughter didn't like it, the mother bought something else and told me I could keep the silk as payment. But if you'd rather me wear the muslin—'

'No, no, the blue will look marvellous against your complexion,' Lavinia said, putting the cream gown aside. 'Perhaps I *should* let you make your own gowns. This is every bit as good as what we get from Madame Delors, and unlike her, you really are French. However, getting back to Lady White, you should know that besides being unconventional, she is the very devil at cards. I have played with her countless times and have yet to win more than a dozen hands.'

'Don't tell me she cheats?' Sophie said in delight.

'Outrageously, but she does it so well it is nearly impossible to catch her at it. Is Antoine going with you?'

'He told me he was.' Sophie's smile widened. He hadn't intended to—until he'd heard that Jane Silverton was also going to be there. Then he had suddenly changed his mind and agreed that a card party given by an eccentric hostess would make for a highly diverting evening. He might have missed the carriage ride, but it seemed the lady had intrigued him enough that he was not about to miss a second opportunity to spend time with her.

For that, Sophie decided she could put up with Robert

Silverton's reserve, Mr Oberon's arrogance and the slight-of-hand dealings of their hostess for as long as was necessary.

Chapter Six

Lady White was, in all respects, an Original. Thin as a rail, she wore unrelieved black against which her snowy white hair appeared wonderfully dramatic. Her lips and cheeks were heavily rouged and she wore a heart-shaped patch next to her mouth. She was also draped in a king's ransom worth of diamonds and gold.

'My husband always said jewellery was meant to be worn,' Lady White explained as she strolled arm in arm with Sophie and Antoine through the elegant rooms of her town house. 'And at my age, I'm not sure how much longer I'll be around to show it off. Best do it now while I still have a skeleton to hang it on!'

Then she laughed. Not the delicate tittering of a society matron, but the full-bodied laugh of a woman who enjoyed life. Sophie liked her immensely.

'Tell me, how is it I haven't seen you before, Miss Vallois?' Lady White asked. 'You're far too beautiful to be missed. The young men can scarcely stop gawking at you.'

Sophie laughed, moved to wonder if she had been singled out for the lady's special brand of attention or if she spoke this bluntly to everyone. 'Thank you, my lady, but my brother and I are only recently arrived in England.'

'Ah, yes, to stay with the Longworths. Excellent family. I knew Nicholas as a boy. Devil of a lad. Always falling into some kind of scrape or another, but he turned out well enough. And dear Lavinia. Such a charming woman. You don't see love like theirs very often. It's all about money and land now. Women marry for social position and men to beget an heir. Oh, get away with you, Walter!' Lady White said when a gentleman ventured too close. 'Miss Vallois isn't interested in you.'

As the crestfallen youth slunk away, Lady White whispered in Sophie's ear, 'A second son with four unmarried sisters. Definitely not the type of suitor you wish to encourage. Unlike this fine strapping young man beside you.' Lady White raised her lorgnette and peered at Antoine through the lens. 'Lud, but you're a fine-looking man. Why ain't you married?'

The question could have been offensive, but Antoine just laughed. 'I have been involved in my studies, my lady.'

'To be a doctor.'

'Yes.'

'Quite an occupation. Constantly surrounded by the sick and dying.' Lady White shuddered. 'Haven't the stomach for it myself, but thank God there are those who do.' She stopped to touch the patch next to her mouth. 'They don't train doctors the same way in France as they do here.'

'I understand there are differences, yes.'

'But the body's the same, is it not? Whether one finds oneself on this side of the Channel or the other.'

'I've always thought so,' Antoine said with a straight face. 'But not having examined any bodies on this side of the Channel, I cannot say for certain.'

Lady White stared at him for a moment, then burst out laughing. 'By God, I like the cut of your jib. If I was forty years younger, I'd give these young fillies a run for their money. In fact, I still might.' She gave him an audacious wink. 'Think about it, lad. I've money enough to keep us both in the style to which a handsome young buck like you should be accustomed.'

Sophie glanced at her brother, half-expecting to see him make a bolt for the door. Instead, he bowed and said, 'You do me a considerable honour, Lady White, but I fear I must decline.'

'Yes, I thought you might. The good ones always do. Still, I hope you'll play cards with me.' She rapped him on the chest with her fan. 'I've a mind to find out if your wits are as sharp as your looks.'

'I would be delighted.' Then, in a courtly gesture that was years out of date, Antoine took the lady's hand and raised it to his lips. *'Je suis très heureux de faire votre connaisance, madame. Vous êtes une Originale.'*

Lady White blinked, and then to Sophie's surprise, her eyes filled with tears. 'Oh, you wretched boy. Now you've gone and made an old lady cry and I may never forgive you for that.' She drew a handkerchief from her reticule and dabbed at her eyes. 'But bless you for having had the kindness to say so.' She blew her nose, tucked her hankie behind her fan and then, with a smile and another loud sniff, moved off to greet her other guests.

'Goodness, Antoine, you may wish to think carefully before rejecting her offer,' Sophie whispered. 'You would never have to work again if you agreed to become her—'

'Thank you, Sophie, I think the less said about it, the better.' But clearly the idea of becoming the *cher ami* of such a woman was more than even Antoine could keep a straight face for, and after a moment, they both burst out laughing.

They were still chucking about it a few minutes later when Robert and Jane Silverton came over to join them. 'What are you two having such a jolly time about?' Jane asked.

'Lady White,' Sophie said. 'You were right in saying she is a treat. She says what she thinks and worries about it later.'

'I'm not so sure she does worry,' Mr Silverton said. 'I don't think she cares a whit what anyone thinks.'

'Well, *I* think she's marvellous,' Sophie said. 'You have to admire a woman who has the courage to speak her mind.'

'Even though society is likely to condemn her for doing so?'

Sophie slowly turned to look at him. As always, Mr Silverton was impeccably turned out. His double-breasted coat, cut square across the front and decorated with a row of gilt buttons, fit him to perfection. Beneath that, a fine cambric shirt clung to a broad chest and around his neck, a perfectly tied, perfectly white linen cravat. A powerful man, in the civilised clothes of a gentleman. Were his thoughts a reflection of the same?

'It takes courage to fly in the face of convention, Mr Silverton,' Sophie said. 'Especially in a society so rigid about what it will and will not allow.'

'Are you saying French society is more lenient than English?'

'No. I'm just saying that in general, women do not benefit from its strictures. The only women who possess any kind of freedom are those who are titled in their own right, independently wealthy or widowed. It seems very unfair.'

'Well said, Miss Vallois,' Jane said with approval.

'And you, Miss Silverton?' Antoine asked. 'Do you mind being criticised?'

'One always minds to a certain degree, but fortunately, I am not as closely scrutinised as others. My affliction absents me from the rest of the pack.'

Antoine glanced at the cane in her hand. 'How did you come by your injury?'

'An unfortunate childhood accident. A badly broken foot even more badly set.'

'But it does not prevent you from getting about.'

'Nothing could do that,' she told him. 'I am most determined when I set my mind to something.'

'I can vouch for that,' Mr Silverton said. 'Shall we play cards?'

Sophie wasn't sure how it happened, but a few minutes

later, she found herself at a whist table, partnered with Robert Silverton against Lady White and a young lady by the name of Miss Penelope Green. Antoine and Jane had moved away to play vingt-et-un at another table.

'I hope your brother is skilled at cards, Miss Vallois,' Mr Silverton said as the hand was dealt. 'My sister is a Captain Sharp of the female variety.'

'Antoine plays well enough,' Sophie said, picking up her cards. 'It is my skills as a partner you may find lacking.'

'Nothing to it, my dear.' Lady White raised her arm, causing a battery of bracelets to jangle. 'You simply try to take as many tricks as you can by remembering which cards have already been played. That's why I like this game. It requires the use of one's brain. I'm not sure you young whelps know how to do that.'

Sophie said nothing, but when she raised her eyes and met Mr Silverton's over the top of her cards, she saw that he was grinning broadly. 'I shall endeavour to do my best, Lady White.'

'You'll have to if you expect to escape this table unscathed.' Lady White turned up a card. 'Hearts are trump. Your lead, Mr Silverton.'

Over the course of the evening, Robert learned quite a few things about Miss Sophie Vallois. He learned that while she was blessed with beauty and refinement, she also had a lively sense of humour and a tendency towards speaking her mind. He learned that when she was silent, it was not because she could think of nothing to say, but because she preferred to weigh her words before offering them up for public discussion. She never forced herself into a conversation, but when asked a question, responded with wit and intelligence. In short, it was hard to find anything to criticise about the lady, yet he still found himself maintaining a distance.

'Are you enjoying your time in London, Miss Vallois?' he asked after Lady White and Miss Green had excused themselves to partake of refreshments.

'I am. It is, of course, very different to the life Antoine and I lead in France.'

Assuming she referred to the customs and language of the two countries, Robert said, 'Have you always lived in Paris?'

'Only for the last two years. Before that I lived near Bayencourt.'

'I'm not familiar with the town.'

'It's a small village in the north of France. My father was born there.'

'And your mother?'

'In Provence.' Miss Vallois smiled. 'Mama always said she would never move to the north, but when she met my father, that was that. I went to Provence with her when I was ten and liked it very much. The lavender fields were beautiful.'

Robert nodded, picturing a young girl running through the lush purple fields. He imagined a slender figure in a white dress, with silver-blond hair flying out behind and laughter ringing across the fields. It made for an engaging scene. 'You speak English exceptionally well for someone who's never been outside France,' he observed.

'I was employed for some time by an English lady who hired me to teach French to her daughters. In turn, I was tutored in English with particular emphasis on pronunciation and diction. I was forbidden to roll my r's, drop my h's, or say *zat* instead of that. The lady was something of a...' She looked to him for help. 'A *termagant*?'

'A termagant.' Robert smiled. 'Yes, it is the same in both languages.' So, she had been a governess. That, he supposed, explained her polished manners and her refined way of speaking. 'I would venture to say if their French is half as good as your English, you did an exceptional job.'

Miss Vallois wrinkled her nose. 'I fear I did not. The eldest daughter was not interested in learning the language and took pains to tell me so on a regular basis. But the younger one was very sweet and more than made up for her sister's deficiencies.' She looked at him with renewed interest. 'Have you ever been to France, Mr Silverton?'

The question stabbed at his heart. 'Briefly. I held a commission in the cavalry, but sold it when my eldest brother was killed.'

'Yes, I'm so sorry. I cannot imagine what that must have been like,' Miss Vallois said. 'If I were to lose Antoine, it would be like losing a part of myself. I don't know that I would ever feel whole again.'

Robert stared at her, aware that in a few simple sentences, she had summed up exactly how he'd felt at the time of Michael's death. He'd been shattered, his world cast into darkness by the death of the one person he'd been closer to than anyone else. 'There are still times I don't feel whole. Even now, when I walk into a room, I expect to see Michael there. To be able to walk up to him and laugh over some amusing and totally inconsequential event.'

'Were you close growing up?'

'Inseparable. He was only two years older than me so we shared many of the same interests. He taught me how to ride and he was there when I took my first bad spill in the field.' Robert's mouth twisted. 'It was my first time hunting and, caught up in the excitement, I tried to take a gate at full tilt. I don't remember hitting the ground, but I remember Michael picking me up and carrying me back to the house. He called for the surgeon and stayed with me while my arm was set.'

'That must have been painful.'

'It was, but it hurt a great deal less than my father's indifference.' Robert tried to keep the resentment from his voice. '*He* was more concerned about my horse. Said I could have ruined a prime bit of blood. I wanted to lash out, but Michael put his hand on my good arm and said it wasn't worth it. Told me I'd only regret it in the morning. And, as always, he was right.' Robert stopped, swallowing hard. 'I never expected Michael to die in the war. When the letter came informing us that he'd been killed, I thought it must be a mistake. I didn't want to believe it. To me he was…indestructible.'

'I don't think we ever really believe that someone we love will fall. I suppose that's the best part of the human spirit,' Miss Vallois said. 'The unshakeable belief that the worst will never happen to us or to those we care about. I sometimes wonder if we would venture into the unknown at all if we did not hold that belief true.'

'Indeed. We are fragile in body, yet indomitable in spirit,' Robert murmured. 'And how fortunate that is the case.'

He hadn't expected her to reach out. But when he felt the gentle pressure of her hand on his arm and looked up to see compassion in the depths of those remarkable blue eyes, he knew the sympathy she offered wasn't feigned. Whatever she thought about him as a person was secondary to her need to offer reassurance and warmth. He found that strangely comforting.

'Ah, Silver, thought I'd find you here,' Oberon said, blundering in and destroying the mood. 'And Miss Vallois. I'm so pleased you decided to heed my advice and come.'

'Mr Oberon.' The lady slowly withdrew her hand. Robert was surprised at how keenly he felt its loss. 'As it turned out, Lady Longworth had not made other plans and agreed that it would make for a pleasant evening.'

'Excellent. The company is not always the best, but the variety of entertainments more than makes up for it.' Oberon put his hand on the back of her chair and leaned down to whisper, 'I hope you received the small floral tribute I sent to the house.'

A delicate pink blush stained her cheeks. 'Yes, the roses were beautiful, thank you.'

'My pleasure. They will always pale in comparison to you, of course, but I wanted you to have a token of my affection and esteem.'

Robert drummed his fingers on the table. So, Oberon

had already begun sending gifts. He should have known. The wolf would waste no time in getting the hunt underway. Damn him.

'And how fares your luck at the tables tonight, Silver?' Oberon asked, straightening. 'You should know, Miss Vallois, that Silver has the luck of the Irish when it comes to cards. In fact, he's something of a legend in the gambling hells of London. There's not many who'll wager against him.'

'It's all in the turn of the card,' Robert said, his voice cool. 'Most games are pure luck.'

'Speaking of luck, Butterworth was wondering how you were faring in that matter we were speaking of the other day.'

Robert purposely kept his eyes down. 'You should know better than to ask.'

'Fair enough. Are you going to ask me how I go on in *my* endeavours?'

'Which endeavours would those be, Mr Oberon?' Lady White demanded, returning to the card table. 'I'm sure we would all like to know.'

Oberon's mouth thinned. 'You'll forgive me, but they are of a private nature and not meant to be shared.'

'Then I wonder at you bringing them up at all. Especially in front of Miss Vallois, with whom you can have only the slightest of acquaintance.'

Robert reached for the deck of cards and slid them across the table. Point to Lady White. She obviously had no qualms about giving Oberon a set-down in front of others. Unfortunately, he was nothing if not adept at turning a floundering situation to his advantage. 'You are right to admonish me, Lady White. Miss Vallois, pray forgive my poor manners. Perhaps I can make it up to you by offering to take you to an entertainment tomorrow evening. I understand *Don Giovanni* is playing to great reviews at the Covent Garden Theatre.'

'The theatre!' Lady White said huffily. 'In my day, such things were not considered suitable entertainment for a young lady of refinement. Have you secured the Longworths' agreement to the outing?'

'Not yet, though I have no reason to believe Lady Longworth would withhold it,' Oberon said. 'I hear tell that as a girl, she saw Mary Robinson play Perdita and was much moved by the performance.'

'Of course she would be moved.' Lady White deftly shuffled the cards. 'Mrs Robinson gave an outstanding performance. Pity she was such a trollop. Made a complete fool of herself over the Prince, and he no better.' She cut the cards and began to deal. 'The theatre can offer a most enjoyable experience if the performers are worth their salt. My sister once entertained thoughts of a career on the stage. Nearly put my father in the grave. But she was very good at that sort of thing.'

'Acting, my lady?' Miss Vallois enquired. 'Or of provoking her father?'

The question was so unexpected that Robert burst out laughing. Even Lady White chortled. 'So, there is spirit beneath that pretty exterior. Good. I cannot abide humourless people. So, shall you go to the theatre with this rapscallion, do you think?'

Robert raised his head in time to see an impish smile

lift the corners of Miss Vallois's mouth. 'Yes, I think I shall. If Lady Longworth does not object.'

'I don't suppose she will if you take that handsome brother with you,' Lady White said. 'No doubt he would enjoy a good love story. He's the stuff of which they're made.'

Oberon was quietly fuming. 'I thought it would make a pleasant evening for Miss Vallois and myself,' he said stiffly.

'I'm sure you did. But if I were in Lady Longworth's shoes, I would much rather have Miss Vallois go with a large contingent of friends.' Lady White levelled a keen glance in Robert's direction. 'You should go too, Mr Silverton. Do you good to get out. And take that delightful sister with you.'

'I might just do that,' Robert said, beginning to enjoy himself. 'Jane adores the theatre.'

'Excellent. The more the merrier, eh, what?'

Robert risked a quick glance at Oberon, whose hopes for a romantic evening were now well and truly shattered, and tried not to laugh. 'As you say, Lady White. The more the merrier indeed.'

Not surprisingly, Lady White and Miss Green took four of the next five hands and though Robert knew the woman cheated, he couldn't bring himself to expose her. Not when he was so in charity with her for having totally disrupted Oberon's plans. He thought he would have been ambivalent about the man's intentions to court Miss Vallois, but the more time he spent with her, the more he realised how wasted she would be on such a man. A man without sensitivity or the capacity for love. A man to whom winning meant everything...

He heard a noise—and looked down to see that he had snapped the stem of his wineglass in two.

'Good Lord, Robert, whatever is the matter?' Jane asked, coming up to him. 'If looks could kill, there would be several dead bodies strewn about the floor. Or perhaps...just one,' she said, following the direction of his gaze. 'What has Oberon done now?'

'Nothing. I just don't care for his attentions towards Miss Vallois.'

'Are they inappropriate?'

'He has invited her to the theatre.'

'A trifle bold, but hardly reprehensible. Which play?'

'*Don Giovanni.*'

'Oh, how splendid! I've heard it is a very good performance.'

'Would you care to join us?'

'*Us?*'

'I plan on going as well.'

Jane looked at him in surprise. 'Surely that was not Mr Oberon's idea.'

'No. Lady White suggested we make up a party when Oberon was foolish enough to invite Miss Vallois in front of her.'

'I am amazed he would be so careless—or so obvious in his attentions.'

Intrigued, Robert said, 'Why should he not be obvious?'

'Because as lovely as Sophie is, I doubt she is well

enough born for his father's liking,' Jane said. 'I hear tell he is keeping a very close eye on his son, and on the ladies with whom he is keeping company.'

'I didn't think his father cared so long as Oberon married *someone*.'

'That may have been the case in the beginning, but Lady Jennings told me Lord Mannerfield is growing more and more concerned about his son's wayward nature,' Jane confided. 'He is afraid Monty will be trapped into marriage by some penniless fortune hunter who uses her wiles and her beauty to ensnare him. Word is he is hoping his son marries a title, or a lady with a fortune of her own, neither of which Sophie has.'

'That's true, but I'm not sure how much Oberon cares about that any more. He talks about her incessantly, and you and I both know how single minded he can be when it comes to getting something he wants.'

'But are you sure it's marriage he has in mind, Robert? After all, he was the one who initiated the mistress wager, and we both know he won't give up his stallion without a fight.'

'No, but he stands to lose a great deal more if he doesn't marry,' Robert said. 'And his conversations to this point lead me to believe he is considering Miss Vallois.'

'Well, unless she is secretly the daughter of a French count, I doubt his father will look kindly upon the match,' Jane said bluntly. 'You should do everyone a favour by finding out where she comes from. And if her birth is not what it should be, you should tell Mr Oberon she is not suitable to being his wife. Either that, or court the lady yourself.'

'I *beg* your pardon?'

'Well, why not? I've seen the way you look at her, Robert. And while she may not possess wealth or a title she has everything else a man could ask for in a wife.'

'Have you forgotten that she's not *looking* for a husband?' Robert said. 'She'd rather explore the pyramids in Egypt, or float down the Amazon on a raft.'

'Boat,' Jane said, laughing. 'And, no, I haven't forgotten, but you don't really think she's serious about that, do you?'

'Who knows? The French think differently than we do. But, even if I was interested, what have I to offer her? A tarnished reputation? The knowledge that she would be cut by good society if she were to associate with me? Higher-placed gentlemen than myself have left the country after being given the cut direct, and Oberon tells me Lady Mary is now thinking of suing me for breach of promise. That won't win me any allies.'

'Then *tell* people why you jilted her, Robert!' Jane implored. 'They can't forgive you if they don't know why you did it. I know Lady Mary isn't blameless or you would never have broken it off.'

No, he wouldn't, Robert acknowledged. But after overhearing a conversation between his then fiancée and several of her closest friends, the reasons had become painfully clear. Imagine telling people that your future sister-in-law was repulsive and fit only to live in an institution. Imagine coldly laying out your plans for removing her to the country so that you might never be in the same house at the same time. That was the nature of what he'd heard, and once he had, Robert had known he couldn't go through with it. As his wife, Mary would have had total control of the household and all who lived in it. If she'd wanted to make Jane's life miserable, she could have done so without argument from anyone.

And so, he had brought it to an end…and kept silent as to his reasons. He had no wish to denigrate Lady Mary in the eyes of society, but neither was he about to risk Jane being made to suffer for an error in *his* judgement.

'It doesn't matter,' he said. 'Better I be the one to deal with the fallout than her.'

Jane crossed her arms in annoyance. 'You are too good, Robert. You are in disgrace because of her.'

'Exactly. And if I was to show an interest in Miss Vallois now, she would be tarred with the same brush. Ignored by virtue of her association with me. She deserves a better chance at a future than that.'

'With whom? Your good friend, Montague Oberon?' Jane snapped. 'Seducer of woman and gambler par excellence?'

'That's enough, Jane,' Robert said. 'Cynicism doesn't become you.'

'And martyrdom doesn't become you!'

'I'm not trying to be a martyr. But if I am not willing to involve myself in Miss Vallois's life, I'm better off out of it.'

Robert glanced across the room to where Oberon and Sophie were engaged in a private conversation, and thought about what Jane had said.

Find out where she comes from; if her birth is not

what it should be, tell Oberon she is not suitable to be his wife.

Even if it was that simple, there were still consequences to making known such information. The first being the irreparable damage it would do to Sophie's reputation. If she was discovered to be low born, doors would be closed in her face. She would not be entertained by good society and her chances for making a good marriage would dry up faster than a puddle in the desert. He wasn't willing to inflict that on anyone.

Not even a French girl who didn't appear to like him all that well regardless.

Chapter Seven

The vestibule of the theatre was already buzzing by the time Sophie and Antoine arrived for the performance of *Don Giovanni* the following evening, but she had no trouble in picking out the figure of Mr Silverton in the crowd. He seemed to tower over those around him, his broad shoulders emphasised by the excellent cut of his evening jacket, his snowy white cravat arranged in simple but elegant folds. Mr Oberon stood closer to the door, equally well dressed, but with a superiority of manner that would always set him apart from lesser mortals. 'Ah, Miss Vallois,' he said, coming forwards to greet her. 'What a radiant vision you present. A most fitting tribute to this elegant temple.'

Sophie only just refrained from rolling her eyes. 'You are too kind, Mr Oberon. I think you remember my brother, Antoine?'

'Of course.' Oberon gave him a curt nod. 'I am so pleased you could join us.'

Antoine's greeting was equally cool. *'Mon plaisir.'*

'And here is Silverton come to add his sparkling wit,' Mr Oberon said. 'But where is Jane? I understood she was coming too.'

'Yes, here I am,' Jane called. 'I was just waiting for Lady Annabelle.'

It was then that Sophie noticed the exceedingly lovely young woman walking by Jane's side. She was taller and more slender than Jane, with perfect skin and finely formed features. Her hair was a shade of gold that glistened in the candlelight and her gown of pale pink satin was of the first stare. Pearls glowed warmly at her ears and throat, and her movements were blessed with effortless grace, making Sophie feel like an impostor at the ball—or a cuckoo in a nest of swans.

'I hope you don't mind,' Mr Silverton said, 'but I took the liberty of inviting Lady Annabelle Durst to join our party. Apparently she is very fond of Mr Scott's plays.'

'Not at all,' Mr Oberon said. 'How could we mind so beautiful a lady joining our party?'

'You are very kind, Mr Oberon,' Lady Annabelle said in a low, melodic voice. 'But when Mr Silverton and I met at Lady Chesterton's musicale this afternoon, he told me several of you were attending the performance this evening and I was bold enough to ask if I might come along. *Giovanni* is one of my favourite operas.'

'As it is mine,' Mr Oberon said. 'Pray allow me to make known the rest of the party to you, Lady Annabelle. This is Miss Sophie Vallois and her brother, Mr Antoine Vallois.'

Lady Annabelle nodded pleasantly at Sophie and then

turned to greet Antoine. 'Monsieur Vallois. I understand you and your sister are visiting from Paris. How long do you intend to stay?'

'My sister is remaining for the Season, but I am only here until next week.'

'What a shame. You will scarcely have time to see any of London's many attractions.'

'I will see as many as I can,' Antoine said, 'and let Sophie tell me about the rest when she returns.'

'I am sure she will do an excellent job, but it is never the same as seeing the sights for oneself. Would you not agree, Mr Silverton?'

'I've found that nothing is ever as good as experiencing life's pleasures first-hand, Lady Annabelle.'

When the two exchanged a smile, Sophie was astonished to feel a tiny pinprick of jealousy—a reaction that both shocked and troubled her. She had no feelings of affection for Mr Silverton. His conduct towards her had been anything but encouraging, and given that *her* plans did not include marriage, it made no sense that she should be jealous of the way he looked at another woman. But jealous she was, and the fact the two spoke to one another with such ease only heightened Sophie's awareness of being an outsider. Mr Silverton might have been cut by polite society, but he was still more a part of it than she would ever be.

A few minutes later, the party made its way up the sweeping staircase, stopping to admire the Ionic columns and the elegant Grecian lamps hanging from the ceiling. Sophie pretended to study the elaborate décor, but her eyes lingered more often on Mr Silverton and Lady Annabelle than they did on the gilt-covered wood-work. Mr Oberon might be the strutting peacock, but Mr Silverton was definitely the hawk, darkly handsome in black and white, his waistcoat embroidered with silver thread.

At the top of the stairs, prior to entering the ante-chamber, the party drew to a halt. Sophie noticed Jane cast a covert glance at Antoine, only to look away as her brother stepped forwards to take her arm. 'May I escort you in, Jane?'

'Yes, of course.' She placed her gloved hand lightly upon his arm. 'Thank you.'

Antoine, catching Sophie's eye, started in her direction, but was intercepted by Mr Oberon. 'Miss Vallois, I wonder if I might have the honour—'

And just as smoothly, *he* was intercepted by Lady Annabelle. 'Pray forgive the intrusion, Mr Oberon, but I really must ask Miss Vallois about her gown.' She stepped forwards and slipped her arm companionably through Sophie's. 'It is simply perfection. You must have brought it with you from Paris.'

'In fact, it is one of Madame Delors's designs,' Sophie said, relieved to see Mr Oberon step back.

'Madame Delors? I would never have guessed. I shall have to pay her a visit this very week,' Lady Annabelle said. 'Mama is insisting I have three new gowns made before the Wistermeyers' ball next month and I was at a loss to know where to go.'

And so, they proceeded into the box: Mr Oberon leading the way with Mr Silverton and Jane following,

Lady Annabelle and Sophie coming next, and Antoine
bringing up the rear. Fortunately, there was more than
enough room for the six of them to be seated comfort-
ably and for a few minutes there was jostling as everyone
selected their chairs. In the end, Antoine sat beside Jane
in the second row with Lady Annabelle on his right,
while Sophie sat in the front row between Mr Oberon
and Mr Silverton. And it truly was splendid. Slender
pillars heavily encrusted with gilt separated the boxes,
and from a bracket that extended over the top of each
pillar hung a glorious cut-glass chandelier.

Even more decorative than the trim, however, were
the ladies and gentlemen who occupied the boxes. Sophie
saw the flash of diamonds and rubies, heard the rustle
of expensive silks, and wondered how the crowds in the
two-shilling gallery must feel at seeing such wealth and
opulence all around them. There didn't look to be an
empty seat in the place.

'Do you like opera, Miss Vallois?' Mr Silverton
asked.

Sophie turned her head to smile at him. 'I really
cannot say, never having been to one before.'

'I remember seeing Edmund Kean play Shylock,' he
said. 'It was a stunning performance. Lady White is
correct when she says that much depends on the skill of
the performers.'

'If you don't mind, I would rather *not* hear Lady
White's name mentioned this evening,' Mr Oberon muttered. 'As far as I am concerned, the woman has already
said a great deal too much.'

Sophie quickly looked down, but not before catching

a flicker of a smile on Mr Silverton's face. Had his good spirits to do with Mr Oberon's antipathy, she wondered, or to the unexpected presence of the beautiful Lady Annabelle Durst?

A sudden flurry of activity in the box next to them heralded the arrival of a family well known to Mr Oberon, and when he excused himself to speak with them, Sophie took a moment to glance back at her brother and Jane. They were talking quietly between themselves, Jane looking young and carefree in a becoming gown of pale amethyst silk with clusters of violets tucked in her hair and a delicate strand of pearls around her throat. Her cheeks were unusually flushed, and when she laughed at something Antoine said, Sophie couldn't help but be aware of how happy they seemed to be in each other's company.

'Has your brother made any mention of when he is returning to France?' Mr Silverton asked quietly.

Sophie turned back to find his warm brown eyes fixed on her. 'He has not mentioned a particular day, though I believe he intends to leave next week.'

'He is dedicated to his profession.'

'He is dedicated to *learning* his profession. At the moment, he is apprenticed to a local surgeon and very grateful for the opportunity.'

'It can't be an easy life. Calls at all hours of the night. Injuries of a wide and often heart-wrenching nature. It takes a special kind of dedication to do what he does.'

'That, and a talent for healing,' Sophie admitted, thinking of some of the truly awful things Antoine had encountered. Filthy hospital wards. Soiled linens.

Unsanitary food. It was a wonder he hadn't contracted something himself. 'I am not so blessed.'

'Perhaps not in that area, but you have gifts aplenty in others.'

As if afraid of having said too much, Mr Silverton quickly turned away, but Sophie found her gaze lingering on his profile. Was it her imagination or did his voice seem warmer tonight? Several times he had made a point of touching her when they were together. Nothing to which she could object. A hand at her waist to guide her. A light touch on the arm to draw her attention to something she hadn't noticed. And sitting together here, she was very conscious of his thigh close to hers; of the heat of his body warming her through the thin fabric of her gown—

'—to become a doctor?'

Belatedly, Sophie realised he was asking her about Antoine. 'Forgive me, Mr Silverton, my mind was elsewhere.'

'I was just asking if your father approved of your brother's decision to become a doctor. It is not the usual choice of occupation for the eldest son.'

'No, and…Papa wasn't at all pleased.' Why was she so flustered all of a sudden? Heat was rising in waves, and even now, her heart was beating too fast. 'He…wanted Antoine to stay home and help in the fields.'

Mr Silverton smiled. 'The fields?'

'Yes.' Goodness, why hadn't she brought her fan with her? 'The idea was that…Antoine would take over once Papa got too old, but Antoine never had any interest in farming. Even as a boy he wanted to help people.'

Sophie was about to say more, when Lady Annabelle suddenly leaned forwards to whisper in her ear. 'Forgive my boldness, Miss Vallois, but I do believe your brother is rather taken with Miss Silverton. They seem to be caught up in their own little world.'

Sophie moved uneasily in her chair. Had Mr Silverton overheard the remark? She knew he wasn't fond of Antoine, in which case he wouldn't be pleased at the idea of Antoine and Jane striking up a friendship. 'Perhaps I should ask Jane to sit up here,' she said quickly, slanting a quick glance at Mr Silverton. 'The view of the stage is that much better.'

But he wasn't listening. He was staring straight ahead, his mouth grim, his brow furrowed as though deep in thought. Sophie bit her lip. Obviously, he *had* heard, and it was clear he wasn't pleased about it.

Fortunately, Lady Annabelle's laughter bubbled up like sparkling champagne. 'You can ask her, Miss Vallois, but I have a feeling that tonight, the company in the box has far more appeal for Miss Silverton than the play.'

Robert was dimly aware of the sounds swirling around him. Of Lady Annabelle's bell-like laughter. Of a low murmur of conversation from the box next to them. Of a whistling sound from the stage below. But none of it mattered because what Sophie had just told him caused everyone and everything else to fade into insignificance.

'*…Antoine never had any interest in farming…*'

How simple a statement, yet how utterly destructive…

because it meant Sophie was not well born. She was the daughter of a farmer, a man who laboured in the fields on someone else's land. Her skills with the language had been learned from an English woman who employed her to teach French to her daughters, and her manners and refinement were likely sprung from the same source. Apart from her stunning natural beauty, Sophie Vallois had absolutely nothing to recommend her. And the ramifications of that were inescapable.

Oberon would never consider taking her as a wife now. When he found out the truth, one of two things would happen. He would either stop paying attention to her and look for a well-bred lady to be his bride. Or, he would realise that the object of his obsession, now never to be his bride, would in fact make an enchanting mistress.

It was the latter possibility that had Robert gritting his teeth. Oberon was a master at seduction. He had dazzled lonely widows, shamelessly sweet-talked virgins, and skilfully compromised married women, all in the pursuit of his own pleasure. He didn't give a damn about reputations and once he knew marriage to Sophie was out of the question, his efforts would be aimed in an entirely different direction. He would pay court to her, much as he was doing now, but his *coup de grâce* would be an assignation rather than a proposal of marriage.

He would compromise her. One night was all it would take. One carriage ride into the darkness. And with her reputation in tatters, she would have no choice but to return to France, either to keep house for her brother or to find work in a rich man's home. Oberon might offer to set her up in the house he kept in Kensington for just such a purpose, but how long would it be before his interest in her waned and the next lovely face stepped forwards to take her place? To a man like that, the chase was always more exciting than the capture.

No, the damage was well and truly done. Sophie's unintentional slip had certainly cost her the coronet of viscountess. Only time would tell if it would jeopardize something more valuable.

Despite the undercurrents swirling around her, Sophie thoroughly enjoyed the performance of *Don Giovanni*. Its central character was the quintessential rake, a man who lived to seduce women, and it was his inability to settle on only one that eventually condemned him to an existence in hell. She alternately laughed and gasped, or held her breath in anticipation of the unrepentant Lothario's eventual descent into the underworld. Certainly the crowd seemed to enjoy it. Only once during a poorly enacted scene did a handful of orange peelings make their way on to the stage. Otherwise, the boisterous crowd heartily approved of the drama.

Only Mr Oberon appeared unmoved, his attention fixed more often on her than it was on the actors on the stage below.

'Are you not enjoying the performance, Mr Oberon?' Sophie asked when at last she could no longer ignore the intensity of his stare.

'I have seen the opera before, Miss Vallois, but it does not compare to the enjoyment I am having in watching you.'

'But surely your lack of attention dishonours the talent of the composer.'

'Nothing could do that. But in watching you, I see the joy of one who is hearing the music for the first time. That, in itself, is a pleasure to behold.'

'I think the *story* of Don Giovanni is equally entertaining,' Lady Annabelle observed. 'The composer obviously wishes us to take a message from it.'

'Indeed. That a man should settle for just *one* lady,' Mr Silverton said darkly, 'instead of casting his nets so wide.'

Oberon seemed impervious to the slight. 'That is what we all aspire to do, but the trick is to find that one woman who surpasses all others. One who captures our heart in a way no other can. Don Giovanni never found his lady whereas I...' he stopped to gaze at Sophie '...am hopeful of finding mine.'

A sudden burst of applause drew Sophie's attention back to the stage, and, grateful beyond words for a chance to look away, she likewise began to applaud. What in the world was the man about? To make an admission to a lady in private was one thing, but to say such a thing in a crowded theatre box was quite another. Especially with Mr Silverton glowering at him the entire time. What if he thought her flattered by the man's unwelcome attentions?

Unfortunately, once the cheers came to an end and the theatre began to empty, Sophie knew she would have to make her way back downstairs. But how was she to do that without Mr Oberon claiming her hand like an overbearing master?

To her surprise, it was Lady Annabelle who again came to her rescue. Timing her exit so that she stepped out of the box at the same time as Mr Oberon, Lady Annabelle casually slipped her arm through Mr Oberon's and proceeded to ask his opinion on some of Mozart's other works, in particular his horn and his violin concertos that were becoming so popular. Sophie was quite sure Mr Oberon had no idea he had been manipulated. Why Lady Annabelle had done it was anyone's guess, but at least it had spared Sophie a potentially awkward descent to the vestibule below.

On a happier note, she was pleased to see Antoine helping Jane navigate her way past the chairs, holding her arm in a manner that was neither condescending nor familiar, and Jane was clearly enjoying the attention. Her pretty face was even more flushed than before and Sophie felt sure it had nothing to do with the heated confines of the theatre.

'It would seem my sister is not immediately in need of my help, Miss Vallois. Perhaps you are?'

Sophie turned to see Mr Silverton holding out his arm. Surprised but pleased, she placed her fingers lightly on his sleeve. 'Thank you, Mr Silverton. Are you all right now?'

'All right?'

'You went very quiet earlier. I wondered if I had said something to upset you. Or if Lady Annabelle had.'

It was as direct a question as she could ask—and she was relieved to see him smile.

'No. I was simply…lost in thought.' He turned his head and met her gaze. 'But forgive me for not having told you that you are the most beautiful woman in the room, and that you have been on more than one occasion.'

His voice was low and sincere, and as she fell into step beside him, Sophie marvelled that she had ever thought him lacking in any way. His face might not have the classical perfection of Mr Oberon's, but to her, he would always be the more handsome. In his evening clothes, his stature was enhanced rather than diminished, and when he smiled, his entire face lit up, his eyes coming alive with warmth and tenderness.

How would he gaze upon a woman he cared for? Sophie mused. A woman he loved.

The thought was unexpected—as was her resultant confusion when she realised that, just for a moment, she had pictured herself as that woman. Ridiculous, of course, because Mr Silverton didn't see her that way. To him, she was just a stranger—an unknown woman he had encountered at a coaching inn. One his beloved sister had all but bullied him into taking on a carriage ride and one a meddling hostess had insisted he accompany to the theatre. It was laughable to see herself in the role of the woman he might revere, for while passion could flare in the blink of an eye it took time for true affection to grow.

And love…?

Sophie sighed. Love took the greatest time of all. It was impossible to be in love with someone you had only just met. With someone you were quite sure did not like you.

With someone, she admitted, like Robert Silverton.

* * *

The party dispersed shortly after, and though Robert would have liked to have spent more time with Sophie, he noticed that Jane's colour was still unusually high and decided to order their carriage straight away. He couldn't risk letting Jane wear herself out, knowing it often took days before she was fully recovered.

He waited with Oberon on the road, as servants hailed carriages for their elegant lords and ladies, and sharp-eyed lads of eight or nine watched for unsuspecting victims.

'I think your sister would have preferred to be escorted home by Vallois,' Oberon commented, oblivious to it all. 'They seem to have struck up a friendship.'

Keeping his eye on the street, Robert said, 'Be that as it may, Jane and I came together and we will leave that way.'

'Pity. That would have left me free to drive Miss Vallois home and I would have enjoyed that very much. Since you were determined to spoil my evening with her, it was the least you could have done.'

The idea was so preposterous that Robert actually laughed. 'I did not spoil your evening. It was Lady White's suggestion we all come together.'

'You *could* have said you and Jane were otherwise engaged.'

'But we were not. And it wouldn't have mattered regardless. Lady White suggested Miss Vallois invite her brother and you saw as well as I did how pleased she was by the idea. At that point, I judged there was nothing wrong with my joining the party. And with inviting Lady Annabelle.'

'You take a great deal upon yourself, Silver,' Oberon said distantly. 'If I didn't know better, I would swear you didn't trust me to behave properly with Miss Vallois. But we both know that makes no sense. If I hope to earn the lady's affection, what would be the point in compromising her beforehand?'

A muscle twitched in Robert's jaw. 'In my experience, there is often a great deal of room between intention and action.'

Oberon grunted. 'I'm not sure I like your tone. I thought you would have been pleased with the way I've been courting Miss Vallois. I am still considering offering her marriage, you know, and I believe the Longworths would approve. Why would they turn down the chance of their young friend becoming a viscountess?'

Tell him what you know! Tell him what she is and put an end to this once and for all.

But Robert couldn't bring himself to say the words. Too many questions needed to be asked and too many people's lives would be affected by the answers. He had to be sure of his facts before he said anything. Especially to a man like Oberon.

'They will wish her to marry the man she loves,' Robert said. 'Although Miss Vallois told me to my face that she has no desire to be wed.'

'No desire be hanged! All young women wish to be married, Silver. She was obviously just being coy. And if it's love she wants, I'll make her love *me*,' Oberon said confidently. 'I can be very persuasive when I set my mind to it.'

'I take it you've found no impediment to marrying her?' Robert forced himself to ask.

'I've made no specific inquiries, but I've seen nothing in her conduct that leads me to believe she is anything but what she seems.'

The remark was disquieting. Oberon *never* took anything at face value. In his search to uncover the truth, he turned over every rock, uprooted every tree, until those secrets were ferreted out and exposed. His all-too-ready acceptance of Sophie led Robert to believe that none of that mattered any more. That Oberon didn't care for the consequences…and he found that even more disturbing. It suggested an attachment that wasn't healthy. An attachment that bordered on…obsession.

'Well, as you said yourself, she could be an heiress or an actress,' Robert said casually. 'But if your father requires that you marry a lady of title or fortune, you will have to look elsewhere. Miss Vallois has neither.'

'It matters not since on the day she becomes my wife, she acquires both. My father, for all his lofty intentions, cannot stop me from marrying whom I please.'

'And if his displeasure takes the form of a threat of disinheritance?'

Oberon's smile turned into a sneer. 'As it happens, I have discovered a few things about my father's past he would rather not be made known. Some…youthful indiscretions, if you will, that would be embarrassing for all concerned.'

Robert stepped back as a young boy ran past. 'I'm surprised he told you of them.'

'Oh, you can be sure he did not. But letters kept for the wrong reasons often become an excellent source of information for those who know how to use them. I doubt my mother or the lady in question would appreciate the errors of their youth being made public after all these years.'

Robert stared at the man standing next to him as though he were a stranger. So, the son would blackmail the father with letters written years ago about an affair that would be damaging to all. Oberon knew his world well. A peer might be above the law, but he was not above being cut by good society. The fact Oberon would *use* that information to wilfully destroy his father's reputation and those of several other people, said a great deal about his character—or lack thereof.

'Tell me, Silver, why are you suddenly so interested in my courtship of Miss Vallois?' Oberon asked. 'Surely it cannot be that you have developed feelings for the lady yourself? You, who've sworn off matrimony and despise all things French.'

'I do not despise all things French, and my reputation is such that I have nothing to *offer* a lady,' Robert said. 'But I do not wish to see Miss Vallois hurt.'

'Then you have nothing to worry about for I have no intention of hurting her. Now, why don't you send your sister home and join me for some serious gambling? There's money to be made on greenheads who don't know a trump from a tart.'

'Thank you, but I've no interest in fleecing innocent

young men who haven't the brains to stay out of the hells.'

''Pon my word, sir, that almost sounded like a lecture, and I am not of a mind to take a lecture from you. Act the hero if you must, but don't forget—I *know* the games you've played. I was a willing participant in many of them.'

'Be that as it may, the past is the past. Leave it where it belongs.'

'Leave it where it belongs? Oh, that's ripe coming from you!' Oberon said as his carriage drew to a halt and the footman hurried to let down the stairs. 'A man who still hates *all* Frenchmen because *one* shot his brother in the back. You're the one living in the past, Silverton. Not me.'

Oberon climbed up into the carriage and the moment the door closed behind him, the coachman whipped up the team. Robert stepped back as the stylish equipage passed, his thoughts as dark as the night that swallowed it up. So what if Oberon thought he'd lingered too long in the past? He was the *first* one to admit that Michael's death had prevented him from moving on. It was the reason he had delayed his return to society. The reason he hadn't looked for a wife until a little over a month ago. Anger had plunged him into an abyss of bitterness and despair from which he'd thought there was no escape.

But there *was* life after death, and eventually, his world had begun to right itself. He had emerged from the darkness to pick up where he'd left off, resuming his place in society. Doing the rounds of the civilised gentleman. And if some of the shadows remained, they were no longer a source of despair. He was able to work around them.

And then Miss Sophie Vallois had arrived. Sophie, with her quicksilver smile and her sparkling blue eyes. She had marched into his world and splashed colour on to a drab grey canvas. She had challenged and provoked him. Stimulated and disobeyed him. And she had made him laugh at the idea of a lady wanting to float down the Amazon in a boat. No wonder Jane was her slave. Even old Lady White couldn't get enough of her. She truly was a breath of fresh air.

And if he continued on his present course, he would lose her. It was as simple as that. Oberon intended to do everything in his power to make her see him as an ideal husband, and the only person who stood in his way… was Robert. Because he alone held the ace. Sophie had handed it to him in the theatre tonight. All he had to do now was to decide if, when and how to play it.

Chapter Eight

❧

The sky was grey and overcast when Sophie and her maid set out for Oxford Street the next morning. Not the best time to venture out perhaps, but with Lavinia's birthday the following day, Sophie had no time to waste. She had to pick out a gift today.

Fortunately, she knew what she wanted to buy. The last time she and Lavinia had been out together, they had paused to admire a selection of fans displayed in a shop window. Lavinia had pointed out one in particular and Sophie had agreed it was exquisite. Then, when an acquaintance had hailed them, the fans had been forgotten—until this morning, when Sophie had returned to the shop to buy it.

Now, with the gift tucked safely in its case, she set out for her next destination—only to be forced into the doorway of a gentlemen's clothier when the clouds finally burst and the promised rains came pelting down.

'Miss Vallois, what on earth are you doing out in such dreadful weather?'

Startled, Sophie turned to find herself face to face with Robert Silverton, who was just emerging from within. 'Shopping, as it happens.' Goodness, did the man draw on some secret elixir that made him appear more handsome every time she saw him? 'But I think we will have to cut it short. This rain doesn't look like it's going to let up any time soon.'

'Then perhaps I could offer you a ride home?' He glanced apologetically at her maid. 'Unfortunately, my carriage only has room for two.'

'Don't you worry about me, sir,' Jeanette said. 'A bit of rain won't hurt me. But I'd hate to see Miss Sophie get her fine clothes all spattered with mud. You go on. I'll make my own way home.'

'Here, take a hackney.' He pulled out a coin and pressed it into the maid's palm. 'My conscience will not allow me to see you walk home through a downpour like this.'

Jeanette blushed and bobbed a curtsy. 'Thank you, sir. I'll take those parcels, miss, and put them in your room without her ladyship seeing.'

'Thank you, Jeanette.' Sophie gratefully handed them over, then dashed into the street and quickly climbed into the waiting carriage. 'This is very good of you, Mr Silverton,' she said as they got underway. 'We should both have been drenched had you not come along.'

'I'm glad to be of assistance.'

'How is Jane this morning?'

'She was in good spirits when I left, though I was

concerned about her last night. She is prone to chills, and when I saw how flushed her cheeks had become, I feared she might be coming down with something.'

Suspecting it had more to do with her reaction to Antoine than it did to an illness, Sophie nevertheless said, 'I could mention it to Antoine. He is not an apothecary, but perhaps he could suggest a tonic.'

'Thank you, but Jane has no need of a doctor, especially a—'

He clamped down hard on the words, but not soon enough to prevent Sophie from sliding a startled glance his way. What had he been about to say? That he didn't want Antoine involved because he was still learning his profession? That he was not experienced enough to treat his sister? 'If you are concerned about Antoine's skills, I can assure you—'

'This has nothing to do with ability,' Robert assured her. 'I watched your brother in action. I know how talented he is.'

'Then why did you not finish what you were about to say?'

She waited a long time for his answer. Finally, he said, 'Because to do so would be to reveal something about my past I have no wish to talk about. Or to explain.'

He looked at her then, and Sophie caught a glimpse of a shadow that dwelt in his soul. Of an old wound slowly healing. But what had that to do with his reluctance to accept help from Antoine? Her brother was no more a part of Robert's past than she was. Until a week ago, they'd all been strangers to one another. Yet she couldn't shake the feeling that the root of Robert's animosity lay buried in that past.

Had it something to do with the fact that Antoine was not well born? Sophie hadn't meant to divulge that particular piece of information, but she had been so flustered by her sudden awareness of Robert that the words had inadvertently slipped out. And once they had, there was nothing she could do to take them back. But Robert hadn't learned that truth until last night, and his reluctance to shake Antoine's hand had been evident from the first, when all he'd known about him was that he was French and that—

Sophie blanched. *Mère de Dieu,* surely that wasn't the problem? Robert didn't want Antoine to help his sister… because he was French?

Non, c'était impossible! The war was over. Napoleon had been banished. There was absolutely no reason for Robert to harbour feelings of resentment simply because he and Antoine had been born on opposites of the Channel!

And yet, how else did she explain the tension she felt every time the two men were together? A tension that *had* been there the first time they'd met. She'd never forgotten Robert's hesitation when it came to shaking Antoine's hand. And while he might be willing to compliment her brother's skills when it concerned patching up a gunshot wound, she couldn't forget that he had been brusque, almost to the point of rudeness, when he'd spoken to Antoine outside Nicholas and Lavinia's house that morning…

'You've gone very quiet, Miss Vallois,' Robert observed. 'Have I said something to offend you?'

How did she answer that? If what she suspected was true, he most definitely *had* offended her. But if she was mistaken…

'Do you *like* my brother, Mr Silverton?' she said, knowing the question had to be asked.

She watched his expression change, saw the shutter come down. 'I really don't know him.'

'But you went to his aid the night a man was shot. And you have been in his company on at least two other occasions. Surely that is time enough to know whether you like a man or not.'

'On the contrary, it is barely enough time to form even a fleeting impression.'

Sophie quickly turned away, struggling for the right words; not sure what the right words were any more. 'That day you came to take me driving…when you spoke to Antoine. He offered Jane a compliment and you all but *demanded* that he speak English to her.'

'Of course, because we are in England,' Robert said quietly. 'If we were in France, I would have expected him to speak French, as I would myself.'

To anyone else it might have seemed like a reasonable excuse, but Sophie wasn't fooled. Robert had refused Antoine's help because he was French.

How did she respond to something like that? What was she supposed to say? To find out that a man, of whom she'd thought so highly, should be prejudiced in such a way came as a huge disappointment. While she could understand one man hating another given sufficient cause, to despise an entire nationality over a matter that was clearly restricted to him alone, demonstrated a narrowness of mind of which she could not approve.

'I am surprised at your willingness to be seen with me,' she said quietly, 'given that your dislike of the French is so all encompassing.'

He shot her a dark look. 'I said nothing about disliking the French.'

'You didn't have to. It is the *only* reason you could have for saying what you did.' She turned to face him. 'Why else would you not allow Antoine to offer even the slightest assistance to your sister, even after admitting that he is very good at what he does?'

Robert's jaw tensed, but he returned his attention to the road. 'I would prefer we speak no more about this.'

'But I *must* speak of it! You resent my brother because he is French, yet you are unwilling to tell me why.'

'And *you* seem unwilling to accept that certain matters *are* private and not open to discussion with those not personally involved.'

'Not personally involved? You are speaking of my *brother*, Mr Silverton! That *makes* it personal!'

Sophie hadn't realised they were home until Robert drew the carriage to a halt in front of Eaton Place. But she refused to wait for him to help her alight. She pushed open the door and started to get out.

'Miss Vallois, let me—'

'I will accept nothing from you, sir!' Sophie said as

she climbed down. 'I would not wish to give offence by *forcing* you to take the hand of a Frenchwoman!'

Even through the rain, she saw him flush. 'Don't be ridiculous!'

'I am not the one being ridiculous!' Sophie said, fully aware that she was. For the first time in years, her temper was getting the better of her—and the stupid reasons why made her even more angry. 'I am not the one who has condemned an entire nation for reasons of which you will not speak.'

'I told you. The matter is personal and extremely painful.'

'Very well. Then let our acquaintance be at an end so you will not be forced to think of it every time you look at me! Good day, Mr Silverton.'

She was halfway to the front door when his words stopped her in her tracks. 'My brother was murdered. By a Frenchman. They found him in a deserted barn, ten miles outside Paris.'

The words, torn from his throat, caused Sophie to turn around, the sudden pounding of her heart deafening in her ears. 'How do you know…he was murdered?'

'He'd been bound hand and foot. Someone had put a sack over his head, and his hands were bloodied, as though he'd been fighting. He'd been shot once, in the back of the head. At close range. I don't think I need tell you the kind of damage a bullet fired that close to a person's body can do.'

Sophie pressed her hands to her mouth, trying to shut out the horrific images. *'Mère de Dieu!'*

'He went to France to fight for England, Miss Vallois.

If necessary, to die a soldier's death. Not to be butchered by a man who hadn't the courage to face him. Only a coward shoots his enemy in the back,' Robert said bitterly.

From somewhere deep within, she found the courage to whisper, 'How do you know...it was a Frenchman?'

'Because they found a note stuffed in Michael's pocket. A note, covered in his blood, and hailing Napoleon Bonaparte as the future Emperor of England. No Englishman would write something like that, or shoot a compatriot in the back. I cannot forgive that of your countrymen. God knows I've tried. I'm sorry if that offends you, but you asked for the truth.'

Yes, she had. And as she stood looking back at him, mindless of the rain, Sophie was totally at a loss to find the words that would make sense of such a tragedy. What did you say to a man from whom so much had been taken, and in such a brutal fashion? What could she say that would exonerate her countryman? And why had she not been able to accept that, whatever Robert's reasons for despising the French, they were deeply personal and not meant to be shared?

Drawing his own conclusion from her silence, Robert flicked the whip and the horses set off, the carriage disappearing into the dull, grey morning.

Sophie didn't move. She stood where he'd left her, rain streaming down her face, the wind tugging at her cloak. She should have let him keep his secrets. She had no right to demand answers to questions that were none of her business. And she had been wrong to lash out at him simply because he refused to satisfy her curiosity. He was right. She had intruded where she didn't belong. And only time would tell if he would ever forgive her for that.

It came as no surprise that Robert made no attempt to contact her over the next few days. Why *would* he, given the nature of what had passed between them? Bitter words, spoken in anger, were never easily forgotten, and the petty accusations she had flung at him now seemed exactly that.

How ironic that *both* of them should have been so ill served by her countrymen. Robert's brother had been brutally murdered by a Frenchman, and *she* was staying at the house of a man who had likewise been shot and left for dead by one. Perhaps the French as a whole were a hot-blooded mob who preferred to make peace with swords and gunfire than with cool heads and clear thinking. Only look at the bloodiness of the Revolution. How many innocent people had been put to death during that dreadful time?

Even she and Antoine had not escaped their ire. They had been forced to leave their home when the sentiments of their neighbours had turned against them. When the man she was to have married had betrayed her.

It still hurt to think about that painful time. In her youthful naïveté, Sophie had believed herself in love with Gismond D'Orione. Their parents had agreed that when the time came, they would be married, and there had never been anyone else in her life but Gismond. She had grown up with him. Gone for walks with him.

Experienced her first kiss with him. And because she'd loved him, she hadn't thought twice about telling him about Nicholas.

But Gismond had been afraid. He'd told his father about Sophie finding a wounded Englishman in the road, and about Antoine saving his life, and then his father had told others until eventually, the entire village knew. And when their father had found out, she and Antoine had had no choice but to leave. And so they had, stealing away in the middle of the night without telling anyone of their plans. Antoine had said it was better that way. Safer. They had packed a few clothes, taken some bread and cheese and disappeared into the darkness.

Sophie had never heard from Gismond D'Orione *or* her father again.

It did not make for pleasant memories and when the butler appeared to say that Mr Oberon had called, she was almost glad of the diversion. Even Lavinia seemed more kindly disposed towards him than usual. 'Mr Oberon, how nice of you to call,' she said, putting aside her magazine.

Mr Oberon strolled in, dashing as ever in gleaming Hessians, skin-tight breeches of fawn-coloured doeskin, and a cutaway coat of dark blue superfine. But his waistcoat was unusually subdued and his neckcloth was tied in a simple but elegant knot. 'Good afternoon, Lady Longworth, Miss Vallois. I came in hopes of taking you both out for a drive. The weather has turned fine and I thought it might be pleasant to take a turn about the Park.'

'You are very kind to ask, Mr Oberon,' Lavinia said.

'But I have Mr Harris coming to see me about new curtains. Sophie may go, if she wishes.'

Had it been a few days earlier, Sophie would have declined, having no wish to offer any kind of encouragement to Mr Oberon. But at the moment, she didn't want to be alone. After what had happened, she felt a desperate need to get out into the sunshine, to dispel the darkness of her thoughts by talking to someone who would naturally try to flatter her and make her laugh. If such was a flagrant abuse of his time, she would do her best to suffer the guilt.

'I would like that, Mr Oberon,' she said. 'If you will wait but a moment, I shall get ready.'

Fifteen minutes later, she allowed Mr Oberon to help her up into his dashing, high-perch phaeton.

'I vow I am carrying a ray of sunshine in my carriage,' he said as he climbed into the seat beside her. 'And never did one look lovelier.'

Sophie smiled as she opened her parasol. The carriage gown of buttery yellow muslin had seemed perfect for the occasion, but she had not worn it with a view towards inviting compliments. Mr Oberon needed no encouragement for that. But as if sensing she was not herself, he set out to be more charming than usual. He kept the carriage to a sedate pace and assumed the role of guide, pointing out houses of interest along the way and regaling her with amusing stories as they clipped along. But when after five minutes had passed and the only sound was the steady thud of the horses' hooves, he turned to her and said, 'You are noticeably quiet this afternoon, Miss Vallois. Dare I ask what is troubling you?'

Sophie sighed, aware that despite her best efforts, she had been a less than obliging guest. 'Forgive me, Mr Oberon, I admit my thoughts have been somewhat distracted.'

'I hope with nothing of a serious nature.'

'Serious enough.'

'Does this concern our mutual friend, Mr Silverton?'

Sophie was too unhappy to hide her surprise. 'How did you know?'

'A lucky guess. You seem to enjoy the gentleman's company and given that you were in such good spirits when we parted the other night, I wondered if it might have something to do with him.' He flicked a perceptive glance in her direction. 'Am I close?'

It was hard to know how much to reveal. Was the murder of Robert's brother something one discussed with a man who was little more than a stranger?

It was, if she had any hopes of understanding Robert better.

'Are you familiar with the nature of the tragedy concerning Mr Silverton's brother?' she asked.

'With Michael? Oh, yes, I know all about that. It was a terrible thing,' Mr Oberon said. 'I've always wondered how Robert and Jane got through it.'

Sophie blinked. Compassion? From Mr Oberon? 'I suppose it was because they had each other.'

'I dare say that's true.' Oberon looked at her again. 'I am surprised he told you.'

'He did not wish to.' Sophie averted her gaze. 'I goaded him into it.'

'*You* goaded Silver? I doubt that very much, Miss Vallois. You are anything but pushy.'

'I was the other morning,' she said miserably. And in as few words as possible, she told him of her conversation with Robert and of its distressing outcome.

'Ah, I see why you are downcast. You wish to have Robert's good opinion and fear now you may have lost it.'

'I am not as concerned with what he thinks of me, Mr Oberon, as I am with knowing how clumsily I brought back the memory of something he obviously wishes to forget.'

'But if we are speaking honestly, just being around you is likely to do that. Your delightful accent, slight as it is, betrays your origins and will always come between you.'

The words cut like a knife, partly because Sophie knew them to be true and partly because they had been uttered by someone who knew Robert much better than she did. 'You do not think he would ever be able to see beyond it?'

'I think it unlikely,' Oberon said. 'Robert has very strong opinions about the French. I'm telling you this because he and I have been good friends for years. We were even closer before his brother was killed. But all that changed after Michael's death. And it didn't help that his father committed suicide not long after.'

Sophie gasped. 'Suicide?'

'Not many people were willing to come right out and

say that, of course, but I believe Sir William took his own life,' Oberon said. 'He was never the same after word came back from France that Michael had been killed. He'd been so proud of his eldest son. Michael was a captain and his father thought him the best of all men. He loved Robert, but Michael was the apple of his eye, and he took his death very hard. He shut himself away for weeks on end, refusing to see anyone. The gambling started shortly thereafter. Robert tried to stop him, but his father would have none of it. It was an addiction, you see, and Sir William could no more stop himself from gambling than he could bring his eldest son back from the grave. The family carried on as best they could, but it was impossible to ignore the fact that he was getting worse, as was their financial situation.

'Ironically, it was Robert who saved the family from total ruin,' Oberon went on. 'He had a knack for winning and was able to recoup much of what his father lost. But it was a dreadful situation and everyone feared for the outcome. Then, some months later, Sir William said he was going north to a hunting lodge in Scotland. It seemed a sudden decision, but he told Robert he was meeting friends for some shooting. Many of us hoped it was a sign Sir William was on the mend, but as it turned out, nothing could have been further from the truth. One of the gamekeepers found him in the far woods a few days later. Some say it was an accident, but I don't believe he ever had any intention of coming back.'

'How terrible!' Sophie said in a hushed voice.

'It was. And not long after, Lady Silverton fell into

a dreadful decline. The doctors said there was nothing they could do. That she had lost the will to live.'

It was almost too much to bear. Sophie tried to imagine how devastating three deaths in close succession must have been for Robert and his sister, but it was completely beyond her. 'I cannot imagine how they endured it.'

'Neither can I, but I know it was the start of Robert's bitterness towards the French. I suppose, in many ways, he blames them for the loss of his entire family. Naturally, I tried to make him see that despising an entire nation over the thoughtless actions of one lunatic made absolutely no sense, but he couldn't see it. Wouldn't see it, I suppose. And he resented me for having tried to change his mind.'

'I'm sorry to hear that,' Sophie said, gazing at the road ahead. 'It isn't fair that you were made to suffer for trying to make him see reason.'

'Robert was set on a course from which I could not dissuade him,' Oberon said regretfully.

It was everything Sophie hadn't wanted to hear because, with every word, Mr Oberon confirmed that her chances for any kind of reconciliation with Robert were virtually non-existent. 'I wonder that his sister does not share his antipathy towards the French,' she said at length. 'The first time we met, she told me how much she was looking forward to speaking to me of Paris.'

'Jane is not as hard as her brother. She's had her own challenges to deal with and in overcoming those she has learned the meaning of tolerance. Dealing with disappointment at such an early age has enabled her to look more kindly, perhaps with more forgiveness, upon the world.'

Sophie turned her head to look at him. 'You surprise me, Mr Oberon. I would not have expected such compassion from you. Or such understanding.'

He smiled, the brim of his hat shading his eyes. 'I am often judged more harshly than I deserve, Miss Vallois. But I do not trouble myself over it. Trying to correct the opinions of others serves no useful purpose. It is enough that those of whom I think highly know who I am.' He turned to look at her. 'I hope I may consider you one of those people.'

It seemed impossible to believe, but Sophie realised her opinion of the man had changed. How could it not given everything she had heard today? 'You may consider me so, Mr Oberon. And thank you for telling me more of Mr Silverton's sad story.'

'You understand, of course, that he would not wish to know I had told you of it,' Oberon said, returning his attention to the road. 'Robert is a proud man, and proud men do not like their weaknesses being shared with others.'

'I will, of course, make no mention of our conversation,' Sophie assured him. 'I am well aware of how deeply I hurt Mr Silverton. I have no desire to make matters worse.'

'Thank you. I value Robert's friendship too, what little I have left of it. He is, in all ways, an admirable man, as I told you the second time we met.'

'Yes,' Sophie whispered. 'Quiet, honest and steady as a rock.'

She felt his gaze upon her, but did not turn her head. 'You have an excellent memory, Miss Vallois.'

'For some things, Mr Oberon.' An image of Robert's face appeared in her mind: the firm line of his chin, the broad sweep of his forehead, the smile on his lips when he was pleased or amused. A smile she was afraid she might never see again. 'For some things.'

As a result of the carriage ride with Mr Oberon, Sophie's spirits were only marginally restored by the time she and Antoine joined Nicholas and Lavinia for a soirée at the home of Sir David and Lady Hester the following evening. Everything Mr Oberon had said convinced her that the gulf between her and Robert was too wide to bridge. Even the sound of her voice would remind him of that painful time in his life. How could anyone enjoy a friendship under such strained conditions?

Fortunately, Antoine more than made up for her lack of good spirits as a result of having spent the best part of the day at Nicholas's club.

'I must admit you were right in everything you said about Nicholas,' Antoine commented as he and Sophie stood by the edge of the dance floor later that evening. 'He has introduced me to several of his closest friends and they are all excellent fellows. Lord Marwood invited me to come shooting with him, and Mr Kingsley said we would be most welcome to pay a call on him and his wife, either here or at their country house.'

'I'm happy for you, Antoine,' Sophie said, wishing she could find the strength to match his enthusiasm.

'You are moving with a very smart crowd and seem to be enjoying it.'

'It has all been Nicholas's doing,' Antoine said, looking out over the floor. 'If it were not for him—'

He stopped so abruptly that Sophie turned her head to look up at him. 'If *what* weren't for him?' Then, following his gaze, she saw Robert and Jane Silverton standing at the other side of the room.

In an instant, her breath caught. *What shall I say to him?* To ignore him would be craven, but how did she *begin* to apologise for what had happened the other morning?

'I did not think Miss Silverton would be here this evening,' Antoine said softly.

That was all it took. It was there, in his voice. And in a moment of heartbreaking insight, Sophie realised she was not the only one wrestling with demons. Her brother was in love with Jane Silverton—and Sophie knew it was doomed to fail. Robert would never give his approval. 'I suggest you not stare at her so boldly, dearest,' she cautioned, 'lest people begin to wonder at the nature of your feelings.'

Two spots of colour appeared high on her brother's cheeks. 'There is nothing between myself and Miss Silverton,' he said too quickly. 'I simply enjoy talking to her.'

'Then pray do not stare at her as though you wish you could do more. I am not the only one in the room with observant eyes.'

As if to confirm her fears, Sophie saw old Mrs Templeton smile and nod in their direction, and then lean in closer to her eldest daughter. When she whispered something in her ear, the daughter also turned to look and likewise smiled in that knowing kind of way.

'I suggest you ask Miss Templeton to dance,' Sophie said quickly. 'Inform her that you are oft in the habit of staring at people when your thoughts are actually preoccupied with thoughts of…medical procedures.'

'Medical procedures? What are you talking about, Sophie?'

'Just do as I say unless you wish Miss Silverton to be at the heart of rumours over which you have no control. In fact, you might like to stare at Miss Templeton in just such a way before asking *her* to dance.'

'Now you're talking nonsense.'

'No, I'm not. I may be younger than you, but I understand the rules of the game far better.'

'And what are you going to do while I am playing these games?' he asked drily.

'I am going to speak to Mr Silverton.' Sophie took a long, deep breath. 'I fear I have already said too many things for which an explanation is required and an apology offered.'

Robert had not wanted to come this evening. Not only because the last thing he felt like doing was socialising with people who resented his presence, but because of his last agonising conversation with Sophie. She hadn't deserved the harshness of his reply. When he had begun relating the details of Michael's death, he had seen how deeply she was affected, yet he had still gone on talking, adding detail upon detail until her face had turned white and her eyes had reflected the horror of his words. It had been a heartless thing to do, entirely unnecessary, and if it were within his power, he would have taken back every single word.

But it was not within his power. The damage was done and he had no idea how to undo it. He had started a hundred letters…and thrown them all away. He had stood in the silence of his room and rehearsed the words of his apology. And every one of them had rung hollow and meaningless—

'Mr Silverton.'

And then, she was there, standing before him in yet another new gown—this one sweeping over the curves of her body and revealing just enough of the seductive roundness beneath to stir a man's blood. Her white-blond hair was caught up with a sprig of tiny white roses, and she looked, Robert thought sadly, like spring come to life. A virgin goddess sent to tempt and distract. And she did both…exquisitely. 'Miss Vallois,' he said, fearing the huskiness in his voice would betray him. 'I trust you are well?'

'Tolerably well. You?'

'Tolerably well.'

A moment passed, and, as if realising that was the extent of his conversation, Sophie turned to greet his sister. 'Good evening, Jane. Lavinia and I were sorry not to see you at the musicale this afternoon. The young woman Lady Staynwell engaged to perform was very good. Miss Roundtree, I believe her name was.'

'Yes, I was sorry not to be there,' Jane said, appearing somewhat distracted. 'I understand her mother taught her to play the pianoforte at a very young age. My goodness, it is warm, is it not?' She opened her fan and fluttered it vigorously in front of her face.

Robert, who was actually finding it cooler than usual, said, 'I could fetch a glass of punch—'

'Yes, punch would be excellent,' Jane said. 'But do stay here and talk to Miss Vallois. I am perfectly capable of fetching it myself.' Which she did—walking away with a degree of alacrity that both surprised and concerned Robert.

'Jane must be very thirsty indeed. I don't think I've ever seen her move so fast.' He turned to the lady standing beside him. 'Would you also care for some refreshment, Miss Vallois?'

'Thank you, no.'

The silence lengthened…and became awkward. Robert desperately tried to appear at ease, but as the memory of what happened returned in full force he knew he had to say something. 'Miss Vallois, there is something I must say—'

'No! It is I who must begin.' She paused, catching her lower lip between dainty white teeth. 'I've not been able to stop thinking about…what passed between us earlier in the week. I feel terrible for having caused you such distress and I owe you an apology.'

'You owe me nothing,' Robert ground out. 'You were right to speak to me as you did.'

'Not given what happened—'

'You had no knowledge of what happened and I went at you like a bull at a gate,' he said, feeling the tightness of guilt at the back of his throat. 'That was wrong, and unkind. I saw how it made you feel.'

'It shocked me for the terrible things that had happened to you,' Sophie said urgently. 'It made me see why your feelings towards the French are what they are. And it helped me to understand that your feelings towards my brother, and perhaps, myself, are not so much personal as they are…instinctual.'

'Miss Vallois—'

'No, please let me finish. You owe me no apology or explanation, Mr Silverton. Because it all makes sense now. *Any* reminder of the French, no matter how small, will always bring to mind that which you wish most dearly to forget. It was selfishness on my part that caused me to demand a justification for your reaction towards me, and I deeply regret that.'

He couldn't speak. She was apologising to him when it was he who should have been begging *her* forgiveness. Making excuses for herself when there were no excuses to be made, and tearing herself apart into the bargain. 'You were entirely within your rights to challenge me about my feelings towards the French,' Robert said huskily. 'I was allowing my hatred for one man to colour my opinion of everyone else, and in doing so, I demonstrated not only a blatant disregard for the truth, but a shocking narrowness of mind. It would be like you saying that all Englishmen wear green because you happened to meet *one* Englishman who did. But every person must be judged on his or her own merit, and even a condemned man must have his hearing. I can forgive someone for disliking a man if they know he has done wrong, but not before.' He was relieved to see her smile. More than relieved. Hopeful. 'And now that we have cleared the air and offered apologies that are not required, do you think we might start again...as friends?'

Her expression lightened, the darkness leaving her eyes. Did she feel as relieved as he did? Did the stars suddenly seem a little closer than they'd been a moment ago? 'I do hope so, Mr Silverton. In fact, I should like that above all.'

'Then perhaps, if you are not engaged for the next dance, I might claim the honour?'

'You may, though I should warn you, I am not the best of dancers. My employer taught me how to speak, but she did not think it necessary that I knew how to dance.'

'I don't care.' He looked down at her, wanting to trace the line of her jaw with his fingers, to stroke the sensual curve of her throat. 'I just want to dance with you. And perhaps to talk and to make you laugh. Is that asking too much?'

She shook her head. 'Not at all. I should like to dance, and to talk, and to laugh.'

And when the quadrille came to an end and the minuet began, that was exactly what they did.

Lavinia stood with a group of ladies by a cluster of ferns and tried to pretend an interest in what they were saying. In truth, she was far more interested in what was going on elsewhere in the room. She had watched Sophie cross the floor to talk to Robert and Jane, and then a few minutes later, saw Jane leave and Robert and Sophie take up what looked to be a far more serious conversation. But it wasn't until they laughed, and Lavinia saw the expression on Robert's face, that she realised what was happening.

'Good evening, Lady Longworth,' a smooth voice said beside her.

Danger. Lavinia sensed it immediately, recognised it for what it was, and with the composure of a duchess, turned to face her adversary. 'Mr Oberon. Is it not a pleasant evening?'

'It is an exceedingly pleasant evening and the company equally delightful.' Oberon held the stem of his champagne glass between long slender fingers. 'But how careless of Lord Longworth to leave you all alone.'

'Ah, but I am not alone. I am surrounded by friends and now have you to keep me company.'

'Which I am most happy to do.' He raised the flute to his lips, but his eyes were on the floor. 'I had hoped to find Miss Vallois with you, but I see she is engaged with our friend, Silverton.'

'Yes. She thinks very highly of Jane and is often in her company.'

'Yet, Jane is not with them.'

Years of rigidly instilled training allowed Lavinia to open her fan with no visible sign of concern. 'She was a moment ago, but left to secure refreshments.'

'And found Mr Vallois instead.' Oberon's mouth lifted, little more than a grimace. 'It would appear both the Silvertons are very much taken with your guests, Lady Longworth.'

'Why would they not be? Sophie and Antoine are

both likeable young people. You must have discovered that during the time you spent with Sophie the other afternoon.'

'I did, and as a result, it is my sincere desire to spend *more* time with her. But frankly, I am surprised to see Silverton looking so engaged. His dislike of the French is well known to both of us, I think.'

Hearing an edge to Oberon's voice, Lavinia sensed the need to tread carefully. 'Mr Silverton is, first and foremost, a gentleman. He would never allow his personal feelings to affect his conduct towards a lady.'

'And yet that is precisely what he did, and in doing so he upset Miss Vallois greatly. She spoke of it to me during our drive.'

'Did she? I am surprised. Sophie usually keeps her own counsel.'

'Do not condemn her for it, Lady Longworth. It was obvious to me she was in distress and when I enquired as to the nature, she told me. So now to see them conversing so amiably, I must confess to some surprise. I had believed Silverton firmly established in his intention to keep her at a distance. And given his current standing in society, I am surprised you would approve of their association.'

Lavinia slowly plied her fan, careful to remain impassive. 'I am aware of society's views with regard to Mr Silverton, but he has chosen to keep his own counsel and I respect him for that. Furthermore, if he spoke out of turn to Sophie, he would naturally be regretful of it and I am sure he is attempting to make amends, even now.'

'And succeeding, by all appearances.' Oberon raised

his glass and finished the last of his champagne. 'However, it is of little concern. No doubt you and Lord Longworth are anxious to see Miss Vallois settled in the most advantageous manner possible.'

Lavinia waved at an acquaintance across the floor. 'My husband and I are more concerned that she is happy, Mr Oberon.'

'Of course, but surely you agree that the suitability of a husband *must* be a factor in the final decision. Love is all very well, but it is nothing compared to the benefits that wealth and position can bestow. Benefits someone like myself, for example, would be in a position to confer.'

It took every ounce of acting skill Lavinia possessed to appear calm in light of his admission. 'You, Mr Oberon?'

'Surely you are not surprised by my interest. I have taken no pains to conceal my admiration of Miss Vallois.'

'But you have spent so little time in her company.'

'Sometimes very little is required. Besides…' his smile grew smug '…after our drive in the park, I believe she now looks upon me with more favour than she did in the past. And only think, Lady Longworth, if Miss Vallois were to become my bride, she would become your equal in society.'

His *bride*. 'I am well aware of what you would be able to give her, Mr Oberon,' Lavinia replied quietly, 'but I think it only fair to tell you that Miss Vallois has no interest in marriage.'

Oberon laughed. 'Yes, so Silverton informed me. But

you and I both know that's not true. All young ladies wish to be married. Even poor Jane.' Oberon glanced towards the refreshment table where she and Antoine were still chatting in a most amiable fashion. 'Pity. She is so obviously smitten, yet he, by virtue of being French and what he hopes to become, can offer her nothing. And soon he returns to Paris. No doubt thoughts of marriage are far from his mind.' Oberon smiled. 'Please give my regards to your husband, Lady Longworth. And perhaps you might tell him…' he took a last look towards Robert and Sophie '…tell him there is something I wish to discuss with him at his earliest convenience.'

Chapter Nine

Robert was reading the newspaper when Jane finally came down the next morning. She wore a morning gown of pale lavender and the soft colour put roses into her cheeks and deepened the green in her eyes. 'Good morning, Robert.'

'Jane.' He put down his paper. 'You look in fine spirits today.'

'I slept better than I have in days and awoke to the sound of a robin singing outside my window.' She helped herself to coddled eggs and toast from the sideboard. 'Did you enjoy yourself last evening?'

'Very much.'

'Sophie looked so very lovely. I would never have thought to dress up a plain white gown with lace in quite that manner. But it was most flattering.'

Robert decided it best to withhold comment. As far as he was concerned, Sophie could have draped herself in burlap and still looked beautiful.

'She dances quite well,' Jane said, spreading a thin layer of marmalade on her toast. She took a bite and paused in thought. 'Do you think I would have been a good dancer had I not been troubled with this wretched foot?'

'I think you would have been a very good dancer if it was something you enjoyed doing.'

'Does that matter? You do not particularly enjoy dancing, yet you are very good at it.'

'Sometimes we do things whether we like them or not.' Robert remembered the long hours spent with his tutor learning the intricacies of the steps so he would not embarrass himself when the time came. 'Dancing is a necessary part of a gentleman's education.'

'Mr Vallois acquitted himself very well,' Jane commented in an offhand manner. 'I saw him partner Miss Templeton in the minuet and she is not an accomplished dancer at all.'

Robert shrugged as he returned his attention to his paper. 'I suspect dancing is as widely done in France as it is here.'

'But one would not expect a man who intended to become a doctor of having time for such frivolous pastimes. Although Mr Vallois does not strike me as being like other doctors.'

'How many other doctors have you known?'

'You know what I mean. Mr Vallois is passionately interested in a wide variety of subjects, not only in the study of medicine. He can speak intelligently on matters pertaining to science and archaeology, and he is very well read. He can recite Shakespeare as well as any actor on the stage today.'

Aware that Mr Vallois's name was coming up a little too often for his liking, Robert said tersely, 'A talent that will no doubt prove useful in his chosen career.'

'That was unkind, Robert.'

He looked up. 'Was it? I thought I was simply being honest.'

'Why do you not like Mr Vallois? Apart from that one occasion when he paid me a compliment to which *you* took exception, he has been the perfect gentleman.'

'I never said I didn't like him.'

'You didn't have to. I can tell from the way your voice changes when you speak of him. It's because he's French, isn't it?'

'My voice does not change when I speak of him,' Robert said, putting the newspaper aside. 'But he is due to return to Paris at any moment, so there is no point in *you* losing your heart to him.'

'I have not lost my heart to him!'

'Then why does *your* voice change every time you speak of *him*?'

Jane said nothing, obviously loathe to answer a question to which Robert already knew the answer. 'It wouldn't work, Jane,' he said more gently. 'What Antoine Vallois wants from life and what you want are entirely different. He would not make you happy and I would resent him for not being able to do so.'

'You know nothing about him,' Jane whispered. 'You resent him because he *is* French.'

So, they were back to that, Robert thought wearily. A

subject neither of them wished to discuss and for which there were no acceptable answers. 'If my resentment of the French was an issue, I would hardly be spending time in Sophie's company, now would I?'

'It was a *man* who shot our brother, Robert. I suspect that is how you are able to rationalise your interest in her.'

He folded his napkin and stood up. 'I'm going out. Is there anything you would like me to fetch for you?'

'Yes. A book. From Hatchard's.' She scribbled the name on a piece of paper and thrust it at him. 'If it's not too much trouble.'

He took the piece of paper and tucked it in his pocket. 'It never has been before.'

She had the grace to look embarrassed, but she did not relent. She glanced towards the window, her back as rigid as her voice. 'Shall I tell Cook to expect you for lunch?'

'No. I've sent a note round to Lawrence Welton, asking him to meet me at his club.'

'Mr Welton?' Jane frowned. 'Is he not a close friend of Mr Oberon's?'

'He was, but they seem to have fallen out and I haven't seen Lawrence in weeks. I just wanted to make sure everything's all right.' He bent to kiss her cheek. 'I'll see you later this evening.'

'Fine.'

He stood up, hating the brittle tension between them. What was he supposed to say? That he was *happy* about her affection for Antoine Vallois? That he *liked* the idea of her marrying a Frenchman and possibly moving away to France? It would take Edmund Kean himself to make that performance believable. 'Look, why don't you order the trap? It's a lovely day for a drive and it might be pleasant for you to get out of the house for a while.'

For a moment Jane refused to look at him, her expression as stiff as her posture. But Robert knew his sister well. She could no more stay angry with him than he could with her—and as if realising the argument would only serve to prolong an unnatural state of conflict, she gave in with a sigh. 'Yes, it is a lovely morning. Far too nice to waste on pointless arguments.'

'I only want what's best for you, Jane,' Robert said. 'You know that, don't you?'

She looked up at him and eventually nodded. 'Yes, but sometimes I wonder if either of us knows what that really is.'

Lawrence Welton did not arrive at Watier's at the specified hour, nor within the half-hour Robert waited for him. Both struck him as strange, given that Welton was normally a very punctual fellow. But finally giving it up as a bad deal, Robert turned and headed towards St James's. He'd send Lawrence a note later, suggesting they reschedule.

He was just passing White's when he heard someone hail him. 'Mr Silverton!'

Turning, he saw Lord Longworth crossing the street in his direction. 'My lord.'

'I'm just on my way in for some lunch. Care to join me?'

Robert inclined his head. 'That would be most agreeable.'

Being a predominantly Tory club, White's was not an establishment Robert frequented. But Longworth was greeted by several gentlemen whose names were well known in society and then shown with some deference to a table next to the tall window. After ordering a bottle of claret, Longworth said, 'I was supposed to have lunch with Mr Oberon, but he sent word he would be unable to attend.'

'Really.' Robert smoothed the linen napkin across his lap. 'It would appear his loss is my gain. But I am surprised by your invitation, given my current standing in society.'

'Yes, well, I expect that will resolve itself soon enough,' Longworth said. 'Once Lady Mary marries, all will be forgotten and society will find someone else to pick apart—' He broke off as the butler arrived with their wine, and waited until after he'd left to continue. 'Besides, you've had far more serious matters to contend with. Tell me,' he said casually, 'with regard to Michael, did you ever find out how your brother came to be where he was?'

'You mean in a deserted barn miles from anywhere?' Robert shook his head. 'Very little information was made available to us. I know my father tried to get details, but it was almost as though no one wanted to talk about it. Other men were given heroes' burials, but it seemed to me Michael's death was hushed up.' He raised the glass to his lips. 'I thought it damned unfair.'

Longworth rubbed his finger along the stem of his

glass. 'There are things you don't know, Robert. Things that couldn't be made public at the time.'

'What are you talking about?'

'I won't go into detail. Suffice it to say we were in a difficult situation in the days leading up to Waterloo. Napoleon intended sweeping into Brussels and had established a presence at both Mons and Charleroi. But from which place would the main thrust be launched?'

'I thought Wellington suspected Mons because it was on the main Paris to Brussels Highway and ten miles closer to Brussels than Charleroi?' Robert said.

'But did that mean his presence in Charleroi was simply a diversionary tactic? We couldn't know for sure. Though Napoleon was outnumbered two to one by the coalition forces by the time he reached Beaumont, Wellington knew better than to underestimate him, especially after what happened at Leipzig. But with no idea how many men Napoleon had, it made it difficult for Wellington to plan any kind of counter-offensive. So, a handful of men were sent out to collect whatever intelligence they could.'

'Sent out,' Robert said, his eyes narrowing. 'You mean, as spies.'

'Exactly. And eventually, a report came back from Mons indicating that Napoleon intended to launch the offensive from Charleroi. Wellington received it in time to plan a counter-offensive and the coalition forces intercepted Napoleon at Waterloo.'

Robert had no trouble following the series of events. The news of Napoleon's defeat at Waterloo had been front-page news and the cause of much celebration. What he didn't understand was why Longworth was bringing it up now. 'What has this to do with Michael?'

'The men selected for that mission were the very best Britain had,' Longworth said. 'They were men who could be counted on to get the job done. And they did get it done, but not without casualties. The reason I'm telling you this now is because I think you need to know why no one told you the truth at the time. You see, Robert…' Longworth looked around, then dropped his voice even further '…your brother Michael was one of them.'

For a moment, shock stole the breath from Robert's lungs. *Michael, an intelligence agent for the Crown?* Impossible! His brother would never have kept such a secret from his family. He had been the most honest, the most decent man Robert had ever known.

And yet, the more he thought about it, the more he realised it made sense. It explained why Michael would abruptly leave London and not tell anyone where he was going. It explained why he would be absent for weeks on end and then suddenly reappear, but not be able to tell them where he had been. His brother an agent for the British Government. Why the hell hadn't he figured it out for himself? 'Why weren't we told?'

'The Department felt it too dangerous, so the men were sworn to secrecy. Most wives never knew their husbands or sons were employed by the government.'

'We never even suspected,' Robert said ruefully. 'And yet, now that you've told me, it all makes perfect sense. But why am I hearing this now? And why are *you* the one telling me?'

'Because I think it's time you knew the truth.

Something went badly wrong on that mission, Robert,' Longworth said bluntly. 'Michael wasn't supposed to be on his own the night he was killed, but the letter that should have gone out advising him the mission had been cancelled was never sent. He was betrayed by one of our own—the same man who killed several of our best agents.' Longworth's blue eyes blazed. 'The same man who tried to kill me.'

Robert stiffened in shock. 'Dear God, *you're* one of them too?'

'Keep your voice down,' Longworth said. 'Yes, I was, and though I didn't work with your brother, I know many of the men who did and they all said he was as brave as any man out there. He did a lot of good before…'

'Before they got to him.'

Longworth nodded, his eyes heavy with regret as he took a deep swallow of wine.

Robert said nothing. It was almost too much to take in. Being told of his brother's true occupation. Of hearing Longworth's admission as to his own involvement in the covert operations. Of hearing how badly the mission had gone wrong… 'Does Lady Longworth know about your involvement?'

'She had to. On my last mission to France, after I was shot by the man who killed your brother, I was found by a young French couple who took me in and saw to my injuries. But when I returned to England, it was with no memory of who I was or what my life had been. Because I was engaged to Lavinia at the time, my commanding officer felt she might be able to help in my recovery, so he told her the truth about what I was doing in France.

We still needed to find the man who'd shot me and murdered a dozen other agents. Eventually, we did.'

Robert sat back, digesting what was turning out to be an incredible story. 'How many people are aware of this?'

'Very few and I'd like it to remain that way,' Longworth said, his tone leaving Robert in no doubt as to the seriousness of the matter. 'Napoleon may be banished, but some men carry grudges for years. I only told you this so you would understand how your brother came to lose his life. The Englishman who shot him—'

'The *Englishman*?' Robert gasped. 'But the note found in Michael's pocket—'

'Was put there to throw us off the track,' Longworth admitted. 'Havermere was a double agent. He'll likely spend the rest of his life serving at his Majesty's pleasure, but before he was apprehended, he took a lot of good men down. Your brother was one of them.'

In that split second, Robert's world turned upside down. Everything he'd come to believe about the French since the night his family had received word of Michael's death shattered like glass. His hatred of the French was completely unfounded. His brother's murderer had been one of their own.

It was nearly two o'clock before Robert said his good-byes to Lord Longworth, but still in need of time to review all he had learned, he decided not to go home, but to take a stroll through the bustling streets. It was easier to hide one's confusion in a crowd than to face a sister who was far too perceptive for her own good. He lost track of time as he walked, his mind going over and over what Lord Longworth had told him. *Michael, an agent for the Crown. His only brother, murdered by an Englishman.* What a fool he'd been—

'Silver! What the devil are you doing? Didn't you hear me calling?'

Pulled from the turmoil of his thoughts, Robert lifted his head and saw Oberon striding towards him. 'No.'

'Bit out of your area, aren't you?'

Robert looked up and realised he was almost at Grosvenor Square. 'I wasn't paying attention.'

'Obviously not. But never mind that. I want to talk to you about Miss Vallois.'

'What about her?'

'Only that I saw you with her last night and wondered what you were playing at.'

The proprietary note in Oberon's voice set Robert's teeth on edge. 'Playing at?'

'You assured me you weren't interested in the girl. That your only concern was that she not get hurt. Yet last night, I could have sworn I saw something between you.'

'What you saw was an apology being offered for the way I spoke to her the other morning. I was endeavouring to set things right.'

'Is that *all* you were doing?'

Robert's eyes narrowed. 'I fail to see what business that is of yours.'

'Perhaps you'll have a better understanding when I tell you I intend to speak to Lord Longworth about Miss Vallois. I would have done it today, but I was held up.

And I would take it as a personal favour if you were to stay away from her. I can't have my future wife associating with people like you.'

People like *him*? Robert bit back the reply that sprang to his lips, saying instead, 'If the lady chooses to seek out my company, I'm not going to turn her away. But speak to Longworth if you must. The choice will ultimately be hers.'

'The choice? Are you saying you intend to go after her?'

There it was. The question, poised like a sleeping cobra. A line had been drawn and Robert knew that if he stepped over that line, the cobra would strike. But the time for doing nothing had passed. 'That is a matter between Miss Vallois and myself.'

The hiss was audible, the creature awakened. 'You're a fool, Silver. What have you to offer her in comparison to me? Not wealth. Not title. Certainly not a position in society. How will she feel when doors keep closing in her face? When the invitations don't come and your social life dwindles to a handful of people as dull as yourselves. I can give her *everything*,' he said. 'Beautiful clothes. The finest jewels. A silver carriage drawn by four white horses, with her very own tiger to ride behind. And in time, people will make their curtsies to the exquisite Viscountess Oberon. You can give her *nothing*. Face it, Silver, Miss Vallois is as good as mine.'

Robert couldn't argue with a word Oberon said. But the fact the man was stupid enough to believe any of those things mattered to Sophie told him how little he really knew about the lady he hoped to make his wife.

'I've always thought,' Robert said quietly, 'that as good as is a *long* way from being a sure thing.'

Oberon's voice hardened. 'I don't like your tone.'

'And I don't like being warned to stay away. Now if you'll excuse me—'

'Not so fast.' Oberon's hand snaked out, his fingers closing on Robert's wrist. 'I've expended a great deal of effort on Miss Vallois's behalf. I've modified my behaviour, changed my appearance, and I do believe the lady has noticed.'

'In that case...' Robert shook him off '...you have nothing to worry about.'

'Don't do this, Silver,' Oberon said, his expression turning dark and resentful. 'Take my advice. Stop now before it's too late.'

'And if I don't?'

'You *will* come to regret it. I can make things very unpleasant for you and those you care about.'

Robert forced himself to look at the man standing beside him. A man he thought he knew. A man he'd once liked. 'If you hurt anyone I care about, I *will* see you burn.'

'Fine.' Oberon stepped back, the cold mask of the gentleman replaced by the face of the cobra. 'Just don't say I didn't warn you.'

Robert was halfway home when he remembered Jane's book. He'd been in such a foul mood after his confrontation with Oberon that he'd forgotten all about it. And knowing it wouldn't sweeten Jane's disposition to return empty handed, he headed back in the direction of Hatchard's—only to find Sophie inside, perusing a selection of books set out on a small table. For a while, he just stood and watched her. She picked up a slim, leather-bound volume and opened it to the first page. While she read, her lips curved upwards, bringing into view the dimples he was suddenly finding so damned irresistible.

He took off his hat and approached, hoping the truce they had established last night might yet be in place. 'Miss Vallois?'

When she looked up, he was pleased to see a warm glow of welcome in her eyes. 'Mr Silverton.'

'I hope I'm not disturbing you.'

'Not at all.'

'You seem to be enjoying the book.'

'Not really.' She closed the volume and set it down. 'The subject matter was not to my taste.'

'Yet you smiled.'

'More for the unusual style of the author's prose than for its brilliance.'

Robert stared down at the floor. Conversation had never been difficult for him, yet when it came to Sophie, he felt as awkward as a schoolboy. 'You enjoy reading?'

'Very much. I share my brother's belief that it is the best way to expand one's knowledge and understanding of others.'

He relaxed slightly. Good. Books. A common interest. 'Have you a favourite author?'

'I confess to enjoying Miss Austen's works at present, though I probably have a better knowledge of the classics.'

'You obviously share your brother's partiality for them,' Robert said drily.

He felt the curiosity of her gaze. 'How did you know Antoine likes the classics?'

'Jane mentioned it over breakfast this morning. I gather they were speaking of it last night.' He stopped and cleared his throat. 'Miss Vallois, you said in the carriage that you'd like to explore the ancient pyramids. Have you had a chance to visit the British Museum?'

'Not yet.'

'Then perhaps it's time you did. Though not as atmospheric as wandering through the desert, the Egyptian display is most impressive and I would be happy to show it to you.'

Her smile left him breathless. 'Thank you, Mr Silverton, I'd like that very much. Probably better than getting all that sand in our shoes anyway.'

'I dare say.' Unbidden, his mind conjured up an image of Sophie walking barefoot across the sand towards him. Of her sitting on his lap, her arm around his neck as he gently brushed the grains from her feet. He could almost feel the heat of an ancient sun burning through his clothes—and the heat at the thought of holding her in his arms burning him everywhere else—

'Fine.' His voice roughened. 'Shall we say, tomorrow afternoon?'

'Yes.' Her smile was blinding. 'Tomorrow would be perfect.'

They parted at the door and as Robert started for

home, he felt a hundred times better than he had after his dismal confrontation with Oberon. But one thing had become painfully clear. He had to keep Sophie away from Oberon. The man didn't want a wife. He wanted a beautiful china doll he could parade around town. One he could dress up and show off and keep under lock and key. He certainly didn't want a woman with opinions or dreams of her own. He would scoff at her wanting to fly above London in a hot-air balloon. Laugh at her dreams of exploring the pyramids. God only knew what he would say about her wanting to float down the Amazon on a raft…

'Boat,' Robert murmured under his breath. No, Oberon was right about one thing. There *could* only be one winner in the battle for Sophie's heart. And while circumstances might prevent it being him, Robert was damned if he'd ever let it be a self-centred snake like Montague Oberon!

Sophie was barely through the door when Banyon informed her that Mr Oberon was waiting to see her. 'I've put him in the parlour, miss, to await your answer.'

'Thank you, Banyon. Is Lady Longworth at home?'

'She is not and I did inform Mr Oberon of that, but he asked if he might have a brief moment of your time. He said it was on a matter of some importance. Regarding… a mutual friend.'

It was clear from the butler's expression that he was no fonder of passing along cryptic messages than Sophie was of receiving them, but, curious about Oberon's reference to a mutual friend, she said, 'Thank you, Banyon. I'll see him in the drawing room.'

Once there, Sophie paused to take a few deep breaths. Moments later, Oberon arrived. 'Miss Vallois. Thank you for agreeing to see me.'

'Your message was intriguing to say the least. Will you sit down?'

'Thank you, but I don't intend to stay long. I am aware that Lady Longworth is from home, but I came here out of concern for you.'

Sophie arched an eyebrow. 'Am I in some kind of danger?'

'Not of a physical kind, but you could be when it comes to…matters of the heart.'

Tempted to inform him that matters of her heart were none of his business, Sophie said, 'Banyon said you wished to speak to me about a mutual friend.'

'Yes. Robert Silverton. A man for whom I know you hold a special affection.'

Aware of the need to tread carefully, Sophie said, 'Mr Silverton *is* a friend, but nothing more. As you pointed out, there are issues that would always come between us.'

'Nevertheless, given the way I saw the two of you talking at Sir David and Lady Hester's last night, I thought you might have…resolved that issue.'

A warning bell rang. So, he had been spying on her. Watching her while she was talking to Robert. 'What you saw,' Sophie said slowly, 'was Mr Silverton offering me an apology for what had passed between us with regard to his brother's death. An apology I was happy to accept.'

'Has he asked to see you again?'

The words came at her like the flick of a whip. 'I really don't think that's any of your business, Mr Oberon.'

'Ah, but it is, Miss Vallois. Because I came here today with a view to making you aware of two things. One of which you will find very distressing. About Mr Silverton.'

So, he had come to tell tales on his friend. 'I cannot imagine what you could say about Mr Silverton that would make me think ill of him.'

'Not even that his sudden interest in you may have more to do with his hopes of winning my stallion than with any genuine feelings of love or affection for you?'

The statement was so bizarre that Sophie felt shock rather than outrage upon hearing it. 'Kindly explain yourself, sir.'

'Of course. I happen to know that Robert recently entered into a wager. One of his own devising, with the goal being to make the most beautiful woman in London his mistress. And given that he's told me more than once that he has no intention of marrying, I can only wonder at the reasons behind his sudden interest in you.'

Sophie was glad she was standing by the window. It allowed her to pretend an interest in the goings-on of passers-by in the street below. So, he would have her believe that Robert's interest in her was motivated by a desire to make her his mistress? Truly he did not know his friend well. 'I couldn't help but notice that you said

Mr Silverton hoped to win your stallion. Does that mean you were also a party to this wager?'

'I regret to say my name was taken down,' he admitted, 'but I can assure you it was not with my agreement and it certainly wasn't over the acquisition of a mistress. I had already informed Silverton that it was my intention to seek a wife and settle down to married life. At least he had the decency to record my participation as such.'

'So you're telling me that Mr Silverton wagered his ability to find a mistress against yours to find a wife, with the prize being your stallion.'

'I fear so,' Oberon said. 'He's always coveted the beast. He once told me that if an opportunity ever presented itself whereby he might take Thunder from me, he would do so without hesitation. That, I believe, was his primary motivation in suggesting the wager. And to be fair, he did offer up a prize of his own. A rather pretty little ring, but one I know to be a cherished family heirloom.'

Sophie kept her gaze fixed on the view outside the window. 'I am surprised he would risk such a valuable item.'

'I did try to persuade him against it, but he said it meant nothing to him. You must understand, Miss Vallois, Robert is a long-standing knight of the elbow. His passion for gambling runs as hot as the blood in his veins. It became his solace when his world turned upside down, and though he hides his craving beneath a civilised veneer, it is there none the less.'

Sophie let the curtain fall back into place. So, now Oberon would have her believe that Robert was a heartless gambler to whom winning meant everything. A man whose interest in her was of the most scandalous kind. 'What do you think Mr Silverton would say,' she asked softly, 'if I were to question him about what you've just told me?'

'I suspect he would try to justify his conduct to you by whatever means he could. There would certainly be no point in his trying to deny the wager exists. You could verify what I've said easily enough. I simply wished you to hear the details of the thing from me so that if he told you differently, you would be in a better position to judge who was telling you the truth.'

'And you would have me believe that *you* are the one doing that.'

Oberon smiled, managing to look both guilty and humble at the same time. 'I may have been a trifle bold in my conduct towards you in the past, Miss Vallois, but I like to think I have always been honest. And I'm not saying Robert is a bad man for, indeed, he is not. But he has been through a great deal, and sometimes, when a man is pushed to the very limits of his endurance, the darker emotions rise up to consume him. I would not wish to see you become…an unwitting victim of that weakness.'

Sophie tapped her fingers on the sash. It was hard to believe they were talking abut the same man. Yes, Robert had been pushed to the limits, but it was impossible to reconcile the desperate, unfeeling gambler Oberon made him out to be with the caring, honourable gentleman she had come to know and admire. Her intuition told her she could not be that far wrong. Besides, experience had taught her it was never wise to judge a person's conduct until one was in full possession of the facts. Oberon had told her his side of the story. She had yet to hear Robert's.

'You said there were two things you wished to see me about, Mr Oberon,' Sophie said, meeting his gaze. 'The possibility of my becoming Mr Silverton's mistress would seem to be one. Dare I ask about the other?'

He smiled, though his expression reflected an element of chagrin. 'I should have known you would not be so easily persuaded. Your loyalty does you credit, Miss Vallois, as does your willingness to believe the best of the people you care about. I hope I may be counted amongst those people, because my affection for you *is* the other matter I've come to see you about.'

Sophie caught her breath. Surely he was not about to declare himself. 'Mr Oberon, I would rather not—'

'Please hear me out. The only reason I've kept silent about my feelings was a result of being unsure of my place in yours. But now that I know Silverton has not stolen a march on me, the time has come to tell you that I care deeply for you, and that I have ever since we met. It would please me greatly if you would do me the honour of becoming my wife.'

No, no, no, this was not what she wanted to hear! 'How can you ask me such a question after admitting you were also a party to this wager?' Sophie said. 'By knowing you are as anxious to hold on to your stallion as you say Mr Silverton is to win him, I can only question the motive behind your proposal.'

He affected a look of pain. 'My dear Miss Vallois.

Horses are nothing more than commodities to be bought and sold. *You* are one of a kind. And did I not tell you that I became a party to the wager entirely without my knowledge?'

'Yes, but then everything you've told me today is unsubstantiated,' Sophie said. 'I have no proof that the claims you make against Mr Silverton are valid, or that your feelings for me are as honest as you would have me believe.'

'Nevertheless, they are what they are, and only consider what you stand to gain by marrying me. Wealth, status, a title. Everything a woman could ask for.'

But not love, Sophie reflected. He said nothing about being in love with her—because he wasn't. 'Thank you, Mr Oberon. Though I am flattered by your offer, I cannot possibly accept. Apart from the fact I have no wish to marry, I do not love you. And I would *never* consider marrying without love. And now, I bid you good afternoon.'

He didn't look surprised. He didn't even look regretful. As he started towards the door, he actually began to smile. 'I understand. But if you think about it a bit longer, you'll come to realise that in this case, love is not the only consideration. You stand to gain a great deal by accepting my proposal, Miss Vallois, but you stand to lose even more by turning me down. You might like to think about that before giving me your answer. And I *will* call again,' he said as he opened the door. 'Of that you can be sure.'

Chapter Ten

The memory of Mr Oberon's visit stayed with Sophie long after he'd left, as did his ominous parting words. She had no idea what he'd meant by saying she stood to lose much by turning him down, but she wasn't foolish enough to believe he was speaking in jest. What little she knew of Oberon convinced her he was a man used to getting his own way. As such, it was with a definite feeling of trepidation that she accompanied Nicholas and Lavinia to a soirée at the home of Lord and Lady Chiswick that same evening. She felt quite sure Mr Oberon would be there and that he would be watching her every move. As she settled into the carriage for the short ride to Park Lane, she couldn't shake the feeling that something very bad was about to happen.

'So, this is the young lady we've been hearing so much about,' Lord Chiswick said upon being introduced to her. 'I can see why.' He was a large man, with a large nose, large hands and ears that stuck out from two tufts of unruly grey hair. 'You are an uncommonly beautiful young woman. I'll wager the young bucks are beating a path to your door.' His bushy eyebrows twitched as his hand closed hot and heavy around hers. 'I know I would, had you been part of *my* circle thirty years ago.'

'Put the poor girl down, Wallace, you'll give her nightmares,' Lady Chiswick said with a long-suffering sigh. 'You must forgive my husband, Miss Vallois. He is just returned from safari and killing wild animals always tends to fire his imagination. So, are you and your brother enjoying your visit to London?'

'Yes, very much,' Sophie said, disengaging her hand as tactfully as possible. 'There is so much to see and do.'

'London is the finest city in the world,' Lady Chiswick said proudly. 'I wasn't at all impressed with Paris when I went to visit my brother and sister-in-law there last year. The filth was appalling.'

'When did you go?' Lavinia asked.

'December. Wretched time to travel, but my niece horrified everyone by falling in love with some well-to-do Frenchman and marrying him. Shocking mess. Constance insisted I be there to lend the family moral support.'

Sophie felt a chill run down her spine. *Constance…and a December wedding.* It had to be a coincidence…

'Naturally, my brother wasn't at all happy,' Lady Chiswick was saying. 'The moment Georgina left on her wedding trip, he sold the house, packed up all their belongings and brought the entire household back to England. I think he was afraid his son and youngest daughter might do something equally foolish. He vowed none of them would ever set foot on French soil again.'

Sophie closed her eyes. Constance Grant-Ogilvy had had three children: one son and two daughters. The wilful, eldest daughter had been called Georgina, and before Sophie had left their employ, Georgina had hinted that she was in love with a man of whom her parents would not approve.

It *had* to be the same family. And if they were related to Lady Chiswick, they might well be here tonight…

'Sophie, are you feeling all right?' Lavinia asked softly. 'You've suddenly gone quite pale.'

'Have I?'

'Probably the heat,' Lady Chiswick said. 'It always affects the newcomers. Have you smelling salts with you, dear?'

'No! That is, thank you, but…that won't be necessary,' Sophie said haltingly. 'I just need some air.'

'Why don't you take a turn around the garden?' Lavinia suggested. 'The night air should put some colour back in your cheeks.'

'Excellent idea, Lady Longworth,' Lady Chiswick said. 'You'll find the entrance through there, Miss Vallois. I'm sure a few minutes will be all you need.'

Sophie inclined her head, grateful for the opportunity to escape. But as she headed towards the French doors that led out into the garden, she knew she needed more than air. She needed to get out of this house. Now…before anything dreadful happened. She hadn't told anyone of her reasons for leaving Mrs Grant-Ogilvy's employ. Accusing the eldest son of inappropriate behaviour was never a recommended course of action for a servant. After all, what an Englishman did on his own property was nobody's business but his own. Sophie had been told that more than once. Fortunately, Eldon hadn't succeeded in ravishing her. She'd been too quick for him. And several well-placed jabs from her elbow had been enough to cool his ardour, as had the veiled threat that she carried a pistol and knew how to use it.

But the fear that *one* day he might catch her off guard had eventually forced Sophie to turn in her notice, and she had left that very day. As expected, Mrs Grant-Ogilvy had been furious. She'd vowed that Sophie would never find work with a decent family again, and had glee-fully predicted that she would be on the streets within a week—which, of course, she hadn't. With several good clients bringing her custom on a regular basis, and the small amount of money Antoine brought in, they were able to get by. She didn't need the pittance Mrs Grant-Ogilvy paid her, and she certainly didn't need her snooty disdain—

'Miss Vallois?'

Sophie looked up, startled to see Robert coming towards her. 'Mr Silverton. What are you doing out here?'

'I could ask you the same thing.' He walked along a winding path illuminated by candles set in metal boxes. 'Shouldn't you be inside mingling?'

'Probably, but the room grew unbearably hot.' Sophie frowned. 'I vow English hostesses vie with one another to see who can squeeze the greatest number of people into their houses.'

'It is an ongoing competition,' Robert agreed. Stopping before her, he rested his foot on the stone bench. 'I was taking a walk in the lower garden, wrestling with my thoughts.'

Wrestling with his thoughts? Sophie stared into the dark waters of the ornamental pond, convinced that his thoughts couldn't be half as troubling as hers. For one thing, he wouldn't be worrying about a proposal of marriage from an unwanted suitor, complete with thinly veiled threats of retribution should she refuse. He also wouldn't be troubled by the knowledge that her hostess was related to her former employer, and that the latter might well be in the house tonight. And he certainly wouldn't be worrying about the fact that he had discovered her here, alone in a moonlit garden, with thoughts running through her mind that were both sweet…and forbidden.

'I wasn't aware you were here,' she said, adding feebly, 'I didn't see Jane inside.'

'Jane didn't come with me.' He looked pained for a moment. 'We had words the other morning and she decided to stay home.'

'Words? I find it hard to imagine you and Jane having an argument.'

'Nevertheless, it does happen. I am not the perfect brother Jane would have you believe.'

'We are none of us perfect,' Sophie said distantly. 'I am constantly amazed by the number of mistakes I make. I thought as I got older they would diminish.'

His laughter was as soft as the night air. 'We all like to think we improve with age, but somehow, I suspect it's more wishful thinking than anything else. But I cannot imagine a lady who wishes to float down the Amazon in a boat, or ride in a hot-air balloon, being overly concerned with mistakes.' He straightened, then came to sit down beside her. 'Jane thinks you're marvellous.'

'She does?'

'Oh, yes. You're the closest friend she's ever had. People tend not to want to associate with those who are afflicted in some way,' he said quietly. 'I suppose it's the law of the jungle. Only the strong survive. The weak are weeded out and destroyed.'

'You mustn't speak of her that way!'

'Who better? I know first-hand how cruel people can be, having seen examples of it all my life. Her chances for happiness are few.'

'I think you worry needlessly, Mr Silverton—'

'Robert, please.'

Her heart did a silly little flip. 'Robert. Your sister is a beautiful young woman with a warm and giving nature. She will be loved for those reasons alone.'

'I wish that were the case, but at eight-and-twenty, Jane's chances of marrying well are non-existent and at this stage, her chances of marrying at all are slim. Had she a sizeable portion, I might hold out more hope,' Robert said, 'but much of what we had went to pay off Father's gambling debts. And while we manage well enough, Jane will always be dependent on me for her living. I don't begrudge that for a moment, but I would have liked her to know the sweetness of a husband's love and the joy of holding her own children in her arms.'

Sophie had to turn away lest she reveal too much of

her own longings. 'What kind of husband would you wish her to find?'

'One for whom she can feel a deep and abiding love, and who will love her deeply in return. He must respect rather than pity her, for Jane would hate that above all. And he must take her as she is and not look to change her.'

'Do you believe such a man exists?'

'I have to. For her sake, if not for mine.' Robert reached for her hand and slowly raised it to his lips. 'But thank you for being her friend. It means a great deal…to both of us.' Then, turning it over, he pressed a soft, lingering kiss into her palm.

Sophie inhaled sharply. The caress was unexpected… and disturbingly intimate, as was the warmth of his breath on her skin. The air suddenly thickened and grew hot. And when he looked at her…ah, the way he looked at her…

'Miss Vallois?' called a voice from the house. 'Where are you, child? Miss Vallois?'

Sophie gasped, all but wrenching her hand back. 'Lady Chiswick!'

'Does she know you're out here?' Robert asked.

'I'm afraid so.'

His expletive made her blush. 'Then it's best she not find us alone. We don't need *both* of us being shunned by good society. Come, I'll take you back inside.'

Unfortunately, barely had they stood up before Lavinia, Lady Chiswick and Mr Oberon appeared in the doorway. 'Miss Vallois!' Lady Chiswick cried in horror. 'Alone in the garden with a man? What is the meaning of this?'

'Well, well, if it isn't my old friend,' Mr Oberon murmured. 'Enjoying a moonlight rendezvous in the garden. How terribly romantic.'

'It wasn't a rendezvous!' Sophie said, glad for the darkness that hid her blush. 'Mr Silverton and I met quite by—'

'Mr *Silverton*?' Lady Chiswick wheezed. '*Robert* Silverton?'

'Yes, that's right,' Robert said, frowning. 'Is something wrong?'

'There most definitely is.' Lady Chiswick's eyes went as hard as bits of stone. 'How *dare* you show your face in my house, sir! You were most definitely *not* invited.'

'As a matter of fact, he was,' Mr Oberon said smoothly. 'By your husband. I delivered the invitation myself.'

The lady turned an alarming shade of red. 'My husband does *not* extend invitations to my gatherings, Mr Oberon. And even if he was foolish enough to do so, Mr Silverton should have had the decency to decline.' The lady's voice dropped to a sepulchral tone. 'He is guilty of the *most* unconscionable behaviour towards my goddaughter—'

'Goddaughter?' Lavinia said…and then gasped. 'Oh, dear Lord. Lady Mary Kelsey is your *goddaughter*?'

'Yes, she is, and she has been treated abominably by this man! I want you out of my house, sir. Now!'

'But, surely you are being too harsh, Lady Chiswick,' Lavinia said, quickly drawing the glass doors closed behind them.

'Do not try to placate me, Lady Longworth. If a member of *your* family had been treated in such a manner, you would feel as I do. My poor Mary did nothing to deserve the treatment she received at this man's hands.' She pointed a bony finger at Robert. 'Leave my house at once, sir!'

'*Le bon Dieu*, how can you be so cruel?' Sophie said, shaken by the woman's ferocity. 'Mr Silverton is a gentleman—'

'He is a bounder, Miss Vallois, and you would do well not to waste your time defending him!'

'Miss Vallois is not defending me.' Robert's quiet voice cut through the night like the blade of a scimitar. 'She is speaking from the goodness of her heart and without knowledge of what happened.' He turned to glare at Oberon. 'Unlike some people who know very well.'

'No, he is *not* a bounder,' Sophie said emphatically. 'He would not have ended his engagement to Lady Mary unless he had a very good reason.'

'A good *reason*?' Lady Chiswick was close to apoplectic. 'There is no *good* reason except that he is a selfish and fickle man!'

Sophie's temper flared. 'He is none of those things! He is fine and decent and—'

'Miss *Beaudoin*? What on earth are *you* doing here?'

No one had heard the French doors open, but the commanding voice that rang across the terrace instantly silenced all arguments. Sophie just closed her eyes. She had no need to turn around to see who the newcomer was. She would have recognised that imperious voice anywhere!

'What is the meaning of this, Eudora?' Mrs Constance Grant-Ogilvy demanded of her sister-in-law. 'What is Miss Beaudoin doing here and why is she dressed like that?'

The woman's enunciation would have put an Oxford scholar to shame, and for the first time that evening, Lady Chiswick seemed completely flummoxed. 'I have no idea what you're talking about, Constance. This is Miss Sophie Vallois. She and her brother are here as guests of Lord and Lady Longworth.'

'Sophie Vallois? What are you talking about, the girl's name is Chantal Beaudoin and she is a French seamstress,' Mrs Grant-Ogilvy informed her. 'I employed her to teach the girls French.'

'Well, well, it would seem we have a case of double identity,' Mr Oberon murmured. 'Perhaps we should give the young lady a chance to explain herself.'

Lady Chiswick drew herself up. 'Well, Miss Vallois. What have you to say for yourself?'

Sophie pressed her hand to her stomach, feeling it pitch and roll a thousand times worse than when she'd been on board ship. 'I—'

'You don't have to answer that, Sophie,' Lavinia said. 'It's nobody's business but your own.'

'No, it's all right, Lavinia.' Sophie knew she had no recourse. She had to be honest. 'Mrs Grant-Ogilvy is not mistaken. I *am* Sophie Vallois, but I was using the name Chantal Beaudoin when she hired me.'

'Then you *did* work for my sister-in-law,' Lady

Chiswick hissed. 'And you admit to changing your name. Why?'

'I really don't think that matters,' Robert said, stepping forward. 'It is enough that Miss Vallois told you the truth.'

'On the contrary, I should think the reasons for *pretending* to be someone else always matter,' Mr Oberon said silkily.

'Stay out of this, Oberon,' Robert snapped. 'You've already said quite enough. Miss Vallois, allow me to take you home.'

'Not without answering my question!' Lady Chiswick barked.

Robert dismissed her with a glance. 'With your permission, Lady Longworth?'

'Thank you, Mr Silverton, but I think it's time we all left.' For once, Lavinia's eyes were as cold and as hard as ice. 'I suddenly find the atmosphere oppressive and the company…suffocating.'

Lady Chiswick gasped. 'Well, I *never*!'

Robert walked up to Sophie and held out his arm. 'Miss Vallois?'

His voice was soft, the way it had been when they'd been alone in the garden. In silence, Sophie tucked her hand into the crook of his arm, feeling the much-needed strength of his body beneath her fingers. Warm. Firm. Reassuring. And with Lavinia on her other side, they walked across the terrace and into the house.

'You're doing well,' Robert whispered as they passed through the crowds of milling guests. 'Keep your head up and don't give them the satisfaction of seeing you break.'

Sophie nodded, reminding herself to keep breathing. Thankfully, the further they moved into the house, the fewer people turned to look. Obviously, Mrs Grant-Ogilvy's voice had only carried so far, but by the time they reached the street, Sophie was trembling. Nicholas was already there with the carriage and she let herself be bundled inside, felt a warm rug placed over her knees. As the carriage drew away, Sophie turned to see Robert standing alone on the street and felt her heart break at the expression on his face. It was all out now. Her make-believe castle was in ruins. The dragon had come—and he had come breathing fire.

Antoine and Lavinia were still in the breakfast parlour when Sophie finally came down the next morning. She had passed a restless night and barely touched the breakfast tray Lavinia had sent up. Her stomach was in knots, her mind spinning like a top. So much had happened. Mr Oberon's shocking revelations and equally disturbing proposal. Lady Chiswick's embarrassing discovery of her and Robert on the terrace, followed by the nightmarish appearance of Mrs Grant-Ogilvy.

And Robert, kissing her hand in the garden. Robert, walking strong and confident beside her. How fiercely she clung to that memory. To the remembrance of him putting his hand over hers and squeezing it gently during that long, endless walk. If it hadn't been for him…

'Sophie! Good morning,' Lavinia greeted her. 'Banyon, fresh coffee and toast, if you please.'

'No, just…coffee,' Sophie said. 'Thank you.'

The elderly servant nodded and withdrew. Lavinia turned back and her expression was deeply concerned. 'Did you get any sleep at all?'

'Not much,' Sophie admitted. 'But then I don't suppose any of us did.'

'That wretched Lady Chiswick,' Lavinia said, fuming. 'And that insufferable Mrs Grant-Ogilvy. I wanted to knock their heads together!'

Sophie managed a smile as she sank into a chair. Under normal circumstances, she would have laughed at seeing the usually unflappable Lavinia in a state of such high dudgeon. But given the situation, it was hard to imagine laughing at anything. 'Thank you, Lavinia, but Mrs Grant-Ogilvy was perfectly within her rights to question me. I *was* Chantal Beaudoin when I worked for her, so her confusion is understandable. Imagine if you were to see Banyon dressed in formal attire, pretending to be someone else and hobnobbing with lords and ladies at a society gathering. I dare say you would have had something to say too.'

'But you were there as our *guest*,' Lavinia said. 'You weren't pretending to be someone else.'

'Mrs Grant-Ogilvy thought I was.'

'It's all my fault,' Antoine said unhappily. 'After we left Bayencourt, I thought it would be safer if we changed our names. People were looking for Sophie and Antoine Vallois, not Chantal and Henri Beaudoin. And, when the months passed and nobody came, I saw no reason to change them back. I only did so after Sophie left

Mrs Grant-Ogilvy's employ so it would be easier if she wanted to find work.'

Sophie closed her eyes, feeling a return of the headache that had plagued her for the past three hours. She couldn't help wondering how Robert was feeling this morning. He had been humiliated too. What he was thinking now? Was he remembering the events of last night and wishing he'd never met her? Or was he remembering, like her, the sweetness of that kiss…?

'Is Nicholas home?' She pushed the memory away, aware that it hurt too much. 'I should speak with him as soon as possible.'

'He's in the library, but won't you have something to eat first?'

Sophie glanced at the plates of food set out along the sideboard and shook her head. Even if she had any appetite for food, it was more important that she speak to Nicholas. A piece of toast and a helping of eggs wasn't going to make explaining last night's débâcle any the more palatable.

Nicholas stood up as soon as she entered, the lines on his face reflecting the depth of his concern. 'Sophie, dear girl. How are you?'

'I've been better,' Sophie admitted as she closed the door. 'You don't look to have slept much.'

'What little sleep I did get was punctuated by uncharitable thoughts of those two dreadful women!' he growled. 'I'm so sorry about what happened last night. I would have done anything in my power to have prevented it.'

'There was nothing anyone *could* have done, Nicholas.

Who was to know that Lady Chiswick was Mrs Grant-Ogilvy's sister-in-law? *And* Lady Mary Kelsey's god-mother? Certainly not you or I.'

'No, and I suppose we must be exceedingly grateful that Lady Annabelle Durst and a friend happened to be in the garden when you and Robert were discovered,' Nicholas said, 'or the consequences would have been considerably worse.'

Sophie's brow furrowed. 'Lady Annabelle was *in the garden*?'

'Yes. Didn't you see her?'

'No. And Rob—Mr Silverton made no mention of her being there.'

'Perhaps he didn't know. But apparently, after we left Lady Chiswick's last night, Lady Annabelle made sure everyone knew that she had been in full sight of you and Mr Silverton the entire time, and that nothing inappropriate had taken place.'

It was almost too much to believe. Once again, the lady had come to her rescue. Sophie was beginning to wonder if Lady Annabelle wasn't some kind of…fairy godmother!

'I don't care as much for myself,' she said, 'but I do regret the embarrassment this will surely cause you and Lavinia. Soon all of London will know that I was employed by Mrs Grant-Ogilvy, pretending to be some-one else, and that I had the audacity to mingle with guests at the home of her sister-in-law. To say nothing of poor Mr Silverton's disgrace at the hands of that dreadful Lady Chiswick.'

Nicholas sighed. 'Lady Chiswick has never been one

of my favourite people, but she was perfectly within her rights to ask him to leave, Sophie. He should never have gone there in the first place.'

'But if he wasn't aware of the relationship between Lady Chiswick and Lady Mary, he cannot be held to blame,' Sophie said, stung by Nicholas's unexpected criticism. 'He is not the type of man who would knowingly offend anyone.'

'Nevertheless, ignorance does not absolve him of guilt. What he did to Lady Mary put him beyond the pale.' Nicholas leaned back against the edge of the desk, propping his hands on either side of his hips. 'Had he gone ahead and honoured his obligation to her—'

'But if she was the cause of the rift—'

'Had he gone ahead and married Lady Mary,' Nicholas repeated gently, 'none of this would have happened. A man's word is his bond and a promise, once given, cannot be retracted.'

'Not even if there is just cause?'

Nicholas sighed. 'Sometimes, not even then. However, the important thing is that *you* did nothing wrong, and that you told the truth in the face of a very difficult situation. That took courage and I'm proud of you, Sophie. Lavinia and I both are.'

'Then you're not sorry you invited me to come to London?'

'Sorry? My dear girl, you've brought us nothing but joy and I know Lavinia is dreading the thought of you going home. Frankly, so am I, but I'm not supposed to show it. Now, why don't you go and have something to eat? I'm sure you had nothing before you came to see me and you didn't have much last night. Then, later on, you and I will sit down and have a little talk about your future.'

'My future?'

'Yes. If it's not to be marriage, we must look at alternatives.' Nicholas put both hands on her shoulders. 'We just want you to be happy, Sophie. And we're willing to do whatever it takes to make that happen.'

It was with decidedly mixed feelings that Sophie accompanied Lavinia to the drapers shortly after lunch. She had already received a note from Robert, saying that, under the circumstances, it was probably best they not go to the museum together, and she had quickly sent one back, saying how sorry she was that the excursion had to be postponed. She'd added a postscript that she deeply regretted *most* of what had taken place the previous evening, and hoped he would be able to read through the lines to see that the time they'd spent alone in the garden…and his kiss…were definitely *not* part of her regrets.

Now, as she wandered up and down the well-stocked aisles, trying to pretend an interest in the brightly coloured bolts of fabric, lethargically looking at lace, she was unable to order her thoughts—

'…of course, it's not as though she ever *had* much of a chance of making a good marriage,' a lady standing with her back to Sophie said. 'Her being crippled and all. But it's shocking behaviour all the same…'

Crippled. Sophie's head slowly came up. Two ladies were chatting a few feet away from her. Neither one was known to her, but the fact they were talking about a single, crippled lady made the idea of doing the polite thing and moving away unthinkable.

She edged a little closer, suddenly very interested in a roll of elegant Alençon lace…

'Still, it's only speculation she went to his rooms,' the taller lady said. 'No one's come forward to say they actually saw it happen.'

'But if a gentleman's word can't be taken as truth, whose can? And when I was at Mrs Coldham's yesterday afternoon, three of the ladies were saying there was talk of her meeting that tall dark fellow in the park.'

Sophie's blood ran cold. Surely they weren't talking about *Jane*?

'It will be the ruin of her, of course,' the first lady said. 'She won't be accepted by good society now. Mrs Coldham said as much and no one disagreed with her. I dare say her brother will have no choice but to send her down to the country. And *if* he's fortunate enough to marry, which is doubtful given what he did to poor Lady Mary Kelsey, his wife will have the business of looking after her, and I don't envy her that.'

'Still, it is very sad,' the second lady said. 'I always thought so well of Miss Silverton. She seemed such a genteel young lady, and so well brought up. Certainly her mother was. But judging from the stories, she's not at all what we thought…'

The women carried on talking, but Sophie had heard more than enough. Forgetting her own concerns and dropping all pretence of shopping, she quickly went to find Lavinia, who had been standing too far away to hear any of it. 'Lavinia, I've just overheard the most appalling conversation.'

'Dear girl, whatever is the matter? You've gone as white as a sheet.'

'Come outside. I have no wish to speak of it here.'

Lavinia dropped the bolt of cloth she had been study-ing and the two quickly made their way into the street. Once Sophie was sure the other ladies were still inside, she told Lavinia all she had learned—and watched Lavinia's face go white. 'And you're sure you heard them say Jane's name?'

'Quite sure. At first, when they spoke of the lady being crippled, I hoped they were talking about someone else. But once they mentioned her name, there certainly wasn't any doubt.'

'This is very serious indeed,' Lavinia said. 'They actually *said* Jane went to a gentleman's rooms?'

'They did, though it was only speculation.' Sophie kept her voice low. 'But apparently several people saw her talking to a gentleman in the park.'

'Quite likely, for I know that Jane often takes the trap and drives out on her own. But she would *never* go to a gentleman's rooms. Even the rumour of such behaviour would be enough to ruin her.'

'Unfortunately, that is the rumour now circulating,' Sophie said. 'The ladies said Mr Silverton would have no choice but to take her down to the country.'

'Oh dear, this is dreadful.'

'Are we to tell her?' Sophie asked.

'Not yet. I am expected at a poetry reading at Lady Henley's later today,' Lavinia said. 'No doubt it will be well attended and I shall make discreet enquiries as to how far the rumours have spread. But if it's true, we will have no choice but to tell Jane and her brother. They must be made aware of what is being said and given a chance to refute it. Even so, I fear it may be too late.' Lavinia's expression said it all. 'Jane's reputation may be lost to all hope of salvation.'

Chapter Eleven

Sadly, upon Lavinia's returning home later that afternoon, Sophie discovered it was worse than either of them thought.

'Of course, no one seems willing to say who saw Jane enter the gentleman's rooms,' Lavinia said, hardly able to contain her anger. 'Speculation has it that a well-placed gentleman let it slip at one of the clubs, whereupon it soon became common knowledge at all the rest. Then it found its way into the drawing rooms of society.'

'But why will no one say which "well-placed gentleman" made the comment?' Sophie asked.

'Because that's not the way it's done.' Lavinia pulled off her gloves. 'Some misplaced notion of honour amongst thieves, I suppose. Besides, it doesn't matter. Several other people saw Jane speaking to a gentleman in the park, and when you add that to what I truly believe is an out-and-out lie, the damage is done.'

'Did they say who the gentleman in the park was?'

'Several names were mentioned, but no one could say for certain. And there is no way of knowing if it is the same man whose rooms she is reputed to have visited.'

'I cannot believe this,' Sophie said. 'Who would wish to harm Jane in such a cruel and inhumane way?'

Lavinia sighed. 'I don't know, but I fear we have no choice. We must pay a call on Jane and Robert as soon as possible. They must be made aware of what is being said.' She walked towards the window and drew the curtain aside. She was quiet for a long time. 'I feel terribly guilty for saying this, but it seems one good thing has come out of all this.'

'What's that?'

Lavinia turned and gave her a crooked smile. 'Nobody is talking about what happened at Lady Chiswick's any more.'

Fortunately, both Jane and Robert were at home when Lavinia and Sophie paid their call half an hour later. Jane was reading in the drawing room, and Robert came down shortly thereafter. He was dressed for going out and looked exceedingly handsome in his black-and-white evening attire. Sophie couldn't help wondering where he was going and who he was going to see. Lady Annabelle Durst, perhaps? To thank her for speaking up on their behalf? Or for reasons of his own…

'I'm sorry to be calling so late,' Lavinia said when the four of them were seated in the drawing room, 'but I thought it best not to waste any time.'

'You appear distraught, Lady Longworth,' Robert

said. 'Has this something to do with what happened at Lady Chiswick's?'

'I fear this is actually worse. It seems, Mr Silverton, that someone is out to damage your sister's reputation.' And with as much detail as she could provide, Lavinia told them what she knew of the situation.

The clatter of Jane's cane falling to the floor made everyone jump. But when Sophie saw the girl slump forward in her chair, she quickly ran to her side. 'Jane!'

Lavinia was on her feet. 'Smelling salts?'

Robert nodded. 'I'll fetch them.'

Sophie clutched the girl's limp body in her arms. '*Sapristi!* If I ever find out who did this—'

'Calm yourself, Sophie, we will find out,' Lavinia said. 'For now we must keep our wits about us.'

Sophie nodded. 'Help me sit her back up.'

'Salts,' Robert said, coming in and handing them over.

'Thank you.' Lavinia removed the lid and held them under Jane's nose.

The effect was immediate. The girl's head snapped up and her eyes flew open, only to fill at once with tears.

'No, Jane, you mustn't cry,' Sophie said as Lavinia handed the bottle back to Robert. 'We shall ask the maid for tea—'

'No! I don't want anyone to come in!' Jane cried.

'But you must have something!'

Robert walked to the sideboard and poured a glass of brandy. 'Here, dearest,' he said, handing it to her. 'The fire will put some colour back in your cheeks.'

Jane took the glass and gazed up at her brother

through her tears. 'It's not true, Robert. I swear it's not true. I have never visited any gentleman in his rooms. I would never—'

'I know.' His smile was infinitely gentle. 'It never occurred to me you would. And we *will* get to the bottom of this.'

'Robert, I'm so sorry,' Lavinia said, 'but we thought you needed to know what was being said.'

'I am grateful to you and Miss Vallois for having the courage to come and tell us.' He paused. 'Given what happened at Lady Chiswick's, I would understand you preferring to have nothing more to do with me.'

Sophie and Lavinia exchanged a glance. 'Mr Silverton,' Lavinia said, 'were you aware of the relationship between Lady Mary Kelsey and Lady Chiswick before you went to Lady Chiswick's house?'

'No. I wasn't even acquainted with Lord or Lady Chiswick. I went at Oberon's insistence. He told me Lord Chiswick was most anxious to show me his collection of hunting trophies.'

'Hunting trophies.' Lavinia sniffed. 'God help you if *all* your friends are so caring of your welfare, Mr Silverton. However, having now established that you did not wilfully intend to provoke Lady Chiswick, and with Lady Annabelle's assurances that you and Sophie were not alone in the garden, I think we can dismiss the matter. The fact that people know Sophie was employed by Mrs Grant-Ogilvy is a trifling matter at best. Your sister's defamation is what we must now turn our attention to.'

'At least now I know why I was getting such strange

looks at the club this afternoon,' Robert murmured. A shutter dropped down over his eyes. 'I know it is an imposition, but would it be possible for one of you to stay with Jane for a little while? I have to go out.'

'I'll stay,' Sophie said, disappointed that his social engagement should take precedence over Jane's predicament. 'And it is no imposition.'

His smile rested on her for a moment, the tenderness of his gaze causing her pulse to beat erratically. 'Thank you. I shall return as quickly as possible. Jane, will you be all right without me?'

Wearily, Jane nodded. With a last look at Sophie, he left, closing the door behind him.

'Well, I suppose I had best go and apprise Nicholas of what's happened,' Lavinia said, getting to her feet. 'Perhaps he can find out more details. Send word when you want the carriage, Sophie, but stay as long as you need. Goodnight, Jane. Try to get some rest.'

'Thank you, Lady Longworth, I will.'

With a nod, Sophie closed the door. When she turned back, it was to see a trace of colour seeping back into Jane's pallid cheeks. The brandy, no doubt. 'Don't worry, Jane,' Sophie said, sitting down beside her. 'Your brother will not allow these lies to be perpetuated. This will all be put to rights.'

'Unfortunately, the damage is already done,' Jane said quietly. 'You don't know how society works, Sophie. From what you've told me, it is my word against a gentleman's and society will never take mine over his. I know what they say about me. That I am a cripple and that…I shall never marry. They probably think I had no *choice* but to throw myself at a man in such a way.'

'No one who knows you would ever believe such lies!' Sophie said fiercely. 'I cannot imagine who would wish to hurt you like this.'

'Perhaps Lady Mary has decided to take her revenge,' Jane said. 'If I have no hope of marrying, Robert will be for ever forced to look after me.' She sniffed and reached for her handkerchief. 'I can't imagine what your brother must think.'

'I'm not sure Antoine knows. He and Nicholas were out most of the afternoon.'

'He will hear soon enough,' Jane said, fresh tears welling. 'And he must have nothing to do with me, lest he be the one people believe I visited and his own reputation suffers as a result.'

'But he doesn't even *keep* rooms in London.'

'No one will care about that. They will say he rented a room for the night, or borrowed a friend's home. They will say he compromised me beyond all hope of redemption. Only think what that will do to his reputation.'

'I don't imagine he would care greatly,' Sophie said. 'I've seen the way he looks at you, Jane. And the way you look at him.'

This time when the girl's cheeks reddened, Sophie knew it had nothing to do with the brandy. 'Is it really so obvious?' Jane asked.

'It is to me. I'm not sure it is to anyone else.'

Jane was silent for a time, twisting her handkerchief around and around in her hands. 'I'm so sorry, Sophie.

I think I lost my heart to Antoine the first time I saw him. I'm sure you can understand why.'

Yes, Sophie could, though her acceptance of it made it no better for any of them. 'Has he made you any promises?'

'He knows he cannot. Without my brother's consent, it would be impossible for us to marry and Antoine does not wish to incur Robert's anger. Besides, he has to return very soon to France and I cannot go with him.'

'Oh, Jane, I wish I knew what to say.'

'There is nothing to say. The circumstances are all wrong.' Jane's voice was light, but her eyes were filled with sadness. 'I'm not the first woman to love a man she cannot have and I certainly won't be the last.'

'You make it sound so final.'

'I learned a long time ago that life isn't always fair. But I will have the memory of his love, and I believe he will remember me when he returns to France. I just worry what he will think when he hears these dreadful stories.'

'He will think the same as the rest of us,' Sophie reassured her. 'He will *not* believe these lies. Indeed, he will be as furious as your brother.' She thought about the look on Robert's face as he'd walked out the door. 'And something tells me Mr Silverton in a temper is not a thing *any* man would wish to experience.'

There was only one thought on Robert's mind as he strode into Oberon's favourite hell—and it was not charitable. It became even less so when he found his enemy in one of the upstairs rooms seated at a table with four other men, all of them titled, all of them rip-roaring drunk.

'Silver! What a surprise!' Oberon called around the whore in his lap. 'Hutton, give Silver your chair—'

'I'm not here to gamble,' Robert said. 'I've come for a word with you.'

'Perhaps later. As you can see, I'm very busy—'

'Now!' Robert gently, but firmly, pulled the half-naked woman from Oberon's lap. 'In private or I'll know the reason why.'

In an instant, Oberon's smile disappeared. He glanced at the faces of the men seated around the table, aware of the curiosity burning in their eyes, and said, 'Very well. But you'd better have a damn good explanation for this.'

'Trust me. I do.'

Oberon downed the rest of his brandy. He stood up and led the way out of the room into the darkened corridor. Stopping at a second door, he opened it and they walked into a room that looked to be an office. 'Now, what's this all about—'

'You know damn well what it's about.' Robert slammed the door. 'Someone's been spreading lies about Jane.'

'Really? I can't imagine who would do such a thing,' Oberon said.

'Can't you? A name leaped immediately to *my* mind.'

The cobra reared up, its black eyes as cold as the death it would surely deal. 'Careful, my friend. Damaging stories can be told about a gentleman as well as a lady.'

'So you admit to telling lies about my sister.'

'Who is to say what is truth and what is a lie? Certainly not those who listen with equal fervour to both. But I admit to nothing,' Oberon snapped. 'And if you attempt to put it about that I did, you *will* suffer the consequences. To call the son of a peer a liar is a serious offence.'

'No more serious than destroying the reputation of an innocent young woman.'

'If such is the case, I am sorry for you, Silver. But don't say I didn't warn you.'

It was as good as an admission of guilt—and they both knew it. 'You won't get away with this,' Robert said. 'As God is my witness, I *will* bring you down.'

He left before the man had a chance to respond, fearing that if Oberon said another word, he would call him out on the spot. Duelling might have been outlawed in England, but there were still places where it could be done and circumstances under which it would be forgiven. Robert had a feeling that before this despicable affair was over, he would be intimately acquainted with both.

It was several hours before Robert was of a mood to go home. He wandered through the empty streets, too angry to be of comfort to Jane, too incensed by the nature of injustice done to be pleasant company for Sophie.

Sophie. He couldn't even think about her in the same breath as Oberon, that cunning, immoral bastard. How like him to try to turn this back on Robert. As though it was his fault Jane should be made to suffer. The man had no more conscience than a corpse, and thinking of that brought to mind something else he'd once told Robert…

'I hold people's lives in the palm of my hand and offer them back in exchange for a favour. No one cares if making good on that favour destroys someone else's happiness. All they care about is restoring their own. So it all comes down to choice. The question is…whose happiness will it be? And what price are they willing to pay?'

Certainly not the happiness of the person who'd gambled it away in the first place, Robert acknowledged bitterly.

He was so lost in thought that he didn't see the person stumbling towards him until they actually collided. 'Watch where you're going, man!' Robert grunted, already reaching for the dagger concealed in his sleeve. London after dark was a dangerous place, rife with pickpockets and thieves. But when he looked up to see the face of his would-be attacker, he realised it wasn't a thief at all. It was Lawrence Welton. 'Lawrence, are you all right?'

The poor fellow looked ghastly. His face was riddled with lines and his eyes were two dark, shadowy pools of despair. 'You're not well. Let me call you a carriage.'

Welton looked up, his eyes finally focusing. 'S-Silverton?'

'Yes. I'm going to take you home—'

'Can't,' the man muttered. 'Not…mine…'

Welton had obviously been drinking heavily. He

sagged and would have fallen had Robert not caught him and held him up. 'You need a doctor!'

'Nothing a doctor can f-fix,' the young man said, his words badly slurred. 'Owns it all...'

'Who owns it?'

'Trusted him, you s-see. But it was...all lies. Should have checked...' Welton went on, his eyes glazed, his mouth slack. 'Nothing left.'

Robert's mouth tightened in anger. He'd never seen Welton in such a state. One thing he knew for sure, he couldn't leave the man alone in the middle of the street, at the mercy of pickpockets and thugs. Instead, he hailed a hackney and gave the driver Welton's address. Once inside, he tried to get the information he needed. 'Lawrence, who did this to you?'

'Thought he was...m'friend,' the man mumbled, shaking his head. 'Enemy, more like.' Then he laughed—a rough, grating sound that was filled with despair. 'Stuck a knife in my back.'

'Then you must speak to someone. If you've been cheated—'

'Never prove it...' He unsteadily raised his hand and pointed a finger at Robert. 'Not a friend of yours.'

He passed out soon after—which made getting him out of the carriage even more difficult. Had it not been for the help of Welton's valet, Robert wasn't sure he would have managed. And once inside the house, it took both of them to get the poor man up the stairs and into his bed.

'I'll see to him now, sir,' the valet said. 'Thank you for bringing him home.'

'It's Finch, isn't it?'

'That's right, sir.'

'Is your master in trouble? He mentioned something about…losing it all.'

The valet's face fell. 'So it's happened. I feared it might. But he kept on saying the gentleman wouldn't do it.'

'What gentleman?' Feeling completely in the dark, Robert said, 'Can you tell me what's going on?'

'He wouldn't wish me to, sir,' the servant said, glancing at Lawrence's unconscious figure. 'A proud man is Mr Welton. Far better than those who've used him.'

It was clear that something very bad had happened to Lawrence Welton and that his servant was reluctant to say anything. Robert could appreciate that. He wouldn't wish his own man to divulge anything of a personal nature with regard to his affairs. 'Please give him my best,' Robert said. 'Tell him I'll call round in the morning to see how he is.'

The valet looked grateful. 'Thank you, sir. I'll do that.'

As it turned out, however, Welton was not in town the next morning. He sent Robert a note thanking him for his help and informing him that he was removing to the country for an indefinite period of time. The letter was brief, the handwriting that of a man unsteady of mind and body…

> …no doubt you will hear soon enough that I have been ruined. The details do not matter, the fault is

my own. I should have known better than to deal
with the devil. But I deeply regret that other truths
will never be known and that innocent people
will be made to suffer. Beware the company you
keep, Robert, for serpents hide behind handsome
eyes...

Robert dropped the letter on the table— *'...serpents
hide behind handsome eyes.'* He would have had to have
been blind not to understand that reference.

Oberon!

'Excuse me, miss, but Mr Oberon is asking to see
you,' Banyon said from the doorway of the drawing
room.

Sophie stiffened, the magazine in her hands forgotten.
She hadn't seen Oberon since the night of the fiasco at
Lady Chiswick's and she wondered why he had come
now. No doubt, thoughts of marriage were far from his
mind. 'Please tell him I am not at home.'

The butler sighed. 'He said that if that was your
answer I was to give you this.' He handed her a sealed
note. 'He said it had to do with Miss Silverton.'

Sophie quickly broke the wafer and read the note
through. 'Show him in.' She refolded the note and got
to her feet. 'But come back in five minutes with the
message that Lady Longworth wishes to see me.'

'Very good, miss.' The butler withdrew, concern
etched deep into his normally imperturbable features.

Moments later, Oberon appeared in the doorway.
'Miss Vallois. I hope you will forgive the boldness of

my letter, but I knew you would wish to hear what I had to say about Miss Silverton.'

Sophie nodded, her mouth as dry as old paper. 'I am interested, of course, though I am surprised you would wish to come here after what happened at Lady Chiswick's.'

'Yes, a most unfortunate incident for all concerned,' Oberon said, not quite meeting her eyes. 'Truths revealed in such a way always leave a bitter aftertaste. But I think we shall put that aside for the moment. I've come to talk to you about Miss Silverton and the tragic situation in which she finds herself.'

Sophie's hand tightened on the parchment. 'It is only tragic because it is all lies.'

'Unfortunately, it is the word of a gentleman against hers,' Oberon said. 'A well to do gentleman, so my sources inform me.'

Sophie stilled. 'Do you know who he is?'

'What would you do if I said I did? Beg that I might tell you so you could go and confront him?'

'Most certainly! I would tell him to his face that he was a coward and demand that he exonerate Miss Silverton at once!'

'My word, such passion,' Oberon mused. 'If I were Miss Silverton, I would consider myself fortunate in having your friendship.'

'It is I who consider myself fortunate in having hers,' Sophie answered. 'Someone has told a hurtful and outrageous lie. Jane would *never* behave in such a manner. Surely you know that. You, who have been acquainted with her *and* her brother for such a long time.'

'Yes, I have known them, and I agree they are both exceptionally good people—which is why I've come to see you. I have a proposition for you.'

Her eyes opened wide. 'A proposition.'

'Yes. A few days ago, I asked you to accept my proposal of marriage.'

'Which, given what you learned at Lady Chiswick's, you now wish to retract.'

'Not exactly.' Oberon strolled around the room, his hands linked loosely behind his back. 'Though I was not…pleased to learn of your former employment, I am willing to overlook it. You would not be the first governess to be raised to the position of a nobleman's wife. As to the confusion over your…identity, I seem to remember Jane once mentioning that your middle name was Chantal, and I suspect Beaudoin to be a maiden name, perhaps on your mother's side?'

Sophie suddenly felt cold, as though an icy draught had blown through the room. 'Yes, that's right.'

'So in essence, you told no lies at all.'

'Perhaps not, but what of my claim that I do not love you?'

'*Love*. That is the *least* of my concerns,' Oberon said dismissively. 'An antiquated notion, best left to poets and the publishers of gothic romances. *I* am in need of a wife and *you* are an incredibly beautiful woman who has bewitched me in every sense of the word. Therefore, I make you an offer. *If* I could resolve Miss Silverton's unhappy situation, would you agree to marry me?'

Sophie took a quick, sharp breath. 'Resolve it? How?'

'I am not without influence in society. I know the ears in which to whisper. If I said I could prove the gentleman was lying—?'

'You would do that for Jane?'

'No. I would do it for *you*. All you have to do is say yes. And I will give you three days in which to decide.'

'Three days?' A quiver of fear rippled down Sophie's spine. 'You did not set a time limit on my answer before.'

'I think we both know the circumstances have changed. However, I am willing to make it a week. But do not ask me again.' He turned and slowly closed the distance between them. 'I am far too generous with those I care about—'

'Excuse me, Miss Vallois,' Banyon said, appearing in the open doorway, 'but her ladyship has returned and is asking to see you right away.'

Dieu merci! It had been the longest five minutes of her life. 'Thank you, I shall come at once.' Sophie turned back to her visitor, her mind in turmoil. 'Good afternoon, Mr Oberon. Banyon will see you out.'

The dismissal was plain. Oberon bowed, but the look in his eyes was far from amiable. 'Thank you, but I know the way. And I will call again in one week from today, Miss Vallois. When I look forward to hearing the words that will make me…a very happy man.'

Chapter Twelve

Sophie didn't bother telling Nicholas and Lavinia about Mr Oberon's outrageous offer. What would be the point? They would never advise her to accept it, and in fact would probably have told her she was mad for even hearing the man out! But while refusing his offer was certainly in *her* best interests, what would it do to Jane? *She* was the one who stood to lose everything if the rumours weren't laid to rest.

No, there *had* to be a way around the problem, Sophie reflected as the Longworth carriage rattled and bounced its way to Lady White's town house. The gregarious hostess had again invited the four of them to attend one of her impromptu soirées, and while Antoine had declined, Sophie had accepted with alacrity. She knew that Robert would be there, given that he had once told her that Lady White actually *enjoyed* the notoriety of having him present, and with luck, she might be able to talk to him about her predicament. Maybe he could think of a way to persuade Mr Oberon to help Jane without asking the impossible of her.

It might be grasping at straws, but she was running out of time! She had to convince Mr Oberon to save Jane's reputation without making her agreement to marry him a condition of his doing so. She had to make him understand that marriage without love would be anathema for both of them. Difficult given that he'd already told her love was the purview of poets and penny novelists. But make him understand she would. Because now, more than ever, her future happiness depended on it.

'Nicholas, Lavinia, how lovely to see you both again,' Lady White greeted them. 'And Miss Vallois, looking as elegant as ever. How are you, my dear?' She leaned in close and winked. 'I understand you've been having quite the goings on of late.'

A little embarrassed, Sophie nevertheless managed a smile. 'I'm fine, Lady White.'

'Good, because no one really cares what Eudora Chiswick thinks. She's an insufferable mushroom whose husband only married her because her father made a fortune in trade and the Chiswick estate was falling into total disrepair. You're better than the lot of them and that includes her stuck up sister-in-law, Constance. As for poor Miss Silverton—' Lady White broke off, sighing. 'Now there is a truly unfortunate turn of events. I despaired of the poor child marrying before, but there's not a hope she'll find a husband now. Dreadful state of affairs. I wish I could do something to help. But now, here is our dashing Mr Silverton. I dare say you won't mind spending a little time with him.'

With that, Lady White drew Nicholas and Lavinia away, no doubt to quiz them about exactly what *had* happened on the terrace at Lady Chiswick's, and the details of poor Jane's disgrace.

'She is an incorrigible gossip,' Robert said, 'but she means well. And there are times when we all need the company of those who don't give a damn about society.' His jaw clenched. 'I also knew there was absolutely no chance of running into Oberon here.'

At the mention of the man who held both Jane's future and her own in the palm of his hand, Sophie said, 'I was hoping you would be here tonight, Mr Silverton—'

'I was Robert to you in the garden,' he interrupted quietly. 'Am I not Robert to you any more?'

Sophie felt the familiar quickening of her pulse that told her this was more than just nerves. It went deeper... to a longing she couldn't put a name to. That she was afraid to put a name to. 'Forgive me, but I wasn't sure... after what happened between us at Lady Chiswick's, and I received your note cancelling our outing—'

'Surely you understood why I did that?' Robert said. 'I couldn't allow my desire to see you to add to the stories I feared might already be circulating. We were fortunate Lady Annabelle spoke up on our behalf, but if people saw us together, they would suspect there was... something more. I couldn't risk having you share in my humiliation.'

'But when Lavinia and I came to see you the other night, you left so abruptly,' Sophie said.

'Yes, to see Oberon. I had to meet with him, and it was not pleasant.'

'Oberon!' Sophie said, the name torn from her. 'I am sick to death of Mr Oberon! Robert, there is something I must speak to you about and it is awkward in the extreme. But I don't know who else to turn to.'

'Come,' he said, lightly putting his hand on her waist. 'I know of a place where we can talk.'

And he did. A few minutes later, Sophie found herself seated across from him at a table in a small alcove just off the drawing room. Five card tables had been set up in the main part of the room, and several foursomes were already engaged in play. Conversation was brisk, laughter was frequent, and though Sophie and Robert were separate from the rest, there was no question of their being alone. Robert was right. Neither of them could afford a repeat of what had happened in the garden at Lady Chiswick's. Lady Annabelle Durst would not be waiting around the corner to save them this time.

'Well, Miss Vallois?'

Sophie bit her lip. Where did she start? There was so much to say. 'This is not going to be easy to tell you, but earlier this afternoon, Mr Oberon came to see me.'

She saw his hands tighten on the table. 'And Lady Longworth didn't throw him out on his ear?'

'Lavinia wasn't home. And I did ask Banyon to send him away, but Mr Oberon said he had news that would be of interest to me.'

'And had he such news?'

'He did. He told me he intends to find the man who started this terrible rumour about Jane and to use his position in society to make the man confess to lying.'

'Did he indeed?' The words were carefully noncommittal, but Robert's eyes glittered like shards of ice. 'A generous offer. What did he ask in exchange for this boon?'

Sophie swallowed, knowing this was going to be the hard part. 'My acceptance…of his proposal of marriage.'

Robert's face went as still as death. 'Tell me you didn't agree.'

'Of course not! I was too shocked by what he suggested even to think straight. So he told me he would give me time to consider my answer.'

'How long?'

'One week.'

'Do you need that long to decide?'

'Of course not. I do not love Mr Oberon and I certainly don't want to marry him. But he has the power to restore Jane's good name, Robert, which is why I cannot simply dismiss this out of hand. I have been desperately trying to think of a way around it.'

'Jane would be the *last* one to wish you to marry for such a reason,' Robert said harshly. 'And as much as I love my sister, restoring her reputation is no reason for you to throw *your* life away. Oberon is not a kind man.'

'Yet he has offered to set this terrible matter right.'

'Perhaps because he was the one who set it wrong in the first place.'

Sophie gasped. 'Surely he would not do something so reprehensible. He is your friend.'

'He *was* my friend. I have since come to learn

that friendship means something entirely different to Oberon.'

Their eyes met across the table, and Sophie saw how deep Robert's enmity went. 'He said something else. About a wager made some time ago, involving his stallion and a ring belonging to your family. Do you know what he was talking about?' She saw his shoulders stiffen and knew she had her answer. 'I see that you do.'

'There would be no point in my trying to deny it. The wager is written down in a place where any gentleman in London could see it. But I am far more concerned with what he told you *about* it than with the fact that it exists.'

'He said you were looking for the most beautiful woman in London to be your mistress,' Sophie said quietly. 'He said the wager was your idea—'

'*My* idea?'

'Yes. He believes gambling is your way of dealing with what life has thrown at you.'

There were times, Sophie realised, when words were not enough to describe the depth of anger in a man's soul. This was one of those times. 'I trust Oberon mentioned that he was also a party to this wager?'

'He did, but he said you put his name to it against his will.'

His anger became a cold, dangerous fury. 'By God, even I had not thought him so devious. For what it's worth, the wager was *not* my idea and I did *not* agree to participate in it. Oberon has told you a monstrous lie, and I suspect a good many others as well. But only one thing matters right now, Sophie. Do you believe him? After all, it is my word against his.'

'Yes, it is, and I do *not* believe him, Robert. How could I, knowing what I do of you?' She looked down, reluctant to meet his eyes. 'Knowing what has…passed between us. But neither did I wish to keep my knowledge of the wager, or anything else he said to me, a secret from you. I would have honesty between us, if nothing else.'

'If nothing else.' Robert stared at the table, as if to see answers magically appear in the surface. But there were no easy answers. They both knew that.

'Sophie,' Robert said finally, 'this is neither the time nor the place, but I must say something because this cannot go on a moment longer.' He looked up, and his burning gaze held her still. 'If I was to secure Lord Longworth's approval, would you allow me to speak to you?'

For a moment, it was as though her brain shut down. As though his words failed to penetrate the fog swirling around her. He wished to *speak* to her? But…a gentleman did *not* ask to speak to a lady unless he intended to speak of marriage. And he had already told her he had no intention of marrying. Besides, there was the issue of her being French—

'Your hesitation leads me to believe you are not as firmly fixed in your affections as I had hoped,' Robert said slowly. 'If that is the case—'

'No, I know exactly where my affections lie.' Sophie pressed her hand to her throat, aware that her heart was beating so loud he must surely hear it. 'But I thought… that is, we have both stated our intentions not to marry.

And yet…' She looked at him and her breath cut off. 'Here we are.'

To her surprise, he smiled. 'Yes, here we are—and you still haven't answered my question.'

Laughter erupted from one of the card tables. Sophie heard the clink of a glass and the muted sounds of a string quartet coming from another room. Candles sputtered and perfume wafted and, wonder of wonders, Robert wished to speak to her. 'Yes, I would allow it,' she said. 'Most happily, I would.'

It was not triumph she saw in his eyes. It was…peace. He reached for her hands and drew them to his lips, oblivious to anyone who might be watching. 'Do not consider Oberon's offer. Ignore him. Stall him. Lie to him, if you must, I really don't care. All I know is that he *is* the man behind these rumours, and that once I have proof, I'm going to expose him for the blackguard he is. He'll never bother you again, Sophie. On that, you have my word!'

It was with that same sense of purpose that Robert set out the following morning. His brief conversation with Lord Longworth before he'd left Lady White's had resulted in the meeting he was about to have, and over the last few hours, he had gone over the details of what he wanted to say. In light of recent developments, matters had reached a point where something had to be done.

Oberon had betrayed him. Heartlessly. Unemotionally. Irreparably. He had lied *to* him and told lies *about* him—and to the only woman who had ever mattered. For that, Robert would make him pay. He was shown into Lord Longworth's library and found the gentleman waiting for him. 'Good morning, my lord.'

'Robert.' Longworth waved him into a chair. 'Can I offer you something in the way of refreshment? I fear it's a bit early for brandy.'

'Thank you, but I won't take up much of your time. I've come to speak to you about Mr Oberon and Miss Vallois.'

'Have you indeed?' Longworth sat down in the chair opposite. 'What is it you wish to say?'

'I am aware that Oberon has spoken to you about his interest in Miss Vallois and that you have given him your permission to speak to her. I would ask you now to revoke that permission at the earliest possible opportunity.'

A brief hesitation. 'I take it you have a good reason for asking?'

'I have two. The first is that I believe Oberon to be a liar and totally without character. The second is that I am in love with Miss Vallois and wish to marry her myself.'

Longworth's brows rose. 'Perhaps not too early for that drink after all.' He got up and crossed to the sideboard. Pouring two glasses of brandy, he handed one to Robert, tossed back his own and sat down again. After a moment, he said, 'You've made some very strong statements. Would you care to back them up with fact? Apart from your feelings of affection for Sophie. I think I understand those well enough.'

'I do not make the claims lightly, my lord, but because of something that happened between Oberon and myself a few weeks ago, I believe he is behind the despicable stories circulating with regard to my sister.' And then briefly, but succinctly, Robert told the man everything. His conversation with Oberon at the Black Swan, the nature of the mistress wager, and the depth of his concern about the other man's growing obsession with Sophie. The only thing he left out was Oberon's most recent proposition. Judging from the expression on Longworth's face, Robert suspected Oberon would have been facing pistols at dawn. As it was, Longworth swore viciously under his breath. 'By God, if what you say is true, the man should be shot!'

'I have every reason to believe it is true, but he will certainly deny it if asked. When I spoke to Miss Vallois yesterday about my concerns regarding Oberon's involvement in Jane's disgrace, I saw how shocked and displeased she was. It was last night at Lady White's that I asked if I could speak to her, if you were to give your approval. I'm well aware that my own position in society does not recommend me in any way.'

'No, I can't say that it does,' Longworth agreed. 'Nor do you have the wealth or position I would have liked for Sophie.'

'Surely I have enough,' Robert said softly, 'for the daughter of a farmer from Bayencourt.'

The look of shock on the viscount's face had Robert bracing for an explosion—but it never came. Longworth's expression of anger slowly gave way to grudging acceptance. 'She told you, yet you said nothing to me. To anyone.'

'I was afraid of how she would be treated by the *ton*

if word of her origins leaked out,' Robert said. 'I know better than most how cruel people can be and I did not relish the thought of Miss Vallois being exposed to ridicule and censure. I also thought that since you and Lady Longworth had not made mention of it, you would not be pleased at hearing it spread around by someone else.'

Longworth sighed. 'Perhaps it would have been better if it *had* leaked out. We might not be in this predicament now.'

'Don't be too sure. Oberon's obsession has no basis in logic. As for myself, while I may not be rich, I'm far from being a pauper. More importantly, I would love her with all my heart.'

Longworth studied him in silence for a moment. Finally, he nodded. 'Very well. If Sophie will have you, you have my blessing. I am more concerned that she be happy than anything else.'

'Thank you, my lord.'

'One thing. If you are able to prove Oberon's misdeeds, come to me at once. He must be held accountable for what he has done.'

'I will not come without proof, though I fear it will be difficult to obtain.'

'Devious men seldom leave well-marked trails for others to follow. And the people they hold in their hands, they hold on to tightly.'

Robert nodded, thinking of poor Lawrence Welton. 'Indeed, my lord. Of that, I am most painfully aware.'

For Sophie, the hours ran all too quickly into days. She lived in a constant state of nervous anticipation, waiting for the next blow to fall. As the countdown to her meeting with Mr Oberon approached, she began to fear that even Robert might not have the power to stop him. And then, three days into her allotted time, another rumour began to circulate throughout the drawing rooms of society. A rumour accusing a certain gentleman of having made up the bold-faced lies about Miss Silverton visiting a man in his rooms, when, in fact, nothing of the sort had happened. Furthermore, if Miss Silverton *had* spoken to someone in the park, it was nothing more than the polite exchange of greetings expected between a lady and a gentleman during the course of their social day. Certainly nothing grievous enough over which to defame her character.

The reason for the man's lies was not made clear, but neither did it seem to matter. Montague Oberon had been heard to speak up strongly in the lady's defence, and with his name behind the rebuttal, no one was going to argue.

'And so, there we have it,' Lavinia said at the conclusion of her recounting. 'It would appear Jane's name is cleared and her reputation fully restored.'

Sophie raised the teacup to her lips. What would Lavinia say, she wondered, if she knew how steep a price Mr Oberon had demanded in exchange? 'Does Jane know?'

'I suspect the news will have reached her by now. It was the only topic of conversation at Lady Orville's this afternoon and given that most of the ladies arrived already in possession of the news, I can assure you it has been widely discussed.'

Again, Sophie could feel nothing but relief for her friend. It was over, the terrible stories finally laid to rest. Jane was once again free to move about in society, knowing that she would be welcome at any house she chose to visit, and that churlish whispers would not follow her wherever she went. That it put society in a dismal light was a fact Sophie could not deny. If people were so willing to believe a pack of lies on the strength of one man's word, what did it say when they were so ready to put it all aside on the strength of another's?

'I fear it is a rhetorical question,' Lavinia said. 'Society is what it is and I doubt it will ever change. People were willing to believe the lies when they were nothing more than rumours, so they could hardly *not* believe Mr Oberon when he came forwards to dispute them and publicly condemn the man who started them.'

Sophie's eyes widened. 'He actually *named* the perpetrator?'

'Oh, yes. And I was deeply saddened to learn of it.' Lavinia looked unhappy. 'I never thought a fine young man like Lawrence Welton would do such a thing.'

Robert was at his club when he heard the news. 'Lawrence Welton?' he repeated in stunned disbelief. 'But that's impossible!'

'Of course it is,' said Captain John McIntosh, the gentleman imparting the information. 'But Oberon was most definite in his naming Welton. He said he had spoken with him a few days earlier and gained the man's confession, after which Welton bolted.'

Robert was too angry for words. So that was what

Welton had meant in his letter. Oberon obviously held a packet of Welton's vowels and Welton's agreeing to become the foil for Oberon's monstrous plan was the price he demanded for discharging them.

'Still, it's cleared your sister's name,' McIntosh said.

'And made Oberon look like a hero into the bargain,' Robert muttered. 'And that bothers me no end. Lawrence would never do something like this.'

'Of course not.' McIntosh drained his glass. 'But he has a weakness for cards and, by his own admission, only a fool gambles with the devil. Well, I'd best be on my way. Good to see you again, Robert.'

'And you. I appreciate the information.'

The captain's smile held more than a trace of regret. 'I'm just sorry it couldn't have been better.'

Robert sat quietly after the other man left, thinking over all that he had heard. So, Jane's life had been made better at the expense of Lawrence's. Obviously that was what Oberon had meant when he'd said he held people's lives in the palm of his hand. He had no qualms about using whomever he pleased in the achievement of his own ends, and this time, his old friend Lawrence had been the expendable one.

But where did that leave Sophie? She was now in the unenviable position of believing herself indebted to Oberon for having restored Jane's good name when nothing could have been further from the truth. Robert knew the entire episode had been a carefully devised plot to strike back at *him* for having dared to interfere, and to put Sophie in a position of obligation to Oberon.

And Oberon's price for revealing the so-called deception was her hand in marriage.

It was unthinkable! An outcome that must be avoided at all costs. Whatever it took, Sophie must not be allowed to become a prisoner to Oberon's tricks. The man was evil, and if Robert was able to do only one thing, it would be to ensure that his sweet Sophie never became prey for the monster.

Robert called on her the same afternoon. He was told that Lord Longworth and Mr Vallois were not at home, but when he advised Banyon it was Miss Vallois he wished to see, he was taken into the morning room where Sophie and Lavinia were sitting quietly doing their embroidery.

'Mr Silverton, what a pleasure to see you,' Lavinia said.

'Lady Longworth. Miss Vallois. I called to apprise you of the good news regarding my sister.'

'Indeed, sir, we have already heard and we are both overjoyed at the outcome. Speaking of which,' Lavinia said, rising, 'I have written a note to dear Jane and would ask that you take it to her. I shall just go and fetch it.' She left, giving Robert a knowing smile as she passed.

Finally, it was just he and Sophie alone. He walked towards her slowly, suddenly anxious as to how she would receive what he wanted to say. 'Well, Miss Vallois, it would seem at least one problem has been put to bed.'

'It has, and I am so very pleased, for Jane's sake. Thank you for coming to tell us.'

'That wasn't the only reason I came.' He halted in front of her. 'I think you know that.'

Her eyes rose to his and then fell, long lashes casting shadows on her skin. But she smiled, and he heard her take a quick breath as she said, 'And what is this other reason?'

As he looked down at her, he wished for the first time in his life that he had been blessed with a poet's gift for words. 'I believe it safe to say that you and I did not get off to an auspicious start that night at the inn. I won't ever forget you telling your brother that you'd rather sleep in the barn than accept an offer of help from me.'

She laughed, but sent him a reproving glare. 'You are not kind to remind me of that, sir.'

Robert smiled. 'No, perhaps not. But I've since come to learn that I was wrong about so many things. We talked in the garden at Lady Chiswick's about making mistakes. Well, I've made more than my fair share with you. I let ignorance cloud my judgement to the point where it almost blinded me to the truth, and you, dear Sophie, suffered for that ignorance.'

'You were only acting on your beliefs.'

'Misplaced beliefs. I saw a man I thought would do me no harm destroy the reputation of my sister and cause a fine gentleman to lose his home and his good name. I saw a woman I…cared deeply about forced into an untenable position as the result of her own desire to protect someone who wasn't able to protect herself. And I let my steadfast belief in my own lack of suitability stand in my way of my telling her how I really felt about her. But all that's in the past. From now on, I intend to tell her every single day how much I love her.' He slowly sat down beside her. 'Sophie Vallois, would you do me the very great honour of becoming my wife?'

He waited, heart in his mouth, for her answer. Never had he believed the seconds could move so slowly. That he would feel himself age as he waited for her response. That he might see his world fall apart at the thought of her saying no. But such was not her response. 'Yes, I will,' she whispered. 'Just as soon as matters can be arranged.'

He felt almost lightheaded with relief. He stood up and held out his hand, drawing her to her feet. 'Lord Longworth already knows of my intentions, but I will speak to your brother immediately upon his return. I would like to have his approval, but I'm prepared to marry you without it.'

Her smile was golden, like the sun emerging after the rain. 'Antoine will approve, as long as he knows I love you. He only wants me to be happy.'

'Then I shall do my best to convince him of it. And I shall arrange for a special license, and we shall be married on the day of your choosing. I want you as my wife as soon as possible.' Then, drawing her close, he kissed her, his lips gently tracing the outline of her mouth. There was no experience to her kiss, but the taste of her nearly drove him mad. And when his tongue teased her lips apart and he delved into the sweetness of her mouth, he was lost.

'Enough!' He set her gently away, blood coursing through every part of his body. 'I have no wish to frighten you.'

Her smile reassured him. 'You don't frighten me, Robert. I want this too. Can you not feel it when you hold me?'

'I feel that, and more.' He reached for her left hand and raised it to his lips, gently kissing the finger that would soon wear his ring. Then, at the sound of approaching footsteps, he reluctantly released Sophie and stepped back. But when the door opened and Lavinia walked in, he knew she saw their happiness.

'Oh, my dears, I am so very pleased for both of you.'

'Thank you, Lady Longworth,' Robert said. 'Perhaps you would be good enough to send me a note as soon as your husband returns. I would speak to him, and to Mr Vallois, at the earliest opportunity.'

'Of course, I shall be happy to do so. As it happens, we are all engaged for dinner with Lord and Lady Otterham this evening, but would you and Jane care to dine with us tomorrow? To celebrate this most wonderful news?'

Robert glanced at the lady who would soon be his wife, and when she smiled, he thought she had never looked more beautiful. 'We would be delighted.'

'Excellent.' Lavinia was positively beaming. 'I am so pleased everything has worked out. I do not think the story could have had a happier conclusion had dear Miss Austen written the ending to it herself!'

Chapter Thirteen

The meeting with Lord Longworth and Sophie's brother went better than Robert could have hoped. Though Antoine was quiet to begin, once Robert convinced him of the depth of his affection for Sophie, he seemed to relax and accept the news, and even to appear happy about it. Longworth had no such reservations. He shook Robert's hand and told him how pleased he and Lavinia were with Sophie's choice, then he assured Robert that they were very much looking forward to having everyone together at dinner the following evening.

Robert thought it an encouraging start.

Given that Sophie was engaged for the evening, he decided to take his sister to Vauxhall, as much to celebrate her good news as his own. It went without saying that Jane's mood had improved immeasurably since learning that her reputation had been restored, though she was deeply troubled at hearing it was Lawrence

Welton who had been falsely named as the villain in the piece.

'I would not have believed it of Mr Welton, even if you hadn't told me the truth,' Jane said as they strolled arm in arm down the Grand Walk. 'He always struck me as being such a fine, honourable young man.'

'He is,' Robert said, tipping his hat to an acquaintance. 'Unfortunately, no one is going to challenge Oberon over it. Everyone's afraid of him.'

'With good reason.' Jane was silent for a moment. 'I would not have thought him so evil. Arrogant, perhaps, and vain, but not cruel and hurtful. To destroy a man in such a way…'

'If you could have seen Lawrence that night, you would have understood my desire to call Oberon out.'

'And yet, what crime could you have accused him of, Robert? Nothing was known for certain. You could not have laid the blame for the rumours at his feet, any more than you could have accused him of lying to you when you asked him about them. But it is truly unfortunate that Mr Welton chose to leave London when he did,' Jane said. 'By doing so, he lent credence to Mr Oberon's story.'

'Indeed, but I'm sure that was part of Oberon's strategy.'

'Poor man. I hope he fares well in the country,' Jane said. 'Still, we must not dwell on it when there is so much happier news to celebrate. You are to be married to dear Sophie and I am so very pleased for you.' Then, he felt her stiffen. 'Robert, look!'

Oberon was coming towards them. He had a doxy on

his arm and was laughing as though he hadn't a care in the world—until he spotted them. Then a cold, calculating look settled in his eyes. Stopping a few feet in front of them, he touched the brim of his beaver. 'Evening, Silverton. Miss Silverton.'

'Mr Oberon,' Jane said, her voice cooling noticeably. 'I understand I am in your debt for having restored my good name.'

Oberon's acknowledgement was perfunctory. 'It was my pleasure. It would have been a crime to allow a good lady's name to be dragged through the mud while the perpetrator was allowed to go free. What say you, Silver?'

'I'm not so sure the perpetrator of this crime will ever be brought to justice, but I'm very glad to see my sister absolved of all wrongdoing.'

Oberon did not smile. 'Not exactly the thanks I had in mind, but it is of no consequence. The only thanks I seek will be found in another quarter. Good evening.'

'Will you not congratulate my brother on his good news, Mr Oberon?' Jane said. 'He is to be married.'

Robert squeezed his sister's arm, but it was too late. The cobra had turned and stood poised, ready to strike. 'Married? Indeed, I had not heard. Who is the lucky lady?'

'Miss Vallois,' Jane said.

Did Robert imagine the soft hiss? ''Pon my word, Silver, I hardly know what to say. You made no mention of this the last time we spoke.'

'There was no need. I thought we understood each other well enough.'

A shadow of anger rippled across Oberon's face, transforming the handsome features into a stone-like mask. 'A moment in private if you please, Silverton.'

'I would rather not leave Jane—'

'I said a moment, sir!'

Robert felt Jane stir uneasily at his side. 'It's all right, Robert. I shall walk on to the Cascade and wait for you there.'

Oberon didn't bother looking at the female at his side. 'Be gone,' he snapped, and she was.

Robert waited until Jane was safely out of distance before remarking, 'How gallant, Oberon. Do you dispense with all of your harlots with such tact and diplomacy?'

'Do not try my patience, Silverton! I am not in the mood.' Oberon took a threatening step towards him. 'How dare you go behind my back and ask Miss Vallois to marry you. She was already promised to me!'

'No, sir, she was not. And do not think I am unaware of the terms you tried to exact from her.'

Oberon's face went white. 'I would have you explain yourself!'

'You promised to restore Jane's good name in return for Miss Vallois's promise of marriage.'

'Which she gave me!'

'On the contrary, you asked her to marry you and gave her a week to consider your proposal. I asked her to marry me today and she agreed.'

For a moment, Robert thought Oberon would strike him, so vicious was the anger that flashed in those obsidian eyes. 'You'll be sorry you did this, Silverton. I will make you pay.'

'There is nothing more you can do. You cannot defame my sister again and you have already destroyed your good *friend*, Lawrence Welton.'

'Lawrence was a fool,' Oberon spat. 'But there are others who can be made to suffer. I will not allow you to stand in my way again.'

'I don't care for threats,' Robert said. 'And it is *you* who would do well to take care. The aristocracy is not above reproach. Society *will* turn its back on *any* man if the crimes are heinous enough.'

Oberon's face could have been carved from stone. His anger vanished, replaced by a quiet loathing that was far more dangerous. 'I *will* bring you down, Robert. And by God, I'll enjoy watching you fall.'

Robert stood his ground, but he felt a chill run down his spine. The façade of the elegant dandy was gone, devoured by the snake and lost for ever. He had no doubt the creature would strike again…and that when it did, it would strike more viciously than ever before.

Sophie was emerging from Clark and Debenham's the next morning when she saw Mr Oberon leaning against a lamp-post, looking in her direction. She was tempted to go back inside, but it was too late. Oberon pushed away from the pole and came towards her. There was a thin smile on his lips, but his manner was as cold as a blast of Arctic air. 'Miss Vallois, what a pleasant surprise.'

'Mr Oberon.' She was eminently grateful for

Jeanette standing quietly behind her. 'I was just on my way home.'

She went to move past him, but was stayed by his words. 'I would have but a moment of your time.'

'Lady Longworth is expecting me—'

'This will not take long.'

'I'm sure it will not. But first, there is something I must tell you—'

'Say nothing. Have your maid stay well behind us and keep your voice down,' Oberon advised. 'I shall walk you the length of this street and then back to your carriage. What I have to say will take no longer than that.'

Aware that there was nothing she could do, Sophie handed her maid the few packages she was carrying and instructed her to follow them at a distance. Then she fell into step beside Oberon and they began to walk.

'It has come to my attention,' he said in a conversational tone, 'that you have agreed to marry Mr Silverton. No, do not answer. Simply smile and nod, as though we were discussing the weather.'

Sophie did, though the knot in her chest tightened until it threatened to choke her.

'It also strikes me that in doing so you have failed to honour your side of the bargain,' he continued.

'I was not aware we had entered into a bargain.'

'Were you not?' He turned to her, his beautiful smile unbearably cruel. 'I thought I'd made it plain. *I* was to restore Miss Silverton's good name and *you* were to accept my proposal of marriage.'

'You said you would *endeavour* to restore her

good name, and you gave me a week to consider my answer.'

'Spare me the argument, Miss Vallois. I was to exonerate Miss Silverton and you were to marry me. Simple. Had you told me at the time that you had no intention of agreeing, the outcome for your friend would have been very…different.'

In that moment, Sophie knew she was dealing with a man without conscience, a man who would not hesitate to use any weapon in his arsenal to secure what he wanted. 'You made me believe you cared as much for Miss Silverton's reputation as I did,' Sophie said, keeping her eyes on the road ahead. 'Now I see it was simply a means of buying my affection.'

'Call it what you will, the end result is that you have accepted Mr Silverton's proposal and do not think to hear mine. Well, I am here to inform you that you *will* hear my proposal, and that you *will* agree to it.'

'That, sir, I cannot do. I have given my promise elsewhere.'

'A promise that need mean no more to Silverton than yours did to me.'

'He asked for my hand and I was free to bestow it. I am not in that position now.'

'And if he had not spoken to you and I had come to you as agreed? Would you have accepted *my* proposal?'

Sophie stopped dead, forcing him to halt as well. 'I would not, sir. I told you I did not love you and that has not changed. If I led you to believe my answer would be yes—'

'Say no more, Miss Vallois. It is I who must now

speak my piece,' he said, taking her arm and forcing her to walk again. 'Perhaps it will help soften your heart towards me.'

'There is really no point—'

'There is always a point, dearest Sophie.'

'Please do not address me in that way—'

He raised his hand to silence her objections. 'It has not escaped my notice that you and your brother are very close. And, indeed, he is a fine fellow for all his being French. But it has also come to my attention, through the most reliable of sources, that in the past he committed an act which, to certain factions of the government, might be viewed as treasonous. No, keep on walking,' he said when her step faltered. 'See, there is your carriage just ahead. We only have a few more minutes in each other's company and there is still much I would have you know.'

'What do you want?' Sophie said, dreading what he was about to say.

'What I want is your agreement to be my wife. I thought after what happened at Lady Chiswick's to make you my mistress, but that would still leave you free to marry Robert Silverton and I'll see *hell* freeze over before *that* happens. So, you will agree to be my wife or I shall make known your brother's doings to certain people in Paris who, I think, would be very interested in knowing the whereabouts of a man who once saved the life of a much sought-after English spy. For if your brother would do that, who knows what other conspiracies he might have been a party to?'

'You're bluffing! You don't know anyone who would wish him harm!'

He smiled, coldly. 'You seem to have forgotten that your former charge, Miss Georgina Grant-Ogilvy, married a Frenchman who just happens to be in an area of government very interested in the activities of men like your brother. And since that illuminating night at Lady Chiswick's, I have taken it upon myself to develop a close and most useful relationship with both the lady and her new husband while they are here in London.'

'You would not dare!' Sophie whispered fiercely. 'Antoine has done nothing to you!'

'Ah, but you, dear Sophie, have. You have bewitched me and I intend to spend the rest of my life showing you how much I love you.'

Knowing that love would have nothing to do with it, Sophie said, 'I will *not* marry you!'

'I think you will. Because you are no longer the only one whose future hangs in the balance.' Oberon turned to bestow an angelic smile upon her. 'If you do not agree to marry me, I shall see to it that the moment your brother returns to France, he *will* be apprehended and clapped in irons. And from what I understand, life expectancy in a French jail can be…alarmingly short.'

'This will *never* come to pass!' Sophie whispered furiously. 'I will tell him of your monstrous plan. If Antoine knows you conspire to trap him—'

'Ah, but you will not tell him or anyone else of our conversation this afternoon, for if you do, I will make life very difficult for two *other* people I know you hold in high regard. In case you fail to realise it, the lives of an English spy and his wife are never completely without danger either. Not to mention dear Robert. Who knows what manner of…accident may befall him?'

Sophie felt the blood drain from her face. 'I don't believe you! Even *you* would not be so vicious as to threaten them in such a way.'

'My naïve child, I would threaten *anyone* who stood in the way of me getting what I want—and I want you. But I prefer to think of it as having the upper hand. I always do, you know,' Oberon said amiably. 'As I once told Silver, everyone has secrets. All one has to do is find out what they are and then put them to use. I make it my business to find out as many secrets as I can, and you would be amazed at how many people's lives I could destroy. Titled ladies and their lovers. Grand dukes and their paramours. Shady businessmen and dissatisfied bankers.' He smiled, as though the conversation was of the most trivial in nature. 'So you see, Sophie, you really cannot win. Refuse me and I will cause you more pain and heartache than you can imagine. Accept, and everything goes on as normal. Your brother can safely return to France, the Longworths can go on as usual, and Robert and Jane will continue with their boring little lives. And you will become my beautiful viscountess and the envy of all society.'

Sophie could think of nothing to say. The proposal was monstrous, as was the creature who uttered it.

'I can see I have given you a great deal to think about,' he said as they approached the carriage. 'So I will honour my original commitment and formally call upon you tomorrow. That is fair of me, don't you think?'

She turned her head away, unable to look at him, so great was her loathing.

'What, no kind words to offer your future husband?'

'If I had words,' Sophie ground out, 'they would not be kind.'

'Ah. Then I suggest you find some. I expect you to convey all appearance of happiness when I inform Lord and Lady Longworth of our betrothal.'

As the world around her began to spin, Sophie placed her hand on the side of the carriage. 'I am surprised at your determination to marry me, Mr Oberon. I would have thought a viscount's son could do better than to marry the penniless daughter of a farmer from Bayencourt!'

'A farmer's daughter?' The look he gave her was one of amused disbelief. 'Come, come, Sophie, surely you do not expect me to believe such a Banbury tale.'

'You mean you didn't know?' She wanted to laugh, even as fear and indecision tore at her insides. 'Your *reliable sources* failed to inform you as to the details of my birth?'

'There is nothing to tell. Your conduct betrays you for what you are.'

'I was born to Gaston and Aimee Vallois in the kitchen of their farmhouse,' Sophie said. 'I grew up helping my mother keep house and sometimes helping my father in the fields.'

'Rubbish! A farmer's daughter would never be able to

speak such impeccable English! She would never appear so elegant in manner and dress!'

'Have you forgotten about my employment with Mrs Grant-Ogilvy? You were there when it all came out. *She* taught me English so that I might speak to her daughters. And because I was often required to accompany the family when they went visiting I was given thorough instruction in deportment, elocution and manners. I may have been taught to behave like a lady, but I can assure you, my origins are quite humble. Only think what society will say when they learn the truth about *that*!' she flung at him.

For a moment, Oberon said nothing, clearly unwilling to believe that she was telling him the truth. His pride and his belief in his ability to control others would naturally prevent him from seeing it as anything but lies. But the longer he looked at her, and the firmer she stood, the more Sophie realised he was coming to accept it. 'So this has all been a sham,' he said, his eyes narrowing to slits. 'An elaborate ruse to trick an unsuspecting public into believing a lie!'

'Not at all. Nicholas and Lavinia never tried to make anyone believe I was anything more than I am. *You* are the one whose motives have been suspect. You've never *loved* me. Your interest in me has always been as a result of my appearance. You said as much the first time we met.'

During the long, tense silence that followed, Sophie felt as though her breath was cut off, her heart thudding noisily within her chest.

'Does he know?' Oberon enquired nastily.

Anxiety shot through her. 'Who?'

'You know damn well who! Silverton! Does he know you're a farmer's brat?'

For the first time, Sophie began to smile. So, the polished veneer was finally being stripped away to reveal the ugliness beneath. 'Yes, he knows. I told him.'

'Yet you did not think to tell me. Pity.'

She knew a fleeting moment of hope. 'Then you withdraw your proposal.'

'I do not!' Oberon's fury nailed her to the spot. 'Nothing has changed, Miss Vallois. I will never let you go so that you can marry him. *Never!*'

With that parting thrust, he left, his steps hard and angry on the cobblestones. Sophie sagged against the side of the carriage. *What had she done?*

'Are you all right, miss?' Jeanette said, hurrying to her side.

'I'm fine.' But Sophie felt the perspiration on her palms; as she climbed into the carriage, her spirits were as heavy as the thunderclouds over her head. What on earth was she going to do? She knew Oberon would make good on his threat. He had done so on every other occasion, and having witnessed what he was capable of, she no longer doubted that he was the one behind Jane's fall from grace. Or that he had done it as a warning— or a punishment—to Robert. The man would stop at nothing to achieve his ends.

And now it was her turn to experience his ire. Just when the happiness she had always longed for seemed within her grasp, it was to be snatched away, like sweets from the mouth of a child.

The monster of her nightmares was real...and his name was Montague Oberon.

'Excuse me, sir, this note was just delivered,' the butler said, holding the tray out to Robert.

Jane looked up from her lunch of bread and butter and cheese. 'Who is it from?'

Not recognising the handwriting, Robert broke the wafer and opened the parchment to see a single line scrawled upon the page.

I must see you. Please come as quickly as you can.
Sophie

Fear lodged like a bullet in his gut. 'Something's wrong.' He got up from the table and kissed his sister on the forehead. 'I have to see Sophie.'

Jane's cheeks paled as she read the discarded letter. 'What does this mean, Robert?'

'I have no idea, but I don't like the sound of it.'

Not long after, he was shown into the Longworths' drawing room. Sophie stood alone by the window, her complexion as pale as her gown, her eyes rimmed with red. She looked ready to shatter into a thousand pieces.

'What's wrong?' he asked as the door closed behind him.

'Thank you for coming so quickly.'

'My darling girl, you have no need to thank me. What has happened?'

'I fear I have had a change of heart, Robert. No, please, stay where you are,' she said as he started towards her. 'Do not make this any harder than it already is.'

'What do you mean you've had a change of heart? Do you no longer love me?'

'My feelings are unchanged,' she said. 'But I can no longer marry you.'

'Why not?'

Her voice shook. 'Mr Oberon—'

'Oberon!' In two strides Robert was across the room. 'What has he said to you?'

'Nothing!'

'Your face betrays you, sweetheart. Come, sit down beside me.'

But she shook her head. 'It's best we not spend time together, Robert. It is too late.'

He put his hands on her arms and realised she was trembling. 'What has he said to make you act this way?' When she didn't answer, he drew her into her arms and held her. 'Tell me, Sophie,' he whispered against her hair. 'I can't help you if you won't tell me.'

'You can't help me regardless. Oberon holds all the cards. There is nothing he will not do, Robert. No one he will not destroy in order to get what he wants. It is simpler…better…if I just marry him.'

'It is neither simpler nor better to marry a man you don't love!'

'But he has the power to destroy everyone I do, and I can't let that happen.' Pulling free of his arms,

Sophie moved like an automaton towards the window. 'I won't!'

Robert searched for the words that would make her change her mind. She was slipping away from him and there was nothing he could do to stop it. 'Can you tell me nothing, Sophie? Nothing that can be of use?'

'Only that he knows things,' she whispered. 'I don't know how he found out, but he knows things that can destroy people's lives.'

'Then we will talk to whoever he is threatening,' Robert said. 'Find a way to refute the lies—'

'They are not lies,' she said sadly. 'He knows the truth and that is even more damaging.'

'Then at least tell me *who* has he threatened!'

Sophie put back her head and laughed. 'Who has he *not*? You. My brother. Nicholas and Lavinia. Everyone I hold most dear in my life. And he will make good on his threats, Robert. I know he will.' She looked at him, and the darkness of despair was reflected in her eyes. 'He will never let you have me. He told me as much. If I walk away from you now, everything will be all right. If I do not…'

'You unleash the monster,' Robert said quietly.

'Exactly. Jane is the only one safe from him now. And poor Mr Welton. He cannot touch either of them again.'

It was more than Robert could bear. To see the woman he loved set on a course of action that would ultimately destroy her was beyond all endurance. Because he knew that if she went ahead with this marriage, she *would* be destroyed. If Oberon was willing to use her so abysmally now, what could she expect of their life together? There would be nothing of love or respect. Their marriage would be about possession and revenge. A partnership made in hell.

A marriage to suit the devil himself.

Chapter Fourteen

Not surprisingly, Sophie's unexpected change of plans was met with expressions of shock and dismay when she told Nicholas, Lavinia and her brother of them shortly after Robert left.

'You are going to marry *Oberon*?' Nicholas said. 'But…you have already accepted Robert Silverton.'

'Yes, and I have just told him I've had a change of heart.'

'But I thought you loved him, Sophie,' Lavinia said in bewilderment. 'You told me as much only yesterday.'

'I know what I said,' she whispered. She had to be strong—and the only way to do that was by studying the welfare of the people standing before her. 'But when I thought about all I would be giving up, I realised how foolish I would be to turn Mr Oberon's proposal down.'

'All you would be giving up?' Antoine said. 'You're telling us you've chosen to become a viscountess and accept all that goes with it? *Pourquoi es-tu de nous mentir, petite?*'

'I am not lying to you!' Sophie said. 'Nicholas, you said you wished me to marry well.'

'Yes, and if I thought it was in your best interests to marry him, I would rejoice in your selection of Oberon as your husband,' Nicholas said. 'But information has come to light about which I cannot be happy, and I would *beg* you to reconsider.'

'I cannot. I've made up my mind,' she forced herself to say in as convincing a tone as possible. 'I *am* going to marry him.'

A heavy silence fell, during which Sophie watched the people she loved struggle to come to terms with the news she had just imparted. It was obvious they didn't know what to say. That all they wanted to do was try to convince her of what a terrible mistake she was making.

Little did they know that she understood better than *any* of them exactly how terrible a mistake it was.

Lavinia slowly got to her feet. 'Well, I had best advise Cook we will only be four for dinner.'

'Three.' Nicholas abruptly stood up. 'I'll be at my club. Antoine?'

Her brother shook his head. 'No, I'll stay.'

'Fine. Then I'll see you both in the morning.' With that, Nicholas left. Lavinia hesitated, looking as though she wanted to say something, then, obviously deciding it wasn't the best time, turned and followed her husband out of the room.

Sophie stayed where she was. She didn't look up. Didn't try to stop them. She knew how disappointed they were, but she couldn't let that matter. She had no choice but to see this through to its painful conclusion.

'So, are you going to tell me what's really going on, *petite*?' Antoine asked. 'What's really behind this change of heart?'

Sophie shook her head, wrapping her arms around herself and holding on tight. 'It is better you do not know.'

'Why? Has he hurt you?' Antoine's eyes darkened with an unspoken threat. 'Because if he has—'

'Please, Antoine, don't ask me again. I have made up my mind and there is nothing you can say to change it. I *will* marry Mr Oberon. And you must see that this is very good for you. Now you can ask Jane to marry you.'

'Marry Jane?' Antoine stared at her as though she were a simpleton. 'Robert will never agree to my marrying his sister now.'

'Of course he will. If he was willing to marry me, he can have no qualms about allowing you to marry Jane.'

'And condone a marriage between his sister and the brother of the woman who jilted him for a man he despises?'

Sophie winced at the harshness of his reply. 'He only wants Jane to be happy. If he knows she will find that happiness with you—'

'And be forced to think about *you* every time he sees me? To be reminded of what he lost every time Jane talks about her sister-in-law?'

'Please don't, Antoine,' she whispered, turning away.

'I'm sorry, Sophie, but I know you're holding something back. You wouldn't do this unless there was a very good reason.'

When she still said nothing, he came around the table and sat down next to her. 'You have never lied to me. Never kept anything from me. Why would you do so now when there is so much at stake?'

'It is *because* there is so much at stake that I must keep this to myself. If it were anything less important, I would tell you.'

Antoine's hands fell away and Sophie suddenly felt cold, and terribly alone. 'Then there is nothing more to say,' he said, getting up.

'There *is*! You must speak to Robert. You must marry Jane!' Lord knew, *one* of them had to salvage something out of this pitiful situation!

But Antoine only shook his head. 'If I had one wish, it would be that Jane and I might never be separated again. But that cannot be. I know what Mr Silverton's answer would be, and it is the right one. After all, what kind of life could I offer her?'

'You could offer her the very *best* life!' Sophie said urgently. 'A wonderful life with the man she loves. What more could Jane ask?'

'Respect. Security. Wealth. All of which she deserves, none of which I can give her.'

'But I am to be married to a rich man!' Sophie cried, grasping at straws. 'I will have money. Money that you and Jane can live on.'

Antoine looked at her for a long time. 'Tell me this is not why you consented to be his wife.'

'Of course not! But if I must marry him—'

'Must?'

Sophie could have kicked herself. 'If I *want* to marry him, why should my family not benefit?'

Her argument fell on deaf ears. Antoine was not to be swayed. 'I will take nothing from him, Sophie. Even if it comes through you. You do not know what they say about him in the clubs—'

'And I beg you, do not tell me!' she whispered, turning away. 'I do not wish to hear it.'

'Why? Because it confirms what you already suspect?'

'It would not be his money,' Sophie tried again. 'It would be mine to do with as I please.'

'You would have only what he gave you. If he decided to give you nothing, you would have nothing.'

'Then I shall ask Nicholas to negotiate a settlement for me,' Sophie said. 'I have heard that such things are done. And I will be given…pin money. To buy dresses and shoes. You and Jane can live on that.'

'And what will you say when your husband asks why you have no new gown to wear to the ball, or bonnets to wear when you go out in society? How will you explain where the money has gone?'

'I will not explain myself.' She raised her chin. 'If the money is given to me, it is mine to do with as I please. And if I wish to give it to you so that you and Jane can be together, that is what I will do! It would be worth all the gowns and jewels in London to see the two of you happy together!'

'Ah, my sweet Sophie.' Antoine struggled for a moment, and then pulled her into his arms. 'It tears me apart to see you so unhappy.'

'I am not unhappy and everything will be fine,' Sophie lied. She closed her eyes and rested her face against his chest. 'You'll see. It will all work out.'

'And how will you feel when you see Robert Silverton in society? How will you feel when you see him with another woman? Perhaps with the children the two of you might have had.'

The image appeared all too clearly in her mind, and Sophie felt her heart break. 'I will wish him happy in his new life and hope he thinks of me with kindness now and then. That is what I will feel, Antoine. Because that is how it has to be.'

The announcement of the engagement between the Honourable Montague John Phillip Oberon and Miss Sophia Chantal Vallois was published in *The Times* two days later and instantly became a source of speculation and gossip in the drawing rooms of society. Much was made of the fact that the son of a peer was marrying an unknown French woman—a woman who had once been a servant to Mrs Grant-Ogilvy. Oberon's mother initially refused to acknowledge Sophie as her future daughter-in-law until her husband had intervened to settle matters. And while he did not come out and publicly endorse the marriage, neither did he forbid it or threaten to disinherit his son if he went ahead with it. When asked how he felt about Miss Vallois, however, his expression grew stony and no response was offered before he abruptly turned and walked away.

Naturally, the polite world drew its own conclusions as to the family's reactions. Nothing was better loved than a scandal and the haste with which Oberon planned his wedding to the beautiful Miss Vallois was remarked upon in several of London's most elegant drawing rooms. There were also those who commented upon the fact that the newly engaged pair did not seem to spend a great deal of time together at the glittering society events to which they were invited, while others said it was only to be expected. Nothing was as tasteless as an overt display of affection.

Robert did not attend any of the parties. Loving Sophie as he did, he could not celebrate her marriage to his enemy. He could not pretend happiness at seeing her wed to a man who was as bestial as the creatures living in the forest. No, that was unkind to God's creatures, Robert reflected. God's creatures were *better* than Oberon. They did not plot revenge against their fellow beasts, or try to cheat them out of what they owned. Truth be known, he would rather spend the night in the forest with a pack of wolves than he would in a fancy ballroom with the Honourable Montague Oberon.

'I say, you're looking rather glum,' Captain McIntosh said, stopping by the table. 'I thought you would have been out celebrating your friend's engagement to the young French lady. I believe Sir David and Lady Hester are holding a masked ball in their honour this evening.'

Robert set his fourth empty glass on the table. 'Oberon and I are no longer speaking and I have no intention of celebrating his good fortune tonight or at any time in the future.' Then, aware that he sounded as miserable as he felt, he made an effort to be social. 'Care to join me for a drink?'

'If you're sure you want company.'

'I'm not at all sure that I do, but I would rather not drink myself to oblivion alone.'

'In that case…' McIntosh sat down in the chair opposite and signalled for the butler. 'Brandy, if you please, Mr Gibbons.'

'And another for me as well,' Robert said.

The remark drew a sympathetic glance from his companion. 'You're going to regret this in the morning.'

'Most likely, but since the morning and its attendant misery are still ten hours away, my concern is not immediate.'

'So you and Oberon have fallen out,' McIntosh said. 'Can't say I'm surprised. I've never had much time for the fellow myself, and I certainly don't trust him. Welton found that out the hard way.'

'Welton should have known better than to gamble with him,' Robert muttered. 'Oberon's a devil when it comes to cards.'

'I wasn't talking about cards. I was referring to the investment swindle Oberon pulled on him.'

Robert looked up. 'I've heard nothing about a swindle.'

'Hardly surprising,' McIntosh said. 'Why do you think Oberon banished Lawrence to the country?'

'I assumed because Lawrence had debts he couldn't afford to pay back and Oberon's price was his name on my sister's defamation.'

McIntosh sent Robert a pointed look. 'Are you sure the two of you are no longer friends? I'd hate to think any of this might get back to him.'

'Trust me, I'd rather see Oberon in hell than shake his hand.'

'In that case…' McIntosh leaned in closer '…I can tell you that Lawrence got into his cups one night and lost a fortune to Oberon. Naturally Oberon assured him he would be happy to take his vowel with no pressure to repay, but when he suggested that Lawrence might take a look at an investment he was putting together that was guaranteed to pay a high rate of return, Lawrence agreed, no questions asked. But when he went to see Oberon about the investment a few months later, he was told the scheme had gone sour and that he'd lost every penny he put in. So Oberon took his house instead.'

'Poor bastard,' Robert said. 'Was there ever really a scheme?'

'Your guess is as good as mine. If there was, Oberon likely played up the potential for profit far beyond any reasonable expectation of return.'

'Lawrence should have made enquiries,' Robert said.

'Of course he should, but Oberon was his friend. Lawrence signed the letter without asking any questions. And I suspect that when it all fell through, that's when Oberon told Lawrence he would forgive some of his debts if he agreed to play a part in a small subterfuge, namely be the foil for your sister's supposed transgression. Lawrence had no choice but to agree. It was either that or end up in debtor's prison.'

'But if Oberon was stringing Lawrence along, pretending to invest his money in a fraudulent scheme, he's guilty of a criminal offence.'

'Aye, but who's to prove it?' McIntosh asked. 'Oberon would sell his own mother if he thought it to his advantage.'

And blackmail his father into the bargain, Robert reflected bitterly.

'Problem is,' McIntosh went on, 'there's not many who'll risk running afoul of him.'

Robert slowly looked up. 'Except someone who already has and has nothing left to lose.'

The Captain's eyes narrowed. 'Lawrence?'

'Who else? If Oberon *believes* Lawrence destroyed, and Lawrence likewise believes himself ruined, perhaps he would be willing to tell us what happened. We need to show that Oberon's investment scheme was fraudulent from the start. If we could find proof of a criminal act, we could use it against him.'

McIntosh sat back in his chair. 'You'd have to prove it beyond the shadow of a doubt. Leave no stone unturned, as it were.'

Robert thought of his beloved Sophie and of the bleakness in her eyes during their last encounter. 'I would raise the Rock of Gibraltar if I thought a clue lay concealed beneath it.'

'Would you now.' McIntosh smiled. 'I wasn't aware Lawrence was that good a friend.'

'He isn't,' Robert admitted. 'Though I would gladly see him cleared of any wrongdoing, there is someone else far dearer to me who stands to lose a great deal more. I would give my life,' he said quietly, 'not to see that happen.'

Sophie did not expect to see Robert again. Though he was never far from her thoughts, the feelings they had for one another and the nature of what had passed between them would make it impossible for them to be easy in one another's company. The debilitating pain she would feel at seeing him, the knowledge that she might have been his wife, would always be there between them.

Besides, she was betrothed to Mr Oberon now and must endeavour to play the part. And so she shopped with Lavinia for wedding clothes and talked of flowers and churches, and showed her ring of rubies and emeralds, an ugly, ostentatious thing drawn from the bowels of the Oberon family vault, to the young ladies who asked to see it, and professed herself suitably pleased with her good fortune. More than that she could not do. She could not feign an appearance of happiness, or act light-headed and giddy as newly engaged girls were supposed to do. Instead, she grew quiet, locking her pain deep within, keeping the secret of her broken heart from those she loved the most.

And then the final axe fell. Antoine was called back to France. A distraught letter from Monsieur Larocque's wife explained that her husband had fallen on broken glass and badly lacerated his hands. She wrote that he was incapable of performing even the most basic of surgical procedures and begged Antoine to return as quickly as possible, saying there were many patients in desperate need of his care.

It had been a heart-wrenching decision for Antoine. Weighted against his desire to stay and see his sister through what would surely be one of the hardest days of her life was an equally strong desire to go back and help those who were in need of his skills. It pained him to know that without his assistance, some of those people might well lose limbs, or their sight—or even die.

Nicholas tried to make him stay, saying he would do whatever was necessary to enrol Antoine in a university where he could begin his studies towards becoming a doctor in earnest. Even Lavinia had pleaded with him not to go, saying that Sophie would be heartbroken if her only brother was not there to see her get married. But Antoine's life was *about* helping the sick. To turn his back on them now would be to deny his life-long calling—and Sophie had no intention of asking him to do that.

And so she told him to go back to Paris. She convinced him that to ignore Monsieur Larocque's cry for help would be poor repayment for everything the man had done for him, and said that if he did not immediately return, she would always wonder about his true desire to be a doctor.

It was of little comfort to her that he agreed. They had been through so much the last three years, growing closer as brother and sister than many wives and husbands ever would. But she knew that going back was the *right* thing for Antoine to do. Not only was he was finding it increasingly difficult not to see Jane, but Sophie knew how he felt about her marrying a man she did not love, a man for whom he could feel no respect or affection.

'There will be no turning back from this mistake, *petite*,' Antoine said the night before he left. 'When you are his wife, you will belong to him. I will not be able to help you. If he wishes it, you will be lost to me for ever.'

And Sophie had walked into his arms and held him tightly because she'd known he was speaking the truth. A man could beat his wife or have her committed to an institution without fear of retribution. When a woman married, she and her husband became one person—and in the eyes of the law, that person was *the* man.

But, marry him she would, because she had made a promise to protect the lives of the people she loved. Surely it was better knowing that Antoine was living the life he wanted in Paris than to sit here wondering if the next person who walked into his surgery might be there to arrest him. Surely it was better knowing that Nicholas and Lavinia were able to move freely about London than to live with the fear that someone might jump out at them from the shadows of a darkened alley.

Surely it was better knowing that Robert was going on without her than to lie awake at night wondering if he would meet an unfortunate *accident*, as Oberon had so casually suggested that morning outside Clark and Debenham's.

How much happiness could she have known with that kind of fear dogging her every step?

* * *

And so it was that on the day Sophie walked out of the drapers after the final fitting of her wedding gown, that she was able to find the strength to look Robert Silverton in the eye after all but colliding with him. To speak to him in tones resembling those of a normal conversation.

'Mr Silverton. Forgive me. I should have paid more attention to where I was going.'

'The fault was not yours, Miss Vallois.' He bent to retrieve one of the parcels she had dropped. 'I should have known better than to walk so quickly along so crowded a street.' He straightened to look at her and she saw the pain reflected in his eyes. 'Especially during the height of the shopping hour.'

Sophie closed her eyes. She had been so close. So close to convincing herself she had the strength to do this. To know that she would not crumble the first time she saw him again. But meeting him like this was her undoing. An inadvertent collision on a busy street served as a bittersweet reminder of all they meant to one another—and all they were destined to lose. And it took every ounce of courage she possessed to pretend an indifference she was far from feeling. 'I trust your sister is well?'

'Well enough.' Robert's voice was quiet, but strained. 'She spends a great deal of time in her room. Writing letters.'

'Yes, writing can be…a pleasant pastime,' Sophie agreed. Poor Jane. The girl's heart was as badly broken as her own. Since Antoine's return to Paris, she had received not a single word from Jane, and the girl had been all but absent from society.

Sophie bit her lip and glanced behind her, hoping to see Lavinia emerge from the shop.

'I was surprised your brother decided to return to France before the wedding,' Robert said, fixing his attention on a nearby curricle. 'I thought he would have wanted to be here to see you…marry.'

'He did, very much,' Sophie said, unhappiness falling like an iron bar across her chest. 'But he received a letter concerning the gentleman to whom he is apprenticed and learned that he himself had been badly injured. His wife begged Antoine to return to take care of his patients. Naturally, Antoine wished to help in any way he could.'

'Of course. Your brother is dedicated to his work.'

'It means everything to him.' Oh, *why* did Lavinia not come out? This unbearably polite discourse was growing more painful by the minute. And then Robert made it even worse.

'I have no right to say this to you, Sophie, but I cannot let you go to Oberon without telling you that I love you with all my heart and that if you ever have need of my help for *any* reason, you have only to come to me and I will—'

'Mr Silverton,' Lavinia said, finally emerging from the shop. 'What a pleasant surprise.'

Robert stepped back. His jaw tightened as he belatedly offered her a bow. 'Lady Longworth.'

'Nicholas and I were talking about you just the other

day. He said he sees very little of you about town these days.'

'I think it merely that our paths do not cross.'

Lavinia smiled. 'Of course. And how does dear Jane go on?'

'She engages herself with writing. I think she pens a novel in secret.'

'A novel! How exciting,' Lavinia said. 'I have always wanted to write a book, but find myself sadly lacking in imagination. No doubt it would be a very dry and boring effort.'

'I'm sure you underestimate your abilities, Lady Longworth.'

Sophie felt him glance in her direction, but knew better than to meet his gaze. It was heartbreaking to see him like this, knowing he would never be more than a passing acquaintance. How would she ever bear it...?

'Well, I suppose I had best be on my way,' Robert said at length. 'Good morning, Lady Longworth. Miss Vallois.'

'Mr Silverton,' Lavinia said quietly, only to breathe a deep sigh a few minutes later. 'Poor man. He thinks he conceals his pain, but it is there for all to see. And dear Jane obviously pines as much for your brother as you do for Robert.'

Dangerously close to tears, Sophie whispered huskily, 'I do not pine for Mr Silverton.'

'Of course you do. Oh, you can say what you like to everyone else, but I know what's in your heart, Sophie,' Lavinia said as they turned and walked in the other direction. 'I too married one man when I was falling

in love with another. And I cared a great deal more for
François than you do for Mr Oberon. And though you
refuse to explain your reasons for marrying Mr Oberon,
I know there *is* an explanation. Oh, no, dear, please don't
cry! I didn't mean to make you cry.'

Sophie shook her head, dashing away tears. 'It was
just so hard to see him again.'

'Of course it was, and I shouldn't have said anything,'
Lavinia said. 'I know how deeply you're suffering. But if
you will not change your mind, there is nothing we can
do but carry on. The wedding is only a few days away
and we still have much to do.'

Sophie nodded, swallowing hard. 'Where are we to
go next?'

'We *should* go to Madame Egaltine's for gloves. However…' Lavinia smiled as tucked her arm in Sophie's. 'I
think we shall call at Gunter's for ices instead. I believe
we are both in need of a little refreshment.'

Chapter Fifteen

~~~~~~

Given the nature of Oberon's crime, Robert suspected there were very few people who would know the full extent of the scheme, or the scope of the financial damage done to Lawrence Welton. Oberon would, but there was no point in looking to him for answers. And while Lawrence might know, it seemed he was unwilling to disclose any details as to what had really happened.

'I signed the papers,' was all he would say. 'I gave them back to Oberon and he assured me he would send me a copy once the lawyer had finalised the details. But he never did. And by the time I realised I had nothing in writing, it was too late.'

The disappointing results forced Robert to focus his attention on two other possible sources of information, the first being the legal firm where the papers had been drawn up, and the second being Mr Stanley Hunt, Welton's man of business. Unfortunately, discreet investigations carried out over the course of the next few days yielded little of use. Having been as effectively deceived by Oberon as his employer, Mr Hunt was deeply embarrassed at being asked about the case and sought to bring the interview to a close as quickly as possible.

As for Sir Thomas Buckley, senior partner with the law firm Buckley, Stevens and Mortimer, the results were equally disappointing. Sir Thomas had worked for both the present Lord Mannerfield and his father for many years; though Robert was not granted an interview with the lofty barrister, he was informed by the clerk who guarded that gentleman's office with the ferocity of a Trojan that much of the work done for the son had been handled by a Mr Adrian Brocknower.

When Robert asked to see Mr Brocknower, the clerk informed him in the most discouraging of tones that the gentleman was no longer in the employ of the firm and that he had no idea where he lived or for whom he might be working—both of which convinced Robert that he had to find Brocknower as soon as possible. A position with a prestigious company was hard to come by. Had Brocknower left of his own volition, or had he been forced out by circumstances beyond his control?

Unfortunately, *finding* Adrian Brocknower turned out to be even more of a challenge. After asking endless questions and checking out three addresses, Robert still had nothing. The rooms were all empty and the landladies had no idea where their tenant had gone. Nor did they care, since, unlike many of the young men who passed through their doors, this one had paid his account in full.

It was enough to drive a sane man to drink and, in a

mood to work off some of his excess frustration, Robert made his way to Angelo's. There were always a number of cocky young men anxious to perfect the finer points of the thrust and salute, and while few of them were up to Robert's level of play, they would serve to take the edge off his anger. Unfortunately, by the time he arrived, most of the better fencers had already paired themselves off, and those who were new to the game were happy to practise their lunges in front of a mirror.

Robert made his way to a bench along the back wall and set down his foil. He'd just have to wait it out.

'Are you engaged to meet a partner, sir?'

The voice was quiet. Refined. A mellow baritone perfect for reciting Shakespeare. Robert turned to find a tall gentleman in fencing garb standing opposite him. The man's hair was almost black, and though his face was partially covered by a mask, Robert knew from what little he could see that the man was a stranger to him. 'I am not, sir.'

'Then perhaps you would care to spar with me?'

Robert inclined his head. 'By all means.'

The man led the way on to the floor, walking with the unconscious dignity of a prince. Robert noticed he kept a distance from the other fencers, but was equally aware that no one seemed to be paying them any mind. 'I don't believe I've seen you in here before,' he said casually.

'I usually practise in private, but I thought this afternoon I might benefit from the company of others.' He stopped and turned around. 'Are you ready?'

Robert up took his position. 'When you are.'

The match was surprisingly good. Robert soon

determined the man's skill to be equal to his own, if not slightly better. He moved quickly, expending no unnecessary effort, but his swordplay was quick and well aimed. He struck three times before Robert managed his first hit, and when they drew even at six, they agreed to take a break.

'You fence well, sir,' Robert said, breathing harder than his opponent. 'It is evident I have been too long from the game.'

'You present an excellent form and style, Mr Silverton,' the gentleman said. 'I think only your physical stamina is lacking.'

Robert reached for a towel and wiped the sweat from his face. He hadn't missed the fact that the stranger had addressed him by name. 'Perhaps you have more time to practise than I.'

'I agree that technique generally improves with regular practice, but I find extra tutelage also helps. There is a gentleman near Covent Garden who gives private lessons.' The stranger pulled out a card and handed it to Robert. 'You will find him at this address. But I suggest you go tonight. And if he asks, tell him Parker sent you.'

Robert took the card, his eyes widening at the sight of Adrian Brocknower's name and address. 'How did you know—?'

'Let's just say it has come to my attention that you have been asking questions about a common enemy. I happen to be in possession of information that may prove useful to you.'

Robert inclined his head. Whoever this Parker fellow

was, he obviously had a grudge against Oberon too. Strange he didn't want to settle it himself. 'I am indebted to you, sir.' He tucked the card securely into his pocket. 'Can I interest you in another match?'

He saw the gentleman's mouth curve behind the mask. 'Always. But I give you fair warning, Mr Silverton. *This* time, I intend to play.'

There was nothing Sophie could do to alter the path upon which she had set out. But when she thought about Robert's last words and realised what the rest of her life was going to be like, she knew she could not go any further without allowing herself one brief moment of happiness. Insanity it might be, but it was surely no worse than the madness she was already contemplating.

As she stepped out of the hackney late that afternoon, she looked up at the house on Portman Square and was aware of feeling strangely calm. Was this how a condemned man felt as he enjoyed the last few hours of his life? Was this heady feeling of freedom common amongst women who were on the verge of betraying their husbands or lovers?

As she walked towards the front door, she took some comfort from the fact that she had not yet stood before God and his angels and sworn fidelity to a man she despised.

The door opened to her knock and, ignoring the butler's quickly concealed look of surprise, she was shown into the drawing room. It was well past the hour for social calls, but Sophie had sent Jane a note advising her of her intention to call, and asking if she could please make sure her brother was there. She had also asked that Jane not tell him she was coming. It was best he had no opportunity to prepare for her arrival.

Jane was waiting for her in the drawing room. She rose as Sophie entered and Sophie saw how deeply she suffered. She seemed to have lost weight, and her beautiful green eyes were dark and haunted. 'Dearest Sophie, I am so glad to see you again.'

'And I you,' Sophie said, kissing Jane on both cheeks. 'But you do not look at all well.'

'I am not,' Jane said with a sigh of resignation. 'But I shall recover, in time.' She glanced towards the door. 'Robert will be down shortly.'

'You didn't tell him I was coming?'

'You asked me not to.'

Sophie nodded. It was only natural that Jane should be curious, but she had no intention of revealing any of what she planned. That would be for ever between herself and Robert. If she was to burn in hell for what she was about to do, she would go to the devil alone.

Suddenly, the door opened and Robert walked in. 'Jane, I thought I heard someone at the—?' He broke off and his face went pale. 'Sophie!'

'Good evening, Mr Silverton.'

For a moment, they stood there: three actors in a play, each waiting for the other to speak his lines. When no one did, Jane walked over to Sophie, kissed her on the cheek and left. And in the seconds that followed, Sophie knew how a prisoner must feel while waiting for the judge to pronounce sentence. She'd had no idea that silence could be so terrifying.

'What has happened to bring you here?' Robert said softly. 'Dare I hope you've changed your mind?'

Sophie stared at his tall, upright figure and wondered how was it possible to be so vibrantly aware of a man, so desperate for his touch that her body quivered at the very thought of it. 'The only thing that's happened is that I've realised what my life is going to be like once I am married to Mr Oberon.' Sophie slowly untied the ribbons beneath her chin and slipped off her bonnet. 'And I knew I could not go to him without seeing you one more time. Alone.'

She heard his harsh rasp of breath. 'Don't marry him, Sophie. I beg you!'

But she only shook her head. 'I will not change my mind, but if the rest of my life is to be lived in darkness, I would ask for one bright memory to carry into it. Give me that memory, Robert,' she said, stopping before him. 'You're the only one who can.'

They were so close that Sophie could feel the warmth of his breath on her face. At one time, she would have thought it impossible that she would be willing to sacrifice everything for one brief moment of intimacy, but she had lain awake too many hours going over what she wanted to say to back down now. Before she'd met Robert, she'd had no idea what it was to truly be in love. Now, she did. And with the thought of losing him, nothing else seemed to matter.

When he didn't move, Sophie placed her bare hands against his chest, tilted her face up to his and kissed him. Kissed him with the desperate longing of one who knows it will be the last time. And though his lips remained stiff and unmoving beneath hers, she didn't back away. If he rejected her, it would not be because she hadn't done her best to seduce him.

But Robert didn't reject her—and Sophie knew the exact moment his resistance broke. She heard his anguished groan and felt his arms come around her, crushing her against him. His mouth covered hers hungrily and she trembled as his tongue slipped between her lips, coaxing them apart. Sensation flowed through her veins like liquid fire. The taste of him was intoxicating, the scent of him enough to make her senses swim. There was only this man, this time, this moment. She felt his hand at her breast, a light, fleeting caress, but it was as though a whirlwind swept through her body.

More. She *needed* him to go on caressing her so that when another man touched her, it would be Robert's caresses she remembered. Robert's face she saw. Robert's love that filled her heart.

'Dear God, Sophie.' His voice was tortured, his breathing harsh. 'If I don't stop soon—'

'I don't want you to stop!' she said urgently. 'Make love to me, Robert. Just once, so I'll know what passion really is.'

She felt his lips against her hair. 'You haven't thought this through, beloved. If you truly intend to proceed with this abysmal marriage, it would be madness for us to be together. You *must* know that!'

Sophie weakly rested her forehead against his chin, her body thrumming with emotion. 'I do. But for once in my life, I don't care. I don't want to be sensible. Please don't ask that of me.'

'I have no choice. I can't do something that will make your life more a living hell than it already is. The body doesn't lie, Sophie,' he whispered. 'Oberon will know you've been with another man.'

'But he doesn't need know it was you!' Sophie gazed up into his eyes. 'He already believes the worst of me. Let him think it happened *before* I came to England.'

'It would not make his rage any the less terrifying, nor would it lessen the punishment he metes out. I cannot do what you ask, Sophie,' Robert said. 'God help me, I would never know a moment's peace again.'

With that, he put his hands on her arms and gently pushed her away.

Sophie closed her eyes, fighting to quell her feelings of disappointment and frustration. He was right, of course. It would be madness to go to Oberon after having made love to Robert. She could tell him what she liked, but she knew he would suspect Robert of being the one, and there was no telling what form his anger and revenge might take. And was the purpose of this marriage not to *ensure* the safety of those she loved?

'Forgive me,' he whispered, standing with his forehead pressed against hers.

Sophie closed her eyes, fighting back tears. 'No. I'm the one who should be asking forgiveness. I was thinking only of what I wanted, without regard for the future. The choice to marry him is my own. I should not have asked you to put yourself at risk by indulging me in such a way.'

'I would indulge you in every way imaginable,' Robert said, his voice heavy with longing. 'There is nothing I want more than to make love to you, Sophie. But not when I *know* what he will do when I'm not there to protect you.'

'Then kiss me goodbye,' she said, gazing up at him. 'And know that whatever he has to take from me, I give you willingly.'

His mouth was not gentle. The kiss was savage. Demanding—and Sophie welcomed it. She buried her fingers in his hair, dragging his head down as she pressed her body even closer to his, seared by the passion that burned between them. This was all she would ever have. One moment in an eternity of loneliness. One moment that would become the memory she would cling to for the rest of her life.

All too soon, it was over. Robert kissed her once more, then gently pushed her away. Numbly, Sophie picked up her bonnet and put it on, tying the silken ribbons beneath her chin. Without looking at him, she turned and started towards the door.

'Sophie.'

She stopped, but didn't turn around. 'Yes?'

'I'm following a lead. I can't tell you more because I don't know what I'll find. But I won't let you go until I've exhausted every possible avenue.'

Sophie nodded, but kept her gaze on the floor. 'Then I will go to bed hoping for good news, my love. Because if you cannot find that avenue within the next twenty-four hours, there will no longer be any need to look.'

Chapter Sixteen

Adrian Brocknower was leaving. That much became evident the moment Robert stepped into the dilapidated room at the top of the stairs, on a street where no self-respecting gentleman would ever admit to keeping rooms. The narrow bed was bare, the wardrobe doors flung back, and there was a portmanteau lying open on the rough wooden floor.

'I'm glad I didn't wait any longer,' Robert said as he watched the sole occupant of the room throw clothes haphazardly into the case. 'Or I would have been forced to add yet another vacated address to my list.'

The young man whirled, his face twisted in fear. 'Who the hell are you?'

'A friend. Parker sent me.'

'Parker?'

'Yes. We met this morning at Angelo's,' Robert explained. 'He gave me your card and said to mention his name. I take it you *are* Adrian Brocknower?'

Hearing Parker's name seemed to have a calming effect on the younger man, but his look was still guarded as he returned to his packing. 'For now, but I won't be much longer.'

Robert quickly took stock of the other man. In his early twenties, he was of middling height and slim build. His dark hair was unkempt and his long, narrow face bore the unmistakable stamp of fear. 'You're running away.'

'Disappearing, actually.' Adrian reached for the small collection of books on the desk and dropped them into the case. 'I don't intend to be here when he finds out what I've done.'

'He?'

'You know who.' Adrian looked up. 'If Parker sent you, he's the reason you're here.'

'All right,' Robert said, crossing his arms in front of his chest. 'What exactly *have* you done?'

Adrian pulled open a drawer and emptied the contents. 'I've uncovered a fraud, haven't I? And I was foolish enough to tell my employer about it.'

'Your employer being Sir Thomas Buckley.'

'That's right. I told him I'd found inconsistencies in the paperwork. Documents that should have been registered left unsigned. Monies that should have been invested. And when I brought it to Sir Thomas's attention, he told me I'd meddled in areas that were none of my concern and said my services were no longer required.'

'He turned you off?'

'On the spot. When I tried to explain I was simply following procedure, he had me escorted from the premises, without a letter of recommendation or my final pay. He also threatened me with legal action if I breathed a word of this to anyone.'

'And have you?' Robert enquired.

'Parker knows. He advised me to write it all down, so I did. All the names, all the dates, as well as how much money each person invested and where it was supposedly allocated.'

'Supposedly?'

'You can't put money into something that doesn't exist.'

Robert's eyes widened. 'So there *was* a scam. No wonder Sir Thomas's clerk didn't want to talk to me.'

Adrian tensed. 'You didn't go round the firm, did you? Asking questions? Looking for me?'

'I did go round, but not because I was looking for you. I was hoping to speak to Sir Thomas,' Robert said. 'But after being politely but firmly rebuffed, I learned that *you* had handled much of the paperwork for Sir Thomas and that made me think you might be the one I needed to see—especially once I found out you were no longer with the firm.'

'Yes, well, that's probably for the best,' Adrian said. 'I wouldn't want to be in Sir Thomas's shoes when word of this gets out. From what little I've heard, Mr Oberon is not a forgiving man.'

'Would he have reason to suspect you?'

'I'm not willing to take the chance. He didn't know Sir Thomas handed most of the paperwork off to someone else, and Sir Thomas didn't think I was smart enough to find anything wrong.' Adrian shot him a derisive look. 'I was only a clerk, after all.'

Robert smiled. It never paid to underestimate one's subordinates. 'Where is this list of information you've compiled?'

'Before I tell you that, I want your word as a gentleman that you won't tell a soul who gave it to you.'

'You have it,' Robert said without hesitation. 'But when Oberon is charged, he's bound to know someone betrayed him. And there aren't that many people in the game.'

'That's why I'm getting out of London. If this all blows up, Sir Thomas will point the finger of blame at me, and by the time that happens, I'll have changed my name and be living somewhere Oberon will never find me.'

'With luck, he won't get out of prison long enough to try.'

Adrian laughed. 'Oberon won't go to prison. His father's a peer.'

'He will if I have anything to do with it,' Robert said quietly. 'He's ruined too many lives to go free.'

'Well, I wish you well with it, sir, but I've seen money and power triumph over justice and truth too many times to believe it works the other way round.' With that, Adrian walked across to the open wardrobe and leaned in. There was a sound of wood splintering, and moments later, he re-emerged holding a slim, leatherbound journal. 'You can read it if you like,' he said, handing it across. 'I never want to see it again.'

Robert took the journal, but didn't open it. 'Why didn't you show this to the authorities?'

'And risk going up against the likes of Lord Oberon? Not a chance. They'd have charged *me* with fraud rather than put the blame where it belonged. No, if you hadn't come along, this book would likely have ended up in the Thames. Or with Parker.'

Robert looked down at the journal. Parker again. He was growing curious about this man who operated in secret and seemed to know things about people most others didn't. 'I'm very glad to have this, Mr Brocknower. Perhaps I can use it to help some of the people Oberon has swindled.'

For the first time, Adrian smiled and in doing so, looked less like the fearful young man circumstances had forced him to become. 'I just want to see justice done. Wealth and privilege don't deserve to be in the hands of a man like that.'

'No, they don't.' Robert put the journal on the bed and pulled an envelope from his pocket. 'I don't know where you're going, but this will either help get you there, or establish you once you arrive.'

Adrian stared at the envelope, his face flushing when he realised what it was. 'I'd like to say I don't need this, but I do. Thank you, sir. I'm glad I had the pleasure of meeting you.'

'The pleasure's all mine, Mr Brocknower.' Robert turned to go, and then stopped. 'By the by, who is this Parker chap?'

'Sir Barrington Parker?' Adrian laughed. 'To tell you the truth, I don't know much about him. He came to see

Sir Thomas a few times and I once heard him mention Mr Oberon's name. I thought he might be a friend of his, until I chanced to meet him in the street and he told me to watch myself around him.'

'Did he say why?'

'No, but I found out soon enough.'

Robert smiled. 'I'll leave you to your packing. I have a few appointments of my own to keep before this night is over.'

Oberon was at his club when Robert caught up with him. Just as well. He was less inclined to commit murder with that many witnesses around. 'Evening, Oberon.'

'Well, well, if it isn't my old friend, Silver,' Oberon said, leaning back in his chair. 'And looking very serious, I might add.'

'I have been engaged on serious business,' Robert said.

'Why don't you join me for a drink and tell me about it?' Oberon invited. 'I shall enjoy spending my last hours as a bachelor in the company of my good friend. Stokes! A brandy for Mr Silverton!'

Robert studied the man with whom he had gambled away more nights than he cared to remember and wondered that he had ever thought him a friend. Now, he could only see him for what he was: a desperate, conniving man who took no responsibility for his actions. One who felt no qualms about destroying other people's hopes and dreams.

A man who would ruin an innocent young woman's life in a twisted attempt to thwart another's.

'So, Robert, what business have you been engaged upon that has you looking so glum?' Oberon asked. 'Although, perhaps before you tell me, I should demand that you settle the terms of our wager. You owe me for not having told me the truth about my bride.'

Robert didn't so much as blink. 'The truth?'

'About her being a farmer's daughter, of course,' Oberon said, laughing. 'What a turnabout, eh? A viscount's son marrying the daughter of an impoverished French farmer. My, how the *ton* would laugh if they were to hear such a tale. How I would be roasted for having allowed myself to be taken advantage of by a beautiful face. But they won't, of course, because I have already concocted a delightful new background for my beautiful bride. Shall I tell you what it is?'

'Oberon—'

'No, really, I insist you listen. You'll find it quite amusing. The young lady is actually the only daughter of the Comte de Shaltiere, a noble Frenchman who, sadly, was killed in a tragic accident just north of Lyon. His wife, the beautiful Comtesse de Shaltiere, died too, leaving Sophie and her brother to be raised by a kindly aunt whose name I cannot remember and who no one is ever going to find.'

'You're wasting your time, Oberon.'

'No, in fact, I am making extremely good use of it,' Oberon said. 'I've had to because you've not been the good friend I believed you to be. A good friend would have told me about Miss Vallois's origins, as I understand you learned of them some time ago.'

'It came up in conversation.'

'And you did not think it important enough to share with me?'

Robert met the belligerent gaze with equanimity. 'My decision not to say anything had more to do with protecting *her* good name than yours.'

'Yes, no doubt you and the Longworths were in collusion. Making sure no one ever found out that the beautiful Miss Vallois was actually a farmer's daughter.'

'There was no collusion and it was never the Longworths' intent to make anyone believe Miss Vallois was something she was not.'

'Then why dress her up in fine clothes and present her as though she were a lady?' Oberon snapped. 'What was *that* if not a calculated attempt to convince society she was well born?'

'Miss Vallois may not be well born, but she is every inch a lady.'

'Rubbish! She is a farmer's brat. The sad consequence of peasants rutting in the fields.'

Robert had to fight the urge to lean across the table and grab Oberon by the throat. 'If you feel that way, why not call the whole thing off?'

'Call it off? What, so that you can march in and marry the chit yourself? Oh, no, Silver, I won't let you trump me in this. There's far too much at stake. Besides, I have my pride.'

'But I *love* her,' Robert said quietly. 'Can you make the same claim?'

'Good God, no, nor would I want to! But she still stirs my blood and I want her in my bed.' Oberon's eyes darkened with lust. 'French women are passionate creatures.

With the right encouragement, she'll quiver like a finely plucked bow. In truth, if it were a simple matter to make her my mistress, that's exactly what I would do. But I'd no doubt find myself facing pistols at dawn with you or Longworth or that bothersome brother of hers. So, I shall marry the wench and make sure the story I've come up with is the *only* one society is allowed to hear. Then I shall bury her in the country with my sister. No doubt she and Elaine will be delightful company for one another.'

A red mist boiled in Robert's head, but when he spoke, his voice was like cold steel. 'And how do you think Lord and Lady Longworth will take to your spreading lies about Miss Vallois?'

'I don't really give a damn. They should have told me the truth when I informed them of my interest in her,' Oberon said in a silken voice. 'But they didn't, did they? They *allowed* me to believe the chit was worthy of my attention, and like a fool, I went to them and asked permission to court her. Imagine! The son of a peer asking permission to address a French peasant. Well, it will do well for them to keep the information to themselves. I can make life very unpleasant for both of them if I choose.'

Robert's voice hardened. 'As you've said, you hold people in the palm of your hand.'

'Indeed. But I grow weary of this conversation. Bring the ring to my house tonight,' Oberon said, pouring himself another glass of brandy. 'I intend having it made into a necklace for my new bride. I shall tell her how I came by it and every time she looks at it, she will think of you. A fitting present, don't you think?'

Robert slowly clenched his fists, aware of an unholy desire to punch Oberon senseless. The man's arrogance was revolting, his certainty that he had won an offence to common decency. But it was his total lack of regard for Sophie's feelings that had Robert longing to throw the existence of the journal in his face and watch him squeal like a stuck pig.

He wouldn't, of course. Adrian Brocknower would never be made to suffer for his honesty. The journal was now in the hands of Robert's lawyer with the instructions that it be kept under lock and key until he returned. That alone enabled him to keep a grip on his emotions. He must for Sophie's sake. To prevent the horror her life would become if she were to marry Oberon.

'I will not give you the ring, Oberon,' Robert said at length. 'And there will be no wedding. You are to release Miss Vallois from her promise and swear never to go near her again.'

After a moment spent gazing at him in astonishment, Oberon threw back his head and laughed. 'My dear Silver, what on earth are you talking about? Of course there will be a wedding. And you will be there to see it. Sitting in the front row with Jane and Nicholas and Lavinia. And once it is over, I intend to get *very* close to my darling wife. I intend to strip the gown from her delicious body and take my time ravishing her—'

'You said more than once,' Robert interrupted, his voice vibrating with anger, 'that everyone had a history. Some histories are good, some contain secrets that are both dark and disturbing. Yours is just such a history, Oberon. And I intend to expose it for all the world to see.'

'Expose me?' Oberon sneered. 'My poor deluded friend, you don't know what you're talking about.'

'Ah, but I do. Because I know what you've been doing. I know about your abominable treatment of Lawrence Welton and your attempts to cripple him by having him pour money into a phoney investment scheme. I also know that what you spend far exceeds your allowance and that you do, in fact, owe a great deal of money. Debts your father knows nothing about. Oh, yes, I've done my own bit of investigating,' Robert said, taking pleasure in watching the colour drain out of Oberon's face. 'And when the world finds out what you've done, you *will* be a broken man.'

'You've taken leave of your senses,' Oberon said, his expression growing uglier by the minute. 'No one will believe you. And you certainly won't find anyone to corroborate your story.'

'I don't need corroboration when I have proof. Proof that is safely in the hands of my lawyer even now.'

For the first time, Oberon faltered, a crack appearing in the smooth façade. 'You're lying! No one knew what I was doing.'

'Unfortunately for you, several people did,' Robert said. 'And records *were* kept. Meticulous records, I might add.'

He knew the moment Oberon began to believe him. It was the same moment the snake reappeared, a desperate creature concerned only with its own survival. 'Who told you?' he hissed. 'Give me his name and we'll talk about my releasing Miss Vallois.'

Robert shook his head. 'I'm afraid it isn't that simple. You see, crimes *have* been committed. The Scottish railway scheme for one. The California land deal for another.'

Oberon's face suddenly went a sickly shade of grey. 'You're bluffing.'

'Are you willing to bet your life on it?'

In an instant, it was over. The cocky, self-assured man was replaced by a quivering coward who knew the cards were stacked against him. Lady luck had turned—and she had turned with a vengeance. 'What do you want?' Oberon growled.

'Write a note. Two lines will suffice,' Robert said, 'agreeing to release Miss Vallois from her promise and guaranteeing that you will never contact her again. Write the same letter to Lord and Lady Longworth. I will deliver them both this evening.'

'And if I refuse?'

'You won't.' Robert got to his feet and signalled for the butler to bring pen and paper. 'You will also place a notice in *The Times*, announcing that the engagement between you and Miss Vallois is over.'

'And if I do all that,' Oberon asked petulantly, 'what is my fate to be?'

'That is for the authorities to decide. I'm sure your father will intervene on your behalf and no doubt he will succeed in getting your sentence reduced. But given what is likely to be revealed about your dealings with others, you may not wish to remain long in London.'

The butler placed parchment and a quill on the table. With a visible display of irritation, Oberon began to write. 'Anything else?'

'Yes. Strike the entry from the betting book,' Robert said. 'The Mistress Wager is now officially and for ever at an end.'

Sophie heard a carriage draw to a halt in the street outside the house just before ten o'clock that evening and went rigid with apprehension. Surely Oberon had not come to gloat. Surely he would have the decency to leave her in peace on this, her final evening as a single woman.

She heard the sharp rap of the brass knocker and then the sound of footsteps as Banyon went to answer the door. Muffled conversation followed, followed by more footsteps, and then still more muffled conversation.

She waited for what seemed an eternity for the drawing-room door to open. Ten minutes later when the mantel clock chimed the hour and the drawing-room door still remained closed, Sophie sank into the nearest chair, relieved beyond measure that the visitor had not come to see her.

How tragic her life had become that she should so desperately fear the thought of callers. That the sound of a carriage should set her nerves on edge. This, truly, was what it was to live in fear. And tomorrow, that fear would take on an entirely new dimension. Tomorrow she would become the wife of Montague Oberon and lose all rights to how she led her life. She would be expected to do as her husband bid. Go where her husband directed.

Say what her husband told her to say. Without thought. Without will. Without choice.

In short, her life would become purgatory. It would have to, for Oberon didn't love her. The expression of disgust on his face had been more than enough to convince her of his true sentiments. Lust would remain, as would the need to chastise and control, but there would be nothing of the gentler emotions in their marriage. No affection. No respect. No forgiveness. There would be fear and brutality and loathing—and there was nothing Sophie could do to prevent it. If she ran back to Paris and tried to lose herself in the crowded streets, Oberon would exact his vengeance on those who stayed behind. Her fate was sealed. She *had* to marry him to ensure the safety of the people she loved.

And Robert?

Sophie closed her eyes, feeling the hot sting of tears as she pictured his face. They'd had so little time together, and now even that was over. His memory would become her salvation. When the days stretched long and the weight of her new life pressed down upon her, thoughts of him would be all that carried her through. She would remember the way it felt to be held in his arms, play over and over the sweetness of his kiss.

And when the night came and with it a suffocating darkness that threatened to blot out all hope, she would cling to the memory of him asking her to be his wife. She would remember that, for a few blissful days, she had actually believed it would come true. Until Oberon had returned—and ground her dreams into dust.

The click of the drawing-room door as it opened

brought Sophie to her feet. She held her breath and pressed her hands to her stomach, willing the tumultuous butterflies to settle. But it was only Nicholas and Lavinia who came in. Nicholas, who had tried to do so much for her and, in the end, had been able to do nothing. And dear Lavinia, who had become like a second mother. She searched their faces, looking for some indication as to what had happened. 'Someone came?' she ventured.

'Yes, someone came,' Lavinia said quietly. 'A gentleman, bringing with him the most wonderful news.'

'*Wonderful* news?' Sophie glanced at Nicholas, hardly daring to breathe. 'Tell me quickly. What has happened?'

'You are not to marry Oberon,' Nicholas said, holding out a sheet of parchment. 'He has withdrawn his offer.'

'*Withdrawn it?*' Sophie flew across the room and took the letter in hands that shook so badly she could scarcely read the words. There were only two lines—but they said all that mattered. 'I am released,' she whispered. 'Oberon no longer wishes to marry me. And he has given his word that…he will not try to see me again.' She raised her head. 'How has this come to pass? What on earth could have made him change his mind?'

'Can you not guess?' Nicholas asked. And when he moved aside, she saw Robert standing quietly in the doorway.

'Good evening, Miss Vallois. I trust you are well.'

'Robert! That is…Mr Silverton. Yes, I think I am.' The letter fluttered to the floor. 'In fact…better than I've been for some time. But I am also very confused.'

Robert strolled forwards, his eyes never leaving her face. 'Then I will do my best to clear up the mystery.'

'Lavinia, I believe our presence is required elsewhere,' Nicholas said, stretching his arm towards his wife. 'These two have much to talk about.'

Lavinia was beaming. 'Yes, of course they do.' But before she left, she stopped to give Sophie a quick hug and whisper in her ear, 'I told you your face would give you away.' Then she joined her husband and the two left the room arm in arm.

As the door closed behind them, Sophie turned to face the man she had thought never to see again. 'Why has he released me?'

Robert bent to pick up the fallen piece of parchment. 'Oberon once told me that everyone had secrets, and he was right. But he intended using yours as a weapon against you and I couldn't allow that to happen. So I started asking questions. I needed to uncover the secrets in his past, and if I could find any, to use them against him.'

'And you found some?'

'Oh, yes, and they were far more incriminating than yours. You see, Oberon had several fatal flaws,' Robert said. 'His insatiable appetite for money, his reckless desire for power and his uncontrollable need to gamble. Taken alone, any one of those vices would be enough to destroy a man. But when all three are combined and you add a complete lack of conscience to the mix, disaster is sure to follow. It was only a matter of time before his wrongdoings caught up with him.'

'What did you find out?'

Robert shook his head. 'The details don't matter. Suffice it to say that he committed a crime for which he will be made to pay.'

Sophie arched a brow. 'Lawrence Welton?'

'Amongst others. The list stretches long.'

'What will happen to him now?'

'That is for the courts to decide. There is no getting around the fact that his father is a peer and that he will do everything in his power to clear his son of the charges. But the harm Oberon has done other people is extensive and will not soon be forgotten. I think it unlikely he will wish to linger in London once word of this gets out.'

So it was true. She was not to marry Oberon—and he was never going to bother her again. Relief bubbled up like a wellspring. 'Then it really is over.'

'It is, and you are free to go on with your life. A retraction of the engagement will appear in *The Times*, and your brother and Lord and Lady Longworth need no longer fear exposure of any kind for their past activities.'

Sophie's eyes opened wide. 'You knew about that?'

'I put two and two together—after a rather enlightening conversation with Lord Longworth.' His gaze was both gentle and teasing. 'If I ever find myself nursing a gunshot wound, I'll know who to go to. It seems you and your brother are quite adept when it comes to patching up wounded Englishmen.'

She started to laugh, not sure whether it was from joy or relief. 'I told you I could be of assistance, but you *would* try to put me in my place.'

'So I did.' His own eyes lightened, his expression

becoming almost boyish. 'You're quite the woman, Sophie Vallois. Marrying Oberon to ensure their safety was an incredibly brave, albeit unspeakably foolish, thing to do.'

'How could I have done otherwise?' Sophie asked simply. 'There was so much at stake. Antoine's future. Nicholas and Lavinia's well-being. Your reputation. Perhaps your very *life*. How could I have married you *knowing* that by doing so, I was wilfully putting all of that at risk?'

'For what it's worth, he couldn't have done anything worse to me than force me to watch you marry him,' Robert said. He came so close that she could see the tiny creases fanning out from the corners of his eyes. 'But now it doesn't matter. No one's life is in jeopardy and you are free to marry whomever you please. Although...' he reached for her left hand and raised it to his lips '...I hope your mind is already made up in that regard.'

Sophie raised her free hand to caress his face, loving the texture of his skin, the rough stubble of beard on his chin. She could scarcely bear to think about how close she'd come to losing him. Of what her life would have been like without him. 'It has been made up for some time. And I cannot see it changing now that we have been given a second chance.'

'Ah, Sophie.' Her name was a benediction, and having her in his arms was a sure sign that all was right in his world. 'When will you marry me?'

'Now. Tonight, if it were possible,' she told him, her eyes glowing. 'But I suspect there are those who would object to the lack of notice.'

'Your brother being one,' he said ruefully. 'He would never forgive me for marrying you without his being here to give you away.'

'Then I shall write to him at once,' Sophie said. 'Apparently Monsieur Larocque is recovering well, and I am told he has taken on another apprentice. As soon as Antoine can arrange to be here, I will become your wife.'

Robert smiled as he lowered his head to nuzzle the soft white skin of her throat. 'Perhaps I shall have Jane write to him as well. Then Nicholas and Lavinia will have *two* weddings to look forward to.'

A soft gasp escaped. 'You would *allow* Jane and Antoine to marry?'

'I think it the only humane thing to do. Jane has been wandering around like a sad little ghost ever since your brother went back to France. How could I enjoy my own happiness if it came at the expense of hers?'

Sophie closed her eyes, loving the warmth of his mouth on her skin though it made it exceedingly difficult to concentrate. 'For what it's worth, Antoine has been miserable too. He is desperately in love with her.'

'Then why did he say nothing to me before he left?'

'Because he felt he had nothing to offer.' Reluctantly, Sophie opened her eyes. 'Jane is a gentleman's daughter, Antoine a farmer's son. What could he give her that would compensate for all he believed she would lose by marrying him?'

'Love,' Robert said simply. 'Love, and the rest will take care of itself. With a little help from me, of course.'

Sophie smiled. 'And what about your other concern? The fact that, like myself, Antoine is French?'

'Ah, Sophie.' Robert pressed his lips to her hair. 'You see a fool standing before you. It wasn't a Frenchman who shot my brother. It was an Englishman working both sides of the war. The *same* man who shot Lord Longworth and left him for dead.'

'Never!'

'He told me as much a few days ago. And for all those years, I carried hatred in my soul for a man who didn't even exist.' Robert looked down at her, searching her face for signs that it was still an issue between them. 'When I think what it nearly cost me—'

'No.' Sophie placed her fingers against his lips. 'This is not the time for regrets. All that matters is that you do not resent Antoine for being French, or for being in love with your sister.'

'How could I resent him when I saw how he felt about her,' Robert said. 'Antoine was the only man who ever really *looked* at Jane. He didn't see her handicap. He saw a beautiful, intelligent woman and he fell in love with her. I couldn't ask for a better husband for my sister.'

'And Antoine could not ask for a better husband for his,' Sophie said softly. 'Thank you, Robert, for everything.'

'It is not your thanks I want, darling girl. Only your love.'

'That you have. But now, I think we should find Nicholas and Lavinia and tell them the wonderful news. It was very good of them to give us this time alone together.'

'I think they knew you were about to receive yet

another proposal of marriage. You will marry me, won't you, Sophie?' Robert asked, gently pulling her back into his arms. 'And stay with me always?'

Sophie smiled. To think that one day soon she would say the words that would make this wonderful man her husband. Was it only a few weeks ago that the idea of marriage had seemed so untenable? That the thought of entrusting her heart to a man she'd met in a crowded coaching inn would seem so utterly implausible?

Hard to believe, but it was—and she wouldn't have changed a thing. Because everything she'd gone through had brought her to this moment. To this conclusion. To this man standing before her. 'Yes, I will marry you,' she said without hesitation. 'And I will stay with you for as long as you wish me to stay. For as long as you love me.'

'Then I expect we're going to be together for a very long time.' His eyes grew dark as he bent his head to kiss her. 'And that we are going to be happy for a longer time still.'

* * * * *

HISTORICAL

HISTORICAL

BOUND TO THE BARBARIAN
by Carol Townend

Sold into slavery, maidservant Katerina promised one day to repay the princess who rescued her. Now that time has come, and Katerina must convince commanding warrior Ashfirth Saxon that *she* is her royal mistress!

THE CATTLEMAN'S UNSUITABLE WIFE
by Pam Crooks

When cattleman Trey Wells's betrothed is kidnapped, blame falls on Zurina Vasco's brother—and a vengeful Trey demands she help him track them down. Trey soon realises Zurina is the only woman for him—but there is much to overcome before he can give her the love she deserves...

RECKLESS
by Anne Stuart

Adrian Rohan has only one pleasure: the seduction of beautiful women. Rich, charming and devastatingly skilled in the art of love, he never fails in his conquests...until Charlotte Spenser...

On sale from 4th February 2010
Don't miss out!

Available at WHSmith, Tesco, ASDA, Eason and all good bookshops

www.millsandboon.co.uk

REGENCY
Silk & Scandal

*A season of secrets, scandal and
seduction in high society!*

Volume 5 – 1st October 2010
The Viscount and the Virgin
by Annie Burrows

Volume 6 – 5th November 2010
Unlacing the Innocent Miss
by Margaret McPhee

Volume 7 – 3rd December 2010
The Officer and the Proper Lady
by Louise Allen

Volume 8 – 7th January 2011
Taken by the Wicked Rake
by Christine Merrill

8 VOLUMES IN ALL TO COLLECT!

2 FREE BOOKS
AND A SURPRISE GIFT

We would like to take this opportunity to thank you for reading this Mills & Boon® book by offering you the chance to take TWO more specially selected books from the Historical series absolutely FREE! We're also making this offer to introduce you to the benefits of the Mills & Boon® Book Club™—

- **FREE home delivery**
- **FREE gifts and competitions**
- **FREE monthly Newsletter**
- **Exclusive Mills & Boon Book Club offers**
- **Books available before they're in the shops**

Accepting these FREE books and gift places you under no obligation to buy, you may cancel at any time, even after receiving your free books. Simply complete your details below and return the entire page to the address below. You don't even need a stamp!

YES Please send me 2 free Historical books and a surprise gift. I understand that unless you hear from me, I will receive 4 superb new books every month for just £3.99 each, postage and packing free. I am under no obligation to purchase any books and may cancel my subscription at any time. The free books and gift will be mine to keep in any case.

Ms/Mrs/Miss/Mr ———————— Initials ————————

Surname ——————————————————————

Address ——————————————————————

———————————————— Postcode ————————

E-mail ——————————————————————

Send this whole page to: Mills & Boon Book Club, Free Book Offer, FREEPOST NAT 10298, Richmond, TW9 1BR